BECAUSE OF YOU

BECAUSE *of You*

BECAUSE OF YOU

Calypso Key Series

ERIN BROCKUS

GREEN SAGE PRESS

Edited by Lawrence Editing Services

Cover design by GetCovers

Ebook ISBN: 978-1-957003-31-3

Paperback ISBN: 978-1-957003-33-7

Hardcover ISBN: 978-1-957003-34-4

Chapter One

Evan

WITH MY FINGERS tapping a steady rhythm against my hip, I hurried as fast as I could. Well, as fast as my bum leg would let me. Worried and irritated in equal amounts, I glanced at the clear blue sky, grateful that at least the weather was cooperating. January mornings in the Florida Keys were unpredictable, but today Calypso Key had been graced with abundant sunshine and a soft breeze. Christmas decorations had been put away and the new year recently celebrated, but some things never changed. I quickened my pace even more.

I traveled along a paved trail that ran down a gently sloping hill from our family estate known tongue-in-cheek as Markham Manor. I lived with my father and grandmother, each of us in private quarters. Continuing south, the path ended at our family-run resort, named after the Key. As I trotted with my leg hardly making a hitch, I spared a quick glance at the Barn, where my oldest brother Gabe lived with his daughter and his new fiancée, April.

My destination lay ahead and toward my right, on the western edge of our small island. Skirting the lobby building, I passed between two of our garden cottages. The paved path continued, manicured shrubs and vibrant flowers in full bloom framing it on either side. The foliage opened to reveal a long, rectangular structure stretching before me. Painted soft pink with rustic wood accents adorning its roof and edges, Orchid was our fine dining restaurant and only open for dinner service. But it would be a terrible waste of resources to let the building sit unused all morning, so Calypso Key Resort's pastry chef, Rea Lipton, used a section of the kitchen to prepare her confections, as well as desserts for both Orchid and Dorado, our casual restaurant.

That wasn't the problem, or the reason I was in a hurry.

The problem was Alfonso Conti, Orchid's executive chef and resident pain in the ass. Though Orchid didn't open until 6:00 p.m., he liked to show up for work early, often before noon. Where he would proceed to harangue Rea, who was trying to get all her baking finished in time.

Which explained the text I had received ten minutes ago, just before lunch.

> Rea: That's it, Evan. Come down here and get Alfonso out of my hair, or you're going to have to clean up the blood. I have lots of knives to choose from.

Orchid's dining area faced the ocean to take advantage of glorious tropical sunsets, but I headed for the single door on the eastern, back side of the building. It slammed open, careening off the wall. Rea stormed out, dressed in a white smock and with her eyes blazing. All five-foot-two of her. Raising her hands, she rhythmically smoothed her short brown hair as she paced back and forth.

Probably trying to calm herself down.

Glancing up, she spotted me, and frustration replaced the anger in her eyes. "Evan, I've had it with him."

I stopped before her, both palms out. "I'll talk to him, okay?"

"And what good will that do? Alfonso needs a personality transplant, not a talking-to."

I didn't disagree, but as the resort's general manager, I had to tread carefully. "Just take a break for a while. I'll tell him to work in a different area of the kitchen and leave you alone."

She exhaled a long sigh. "I'm finished baking. Lainey is coming from Dorado to pick up the donuts and croissants. My desserts for tonight are ready, though I was sorely tempted to smash the coconut cream pie in Alfonso's face."

Rea still had a couple of hours left in her shift, but that didn't matter if she was caught up.

"Do you want to take off early?" I asked. "It's okay with me."

She shook her head. "I'll help out in Dorado. I'm sure they could use a hand with the lunch rush." Then she scowled at me, cocking one hip to the side. "And Alfonso isn't the only one I'm mad at. Carissa told me you've been bringing donuts from Sweet Dreams into the dive shop breakroom every morning. What, mine aren't good enough for you?"

Dammit, Carissa!

I resisted the urge to tug on my beard. Getting mad at the dive shop clerk wouldn't do any good. "Of course they are—your pastries are fantastic. I'm just trying to help a new business in town, that's all. We still sell out of your stuff every morning."

I wasn't about to admit the real reason I kept returning to the small bakery on neighboring Dove Key.

Several months ago, I'd been strolling along Main Street when I entered Liv Jacobson's new bakery. Lured in by the delicious scent wafting out the open door, where the owner herself waited on me. Liv had stunning, long, curly hair and appeared close to my own age of thirty-one. The next week, I'd returned. Then the next week too.

After a month, I could no longer convince myself that my visits were just a convenient stop as I headed to town for other things. Liv's eyes were a warm green, and her round figure promised she'd be soft and perfect in all the right places.

We'd struck up a friendship of sorts. One of those curious, superficial relationships where we were friendly and discussed our days every time we met in Sweet Dreams. She didn't know who I was, and I liked the safe anonymity of our relationship. Being a Markham was complicated enough. Being the lame one was worse.

Except the pink boxes I brought back to the resort had been noticed. First, my brother Gabe had given me a hard time about it. He had moved home to shore up the resort's flailing bottom line and wanted to make sure I wasn't expensing off my donut trips. I'd assured him it was all my own money, blushing furiously as I did. Our sister Maia had noticed the boxes too. And now Rea knew about it.

The pastry chef's frown hadn't lightened much. "Evan, she's competition!"

"Oh, she is not. No one from Dove Key is going to drive here for a damn donut. Or the reverse."

She burst out laughing. "Well, that's not true, is it? You do."

I rolled my eyes, glad my bushy beard hid the red flush igniting my cheeks. "She's not a threat to you, Rea. Your desserts are the best in the lower Keys." Which wasn't a lie. I'd never tasted any of Liv's desserts. Just her morning pastries.

Just that thought sent a hot roll through my core.

But my statement pleased Rea, and a satisfied glint entered her eye. "Yeah, even Alfonso can't bitch too much about that."

"I'll talk to him, I promise," I said as we moved to stand under a nearby shade tree.

"Good luck with that. You might bring along some water for him to turn into wine while you're at it."

I couldn't help laughing. "He can't be the only temperamental chef you've worked with."

"He's not. Thank God the other chefs around here are nicer."

I'd hired Alfonso almost four years ago. He'd just won a major cooking reality show and signing him had been a major coup. He brought a lot of prestige to Orchid, which was why we all put up with him. Though his menus had grown steadily less creative over the years, making me think twice about renewing his contract when it was up in a year. "I'll ask him not to come in before noon from now on, okay?"

Rea pursed her lips but nodded. "That will work—if he keeps his end of the bargain. I don't know why he shows up so early."

"He likes to prepare and plan the night's menu without being rushed."

"As long as he stays away from me." A corner of her mouth rose in a reluctant smile. "Thanks, Evan. Sorry I unloaded on you."

"That's what I'm here for, and I understand your frustration. See you later."

As Rea headed toward the lobby and Dorado, I opened the door to Orchid's kitchen and entered the bright, clean area with its rows of stainless-steel counters. Several walk-in refrigerators lined one wall and two industrial stoves and ovens dominated the opposite.

Alfonso stood in front of one of the counters, leaning over it as he scribbled on a piece of paper. Middle-aged and heavyset, he wore black pants and a white chef's coat with his name and *Executive Chef* embroidered on one breast. His black, curly hair was still loose, meaning he wasn't ready to start cooking.

Which he shouldn't be, since it'll be hours before he needs to start.

Hearing the door open, he glanced up. "Good morning, Evan." Originally from Rome, his English was tinged with an Italian accent.

I nodded back and fixed a pleasant look on my face. "Hello, Alfonso. I've told you before, you don't need to get here so early. Rea enjoys the solitude while she works. She's pretty riled up. What did you say to her?"

Straightening, he scowled at the opposite side of the kitchen, which housed the counters, giant mixer, and neatly stacked baking sheets Rea used every morning.

"She overreacts. I only complained about the flour all over the place. She is a pig." The word came out *peeg*.

I cast my eye over the immaculate area. "She is not a pig, and it's hard to bake without spilling flour. Her area looks spotless now. Did you clean up for her?"

Alfonso reared back, horrified. "Of course not! She can clean up her own disgusting messes."

I stopped across the counter from him and crossed my

arms. "You made her pretty angry, Alfonso. She has a right to work in this kitchen without interference. As long as she cleans up her station, why should you even care?"

"Because it is my kitchen. She is an invader. *Barbara...*" He muttered the last word, his eyes sliding to Rea's prep area.

I stared evenly at him, not rising to the bait. I didn't speak Italian, but I'd heard enough of his insults and curses to know he'd called Rea a barbarian. "No more coming in early, Alfonso. I don't want to see you here before noon."

The chef became animated, gesturing with his hands. "And how am I supposed to plan our nightly menus? Do you think our specials arrive by magic?"

"You've been using the same rotating specials for the last year. You don't need any extra time to prepare them."

Brows lowering, he glared at me. "Are you complaining about my food?"

I couldn't afford for him to storm off. One pissed-off chef was my limit. "No. Your food is excellent as always. But I *am* saying Rea has exclusive access to the kitchen until noon. End of story."

He lifted his chin and eyed me steadily. I looked straight back, not giving an inch. Finally, he nodded. "Very well. But if she leaves the kitchen in ruins, I will *not* be happy."

"I'm sure that won't happen. I appreciate your understanding, Alfonso. Have a good day."

I saved my deep sigh until I reemerged into the bright sunshine. Shoulders falling, I let the soft warmth wash over me. I needed a more pleasant distraction. Strolling beside the back of the restaurant, I headed toward the nearby beach.

Stepping onto the white sand and winding my way through the picnic tables, I moved under crisscrossing strands of party lights. Palm trees whispered above in the gentle breeze. This area was reserved for our weekly beach barbeques, always popular with guests.

My gaze sharpened as my destination came into view. The newly remodeled beach cottage was constructed from cinderblocks to withstand Atlantic hurricanes. That part hadn't changed, but now a fresh coat of white paint covered the L-shaped cottage. I couldn't detect any difference between the original, rectangular structure and the extra section that had been constructed. As I skirted around the side, a fifteen-by-thirty-foot private pool came into view, nestled on the oceanside of the cottage, so the combined unit formed a square shape.

Gabe was just entering the unit, his tall form disappearing behind a sliding glass door. Stepping onto the all-weather deck, I followed him inside. A warm wooden ceiling and white marble floor anchored the open bedroom, and it still smelled of fresh paint. The walls were painted white, photos of the Keys hanging on them. The king-sized bed was dressed in white linens and a mosquito net was pulled behind a stunning wooden headboard, where Gabe stood. He ran a hand over his dark scruff as he studied the bed. My brother bore a very strong resemblance to our father, Warren, with the signature Markham dark hair and height. Of all five Markham children, I was the only one who took after our deceased mother. My hair was light brown, and my eyes were blue. I also took after our dad in my height, though I was a couple of inches shorter than Gabe.

"Admiring your handiwork?" I asked.

Gabe turned around with a faint smile. He had built the bed himself, constructing the frame from mahogany and the headboard from solid teak. The headboard's top was a live edge, rippling and weaving its way across the white wall behind.

"Admiring the whole thing. I'm very pleased with how these cottages came out."

I studied the crisp, modern interior, light years from the shabby chic it had been just a few months ago. The walls had been drywalled, so no trace of cinderblock was visible from inside. A seating area lay on the opposite side of the cottage, with a blue-and-white striped couch and love seat. "Anyone would love to stay in these."

Gabe followed my gaze and nodded. "Your idea to upgrade these two end units into two-bedroom cottages with pools was great. And we finished on time and on budget." Financial aspects weren't my strong suit. But fortunately, they were Gabe's. He fronted his own money to finance the renovations and pay off a disastrous loan our father had been forced to take. In return, he was now the majority owner of the island and the resort.

Which was fine by me. He took the risk, so he deserved the reward.

Gabe caressed the headboard and nodded. "Next on the list is renovating the lobby building and the garden cottages."

Leaning back against the wall, I smiled. "And the beach cottages are done well before your wedding next month. Are you going to use them for guests to stay in?"

Gabe shrugged. "Probably. Neither of us wants a big wedding, but we'll invite a few people from out of town. April wants to invite some of her friends from St. Croix, but I can't imagine we'll need all ten beach cottages."

April Desmond had moved here from the Caribbean island the previous February. She and Gabe had fallen hard for each other and were planning a wedding here on Calypso Key next month.

"You must really be hard up for friends if you want me to be your best man." Despite my teasing, I'd been enormously touched when Gabe had asked me. I glanced at the sparkling ocean in the distance, set against our gorgeous white-sand beach.

He remained serious. "There's no one else I'd rather have next to me. I mean that, Evan."

"Thanks. You're definitely keeping things in the family. I told Hailey I'm expecting the first dance, limp and all."

"Hopefully that will happen. She's been getting cold feet lately, which surprises me a little." Gabe's daughter had recently turned nine and was wise beyond her years. I was surprised she would have reservations about being April's maid of honor. "Really? February tenth will be here before we know it."

Gabe laughed and shrugged one shoulder. "We'll work it out."

I smiled, amazed that my grouchy, surly big brother had undergone such a transformation. He was still nobody's fool, but it was nice to see him smile once in a while.

And if I could only admire the woman I was attracted to from afar, afraid to get closer?

Well, I was used to that. What decent woman would be interested in a boring, limping, glorified hotel clerk? None. That's who.

If only I could convince my grandmother of that.

Chapter Two

Liv

TEARING off a piece of clear tape from the dispenser I held in one hand, I attached the Marathon Hammerheads poster to the bakery wall. "There! That should do it."

"You don't have to do this, Liv."

I turned to frown at twenty-one-year-old Dylan Rutledge beside me. Well, frowned up at him. "You just stop it. You're starting to sound like a broken record, Dylan. I was going to sponsor the Hammerheads regardless. Now that I have a genuine baseball star working for me, it's even more of a no-brainer."

He snorted and brushed a lock of dark-blond hair off his forehead. "I'm anything but a star. It's just a developmental season. Tryouts for the team don't start until March."

We stood in the dining section of my bakery, Sweet Dreams. Eight tables were placed against the white walls, leaving a broad aisle stretching from the entryway to the glass display bisecting the shop.

"And with all the help you'll be getting from coaches,

you're sure to make the team," I pointed out. He was trying to make the Hammerheads regular season team as a pitcher, but he had a great eye for hitting too.

The black poster we'd just hung displayed the team's logo and ferocious mascot, with the upcoming schedule underneath. Marathon was a solid half-hour drive from Dove Key, but I was thrilled to be sponsoring the minor-league team. I couldn't wait to go to a game and see my Sweet Dreams banner displayed in left field. Baseball had always been my favorite sport, though I was anything but athletic myself.

Next to me, Dylan laughed. "I can't believe I got a job working for a baker who loves baseball."

Patting him on the forearm, I marched to pass between the end of the glass counter and the wall of the shop. I inspected the rows of confections in front of us. "See? You and I meeting was kismet."

The athletic young man had been a surprise when I interviewed him last month. But the woman I'd hired previously had been a complete disaster, and I fired her after only two months of employment. So this time, I thought outside the box. I hadn't been disappointed. Dylan was on time, great with customers, and a quick learner. The fact that he still lived with his mother and needed the position to help cover their bills tugged at my heartstrings. The job was a win-win for both of us.

As soon as I finished my sentence, my sensitive nose picked up something wrong. "Oh, crap! The oven again."

I hurried to my commercial-grade oven where cupcakes were baking. The acrid smell increased as I neared. Flipping on the oven's interior light, my suspicions were confirmed.

Dylan peered over my shoulder. "Don't think vanilla cupcakes are supposed to look like chocolate."

I breathed a long sigh as I put on an oven mitt, removed the tray, and set it down. The cupcakes sat on a trivet like a dozen hockey pucks. "They were just fine a few minutes ago!" When I'd purchased the used, but high-end oven a year ago, I couldn't believe my luck. Except now I didn't feel so lucky.

"Wish I could help." Reaching out gingerly, Dylan poked a cupcake. His finger made an audible crackling noise against the burned surface. "But I barely know a screwdriver from a hammer."

I threw a dark glance at the oven, then turned it off. "I'll see if the repairman can get out here today to look at it." I peered inside the oven to see if I could spot anything wrong.

The bell above the door jingled, and we both glanced over. My heart did a weird flopping thing as Dylan moved toward the counter. Which was the main reason I'd hired the young man, so he could help customers and leave me free to continue working.

Or try to work at least. Turning from the oven, I faced the front of the shop.

I had to admit this particular customer made me wish Dylan were on a break or something. My mystery man stepped up to the counter and met my eyes with a warm smile. He was Dylan's height, which had surprised me the first time I'd noticed the two of them near each other. The man had such a sweet, casual air about him that his height was easy to overlook, as if he was trying not to be noticed. His light-brown hair was always short and neat and contrasted with his full, luxuriant beard.

He came by the Sweet Dreams at least once a week, and we'd become friends. Well, kind of friends. He was very attractive, in a mountain man sort of way, which surprised me since I generally liked my men clean-shaven.

My men—ha! Like I have them lined up behind the door.

As he smiled at me, I couldn't help being shy and a little self-conscious about my figure. The woman with the extra padding on her hips owns a bakery?

Yeah, she does.

So I enjoyed keeping my lumberjack a mystery. That way I could fantasize and make up life stories about him without reality rudely intruding. He always dressed casually, but his clothes were neat and in good condition. His shirts highlighted a pair of very broad shoulders.

Maybe he's a teacher, bringing sweets to his students. I bet he's the teacher all the kids hope to get.

We exchanged smiles, his blue eyes crinkling at the corners. I nodded to him while Dylan filled a pink box with a dozen donuts. Mystery Man asked Dylan about the burned smell in the air, and I tried not to cringe. That was the last smell I wanted associated with my business. I glared at my misbehaving oven.

When Dylan explained the problem, Mystery Man cocked his head. "Want me to take a look at it?"

I whipped my head around and approached the counter, shyness forgotten. "You fix ovens?"

The man grinned. "Sometimes. I like to fix stuff."

"Be my guest." I beckoned to him and brought him over to the malfunctioning appliance.

Mystery Man peered around the kitchen. "It's probably the thermostat. Where's your breaker panel?"

"I've had the thermostat replaced twice already." I pointed to the back wall. "And the panel's over there. Thanks so much for the help."

He moved to the panel, walking with a slight hitch in

his step, and flipped the oven breaker off as I gathered supplies to make another batch of vanilla cupcakes. Dylan joined my side.

"You watched me make the last batch," I said. "Maybe you'll have better luck than me. Want to make them?"

Nodding eagerly, my apprentice measured ingredients and added them to the giant stand mixer. Mystery Man had opened the oven door and removed the racks. After pulling a screwdriver from his back pocket, he placed an oven mitt on his right hand. Then he reached inside and started doing something to the back of the oven.

The sound of the mixer activating turned my attention back to Dylan. "Good job. Set it to medium and don't over-beat the batter too much. Let's get the rest of our supplies."

The two of us grabbed everything we'd need for the frosting, and by the time the batter was mixed, Mystery Man was closing the breaker panel. He ripped off a paper towel from the dispenser and approached, wiping his hands. "A wire in the thermostat wasn't fully connected. Hopefully, that will take care of the problem."

I beamed at him. "Oh, thank you!"

He smiled and blushed slightly, which I thought was charming. Then he pointed with his chin at the pink box sitting next to the cash register. "I'll pay you for the donuts and get out of your hair."

"Oh, they are on the house today. That's the least I can do."

He was definitely blushing now. "It was nothing, really. But thanks. I'd better get going."

After picking up the box of donuts, he turned toward us again. "By the way, you should have an electrician look at your breaker panel. Some of those breakers look really old. The whole panel might need replacing."

I still owed the appliance company for oven repairs, so I wasn't exactly eager to hear that news. It sounded *expensive*. So I just smiled at Mystery Man from the counter. "I'll follow up on that. Thanks for your help. And expertise."

Then he was out the door and into the Dove Key morning. Back to wherever he came from. With an internal groan, I realized I'd had the perfect opportunity to learn his name. And I'd blown it.

Liv Jacobson, smooth operator.

But I'd learned something about him. I doubted many teachers walked around with screwdrivers in their back pockets, so now I had a new mystery to ponder.

Maybe he works in construction. A foreman? Architect?

I couldn't say why, but I'd always pictured him as a man in a position of responsibility. Of course I was also in a position of responsibility, and it was time to get back to it. I turned back to the mixer.

Dylan poked his tongue out the side of his mouth as he poured the batter into a cupcake pan, doing a decent job at it. Each mold was evenly filled, and he didn't spill much. After carefully placing the cupcakes in the giant oven, he shot me a big smile, his brown eyes lighting up. "My first cupcakes! I'll be honest, Liv. I'm surprised how much I enjoy this. I applied mostly because the hours are all in the morning and I need afternoons and evenings off."

I returned his smile. I'd noted the increased numbers of young women coming into the shop, no doubt attracted by my handsome young apprentice. I was only nine years older than Dylan, but I'd easily slipped into the role of mentor. "I'm glad to hear it, and I'm glad you applied too! Now, what shall we make next?"

We moved on to sugar cookies. Dylan had already made several batches and was gaining confidence with frosting them. I turned him loose to work unsupervised while I peeked at the baking cupcakes.

They looked perfect. Mystery Man had whipped my petulant oven into submission. I started to work on a peach-blackberry tart, wondering what I could add that would kick the final product up a notch.

Kiwi!

I grabbed several from my walk-in refrigerator and had peeled and sliced one when the front door opened again. A woman with honey-blond hair walked in, bringing a smile to my face. "April! Here for a morning sugar rush?"

April had moved to the area about the same time I had, almost a year ago. But we'd come from opposite directions. While she'd moved from St. Croix in the Caribbean, I'd fled from Boston, tail tucked firmly between my legs. We'd met at a monthly wine and book club we both attended. She was just a few years older than me and we had become friends. April became engaged late last summer, and I enjoyed the updates on her wedding planning.

I was more than a little thrilled that she'd asked me to bake her wedding cake. Though she and Gabe weren't planning a lavish wedding, Gabriel Markham was the eldest son of the most prominent family in this part of the Keys. The cake would undoubtedly help cement my reputation.

And my confidence, which had been in sorry shape when I'd first arrived.

I peeked at the case containing the remnants of this morning's donuts, then popped back up. "There are still a couple of apple fritters left. You want one?"

April shook her head and smiled. She worked as a divemaster for Calypso Key Resort. I couldn't imagine doing that job—just the thought of being responsible for other people underwater gave me hives. But as she met my eyes, her smile faltered, and she brushed her arm with one hand. "I think I'll pass this time. Do you have a second to talk? I actually came in here for a reason."

"Absolutely! Dylan can watch the counter, and the cupcakes in the oven have a while yet, so I've got plenty of time. Come on back."

April walked through the gap in the counter next to the wall and followed me through the bakery. The kitchen area took up most of the real estate, with counters lining both walls and several stainless-steel tables between. We passed the commercial oven, and I couldn't resist turning on the interior light to make sure the cupcakes were baking properly. They were rising nicely and developing golden tops.

My tiny office sat at the back of the shop, near the staircase that led to my second-floor apartment. The office had enough room for a desk and a small seating area, two chairs around a circular table. Several cake decorating books were scattered on top.

I gestured to a chair. "Have a seat. What's up? No problems with the wedding, I hope."

"Well..." April flopped onto the simple metal chair with a padded seat. "It's Hailey."

I eyed her sharply as I sat down. I'd met Gabe's nine-year-old daughter and liked her immensely. Plus, she held a very important position in the wedding. "Oh no! Is something wrong with her?"

April laughed and rubbed her forehead. "No. She's perfectly healthy. Last night, she sat Gabe and me down and explained that she didn't feel it was *age-appropriate* for her to be my maid of honor. That flower girl would be much more proper."

I joined her laughter, unable to resist. "Did she really say age-appropriate?"

"Oh, yes. I think she got cold feet about the responsibility involved, even though I tried to reassure her we were planning a very low-key event."

"Did you talk her into it?"

April arched a brow at me. "She's not Gabe's daughter for nothing. Once she digs in her heels, it would be easier to move a mountain. So now she's officially a flower girl. Which leaves me without a maid of honor little more than a month from the wedding."

My lips formed an O. "What are you going to do? Nix the attendants altogether?"

"I certainly hope not. Gabe's brother Evan is his best man. Which brings me to my visit this morning." Placing her hands together under her chin, April shot me a pleading look. "Would you consider being my maid of honor? I feel terrible—the last thing I want is you to feel like you're an afterthought, Liv! It really would mean a lot to me to have you next to my side."

Warmth spread through my chest as I gave her hand a squeeze. "I'd love to! And don't worry about offending me. I'm honored you asked."

April's shoulders dropped. "Thank you! I've been so worried about this I hardly slept. I promise it won't be too much work."

I waved her off. "Stop worrying! It'll be fun."

Apparently, April wasn't convinced. Her eyes were as blue as the sky outside, and now they narrowed with concern. "Are you sure you're not mad? When Gabe and I talked about attendants, you were the first person I thought of. Then Hailey agreed to do it. I really don't want you thinking you're second best."

I laughed, not at all put out. "Stop it, April! With Gabe's brother being his best man, I can understand why you'd want to keep the ceremony in the family. I'm delighted to swoop in and save the day."

April stood and held out her arms. We embraced, nearly the same height.

I gestured toward the front of the store. "Let's get back. Dylan's doing great, but I shouldn't leave him alone too long. And I need to watch the oven."

As we walked toward the prep area, April glanced at me. "Is your oven acting up again?"

I held a finger to my lips. "Shh! It'll hear you. Now I'll have to sacrifice a chicken or something. The oven was on the fritz earlier, but a handsome and talented customer got it working for me."

I peeked at the cupcakes once more, crossing my fingers that maybe the appliance was fixed for good this time. Dylan was back at his cookies, leaning over in his pink apron with a tube of frosting. His face was a study of intense concentration as he applied a ribbon around the perimeter of the cookie.

"Dylan," I said, holding my arms out from my sides. "I'd like to inform you congratulations are in order. I'm now April's maid of honor."

Straightening, he grinned. "Congrats, then. Guess you might be as busy at this wedding as April will be."

The divemaster laughed. "Yeah, that's true. You're in charge of the cake *and* the bride. You're sure you don't hate me?"

I shrugged. "Depends on how much of a bridezilla you turn out to be."

"Been around one or two of those?" April asked, grinning.

I shuddered, remembering my sister's wedding. "Yes, but I was kidding in your case. You'll be fine. Believe me, if there's something I'm an expert at, it's being a bridesmaid. I've been in several weddings."

"I'll talk to Gabe about us getting together for a drink so you can meet Evan. I'll give you a call with the details, okay?"

"Sounds good. I look forward to meeting him."

Which wasn't altogether true. Gabe was devoted to April and Hailey, but he was also shockingly handsome and intimidating. His brother was probably cut from the same cloth, which didn't fill me with confidence.

Oh well, we only need to interact for a month or so.

I saw April out the door and left it propped open. That helped the scent waft onto the sidewalk and bring passersby into the shop, following their noses. I smiled at the quaint Main Street my bakery stood on. Colorful shops lined the two-lane street, and slanted parking stalls lay on each side. Colorful hanging flower baskets hung from ornate lamp-posts. I sighed, pleased to be an important part of April's big day. As a soft breeze blew my curls off my shoulders, two tourists approached, holding hands. I held out my arm, ushering them into Sweet Dreams.

And if it was my fate to always be the bridesmaid and never the bride? I could live with that. I was living my dream, at home in a wonderful small town and answering to no one. Sweet Dreams was off to a successful start. Life was turning around for me.

I'll keep my suitors imaginary—why complicate things with a real man?

Chapter Three

Evan

AFTER WAKING UP, I took a quick peek out the window, then pulled on a T-shirt and shorts. I lived in the Big House, the Markham ancestral residence for the past one-hundred-plus years. I was the only resident with a bedroom on the first floor. A guest room lay next to mine but was empty.

Growing up, my room had been on the second floor with a nice view of the resort to the south. But when stairs became an impossibility for me at age nineteen, Dad had remodeled a cavernous old parlor into a bedroom with an adjoining bath, adding a state-of-the-art gym next door. The guest room had also been created at that time. I'd kept the first-floor room even though stairs presented no difficulties anymore, simply because the convenience was hard to beat.

As I walked out of my room, I gave the gym a passing glance. I still used it several times per week, and Gabe did too. Thinking about my brother reminded me of the text he'd sent last night after I'd gone to bed. Strolling down the hall, I pulled my phone from my pocket.

> Gabe: Can you meet me and April tomorrow evening at Conch Republic for drinks/dinner? She's found another maid of honor and we figured you guys should meet.

Conch Republic was a brewpub on the neighboring island just to our north, Dove Key, and popular with both locals and tourists. I had to grin as yesterday's memory popped into my mind. Gabe had flopped onto my office couch and issued a long-suffering sigh. He explained that Hailey had backed out of being April's maid of honor. April was planning on asking a friend from her book club and must have found someone. I answered back.

> Evan: Sure. I'll have to meet her sometime. I can be there at 5. That work?

> Gabe: We'll be there. Thanks.

My brows flew up at his quick answer. It wasn't even 6:00 a.m., but he was probably getting ready for a run. Both of us liked early morning workouts.

A gray cat with bright green eyes stood halfway down the hall, and I stopped to scratch behind her ears. "Hi there, Pilar. Hanging out on the first floor this morning, huh?" Purring, she rubbed along my legs. Pilar was strictly an indoor cat, but she had the run of our large home. Two other male cats roamed the rest of the Key, but both were neutered. Pilar would continue the bloodline of our cats, which were descendants of a six-toed feline gift from Ernest Hemingway to my great-grandfather. Pilar was kept safe and sound within the confines of the Big House.

Our expansive kitchen lay at the end of the long hall. One side contained the business end, and a mammoth dining table took up much of the other. Every week, a chef from Dorado rotated through to prepare meals for us. But this early, I had the place to myself. After brewing a cup of coffee into an insulated travel mug, I retrieved a large Thermos from a cabinet and filled it with tap water. Then I headed out the back door.

Calypso Key was roughly circular. The resort took up the southern half, and the Markham residences occupied much of the northeastern quadrant, perched on top of a bluff. Several two-bedroom family cottages sat in a row a short distance from the Big House. My sister Maia and her husband, Wyatt, lived in one with their daughter. As I headed south down the hill, I veered onto a sand path heading west. An extensive mangrove wetland on the northwest portion of the island had been left as nature intended.

A kiosk on the resort beach provided kayaks and paddleboards for guests to use, but I was headed elsewhere. I strolled down the path, pleased my leg was barely stiff, until I reached a small, muddy beach. My two high-end kayaks lay beneath a crude wooden shelter. One boat was sleek and light, the other much heavier. I'd added to its mass, placing lead weights at even intervals along the bottom, and the vessel was perfect when I wanted a hard upper-body workout.

After buckling my life jacket, I grabbed the rope attached to the lighter vessel's pointed bow and dragged it to the shore. The morning was quiet, and the air was nearly still as I paddled into the narrow opening between mangroves. I knew every channel and every hammock of the marsh. The current ones anyway. One of the things I loved most about the saltwater wetlands was how they changed from season to season and year to year. The shallow humps of land called hammocks emerged and retreated with nature's whims.

An osprey alighted from a tree above me, and I paused my paddling to watch the large brown-and-white raptor soar into the sky. The marsh was alive with wildlife, both above and below the water. Fortunately, I'd never seen an alligator. I resumed my course, weaving into smaller channels, which emptied into bigger ones. Eventually, I reached the circular lagoon that was my destination. The water formed a donut around a hammock rising above the marsh. The islet was more substantial than most, rising nearly ten feet above the shore, and was a permanent feature. Sometimes I liked to go ashore at a small beach, but today I continued around the land mass.

Ripples appeared in front of me, and I slowly lifted my paddle out of the water, holding my breath. As I coasted toward the disturbance, two manatees became visible under the surface. A giant smile cracked my face. A small group lived in the wetland, but I didn't see them every time I paddled.

Reaching into the kayak, I lifted the Thermos and unscrewed the cap. The largest of the three manatees approached and lifted his broad, droopy snout out of the brackish saltwater. The shape of his body was clear, an elongated gray blob with a tail that ended in a broad circle. Moving my arm to the side of the kayak, I poured water out of the Thermos and into the manatee's open mouth.

I stopped when he'd drunk half the Thermos. "Don't get greedy, big guy. Maybe the other two want a drink." This was Gray, one of two mature males in the area. Manny was the other and more adventurous than his brethren, even venturing into the canal near the dive shop sometimes.

When no more fresh water was on offer, Gray sank beneath the surface and drifted a distance away.

A smaller manatee approached and lifted its head out of the water. I recognized an old scar on her face. "Morning, Betty." I tilted the Thermos, and she deftly caught the stream of water in her mouth. Maybe I should feel guilty for giving them fresh water like this, but I didn't do it all the time. I figured anything that kept the slow, gentle mammals out of open water and boat traffic was a good thing. Each of these manatees bore long scars on their bodies from coming too close to boats.

Others weren't as lucky.

I appraised Betty more closely. "You look bigger than the last time I saw you. Is there going to be another mouth to feed soon?" I gave her the rest of the water, then she slid back under the surface. I screwed the lid back on the Thermos, and when I looked up again, the two manatees had disappeared. "Guess that was last call. I'd better head back too." Returning the Thermos to the bottom of my kayak, I turned around and paddled back to the landing where I'd started, my soul a little lighter.

An hour later, I returned to the house, showered, and dressed for work in khakis and a white Calypso Key Resort polo shirt. The spicy scent of cinnamon rolls tickled my nose as I entered the kitchen, but my heart did a flip-flop at the sight of my grandmother Nona seated at the table. Our mother had died giving birth to my youngest sibling Maia, and she had been as much a mother as a grandmother to us. Which apparently gave her the right to butt into our lives whenever she felt like it. I loved her to the depths of my being, but that didn't mean she didn't exasperate the hell out of me sometimes.

As I sat across from her, she picked up her coffee cup and nodded to me. "Good morning, Evan."

"Nona. How are you?" She wasn't a young woman, so my question wasn't just a pleasantry, though you'd never guess her age from her spry step and manner.

"I woke up this morning, so things could be worse." She had a penchant for western wear. Today she wore a white shirt covered with longhorn cattle and Wrangler jeans.

I laughed. "Nona, you're going to outlive us all."

"Any more updates with the chef wars?"

I poured a cup of coffee from the carafe sitting on the table as, at the other end of the room, chef Martin prepared my usual breakfast of eggs over easy and hash browns.

Too bad Martin can't take Alfonso's place. "No, Alfonso is following orders for once and leaving Rea to work in peace. She's back to her usual self again."

Nona smiled at me. "You're excellent with staff. It's not an easy job."

"Thanks. I like people, which helps. I dropped a pretty strong hint to Alfonso that he needs to up his game a little. He came up with two new specials, so maybe he's turning over a new leaf."

Nona just snorted and sipped her coffee. She knew him as well as I did.

"How about the little job I tasked you with? Months ago, I might add." She lifted her eyes to give me a very steady, appraising look. My heart sank.

Here we go.

"I might be a hale and hearty eighty-four, but I won't make eighty-five if I keep suffering disappointments like I experienced at my poker game yesterday."

I grasped at the weird subject change with both hands. "A run of bad luck?"

She grinned, and there was something slightly predatory in it. My grandmother was not someone to cross. "Not with the cards. I skinned Eloise alive, and now I have enough money to buy a new turquoise bolo tie. No, I was looking forward to our game so I could talk to Louisa Chatham. Since you mentioned you might ask out her granddaughter."

Shit! So much for the subject change.

I fought to keep my face bland and expressionless. I'd had a casual conversation with Lainey Chatham inside Island Market recently. Desperate to get Nona off my back, hers was the first name that came to mind when Nona had last broached the wedding-date subject. I'd blurted it out even though I wasn't interested in the woman in the slightest. But I'd underestimated the granny network.

Which was a grave mistake.

Once caught, trying to schmooze Nona wasn't an option. She was far too shrewd for that. "I changed my mind, okay? Lainey's nice, but she's not what I'm looking for."

Nona set her mug down with a thump. "What are you looking for? And how would you know it if you found it? Evan, your brother is getting married in a month. This wedding is a major family occasion. One you need to bring a date to. You can't show up stag—it wouldn't be appropriate."

I lifted a brow. "And the woman who *skinned her friend alive* is concerned with appearances?"

She returned my look with interest. "Yes. You don't need to be head over heels in love. Just ask someone out on a date, for heaven's sake."

I crossed my arms. "Fantastic! A pity date. No—even better. A pity plus-one."

"Oh, it wouldn't be like that! You're Gabe's best man, and I expect you to set a proper Markham example. But that's not why I want to see you with someone, and you know that."

"Yes, Nona. I do. Just as you know why I'm not interested in going out with someone who feels sorry for me."

I expected Nona to get angry or slather more guilt on, but she didn't. Instead, she leveled a sympathetic look at me and grasped my hand. Her skin was dry and weathered, yet her grip was strong, completely comforting. My chest tightened, and a lump formed in my throat. I took a deep breath, irritated at my reaction to her concern.

"Evan, you are the only one who feels that way. You are the most kind-hearted of my grandchildren. You're also a very good-looking man with a successful career. The only person who thinks you're not good enough is you. *Please* stop holding yourself back."

Sometimes it was hard for me to believe how athletic I'd been. How easy life had been with my future ahead of me. But all that had been *before*. "It's not that easy, Nona. I don't have a magic switch I can just throw to take the last decade away."

"Of course you don't, dear boy. But you just said it— your accident was a decade ago. More."

But how could I explain the effect those early years had had on me? How much I'd been shattered? I'd been the homecoming king, the guy everyone wanted. And in one day, all that had been taken away. I'd had to endure the pitying looks for years afterward, as I regained the ability to walk using hand crutches, then a cane. How all the girls who'd wanted to be with me now stared at me with pity.

I hadn't been celibate over the years since. But I'd only had quick affairs, mostly with guests I'd never have to see again. I wasn't proud of that, but at times I'd been desperate for human touch. An intimate touch, even if it wasn't emotionally intimate.

Nona leaned toward me. "Gabe has a new life, after he'd completely given up on love. Because he met the right woman. You deserve the same chance. That's all I'm saying. And stop building my request into Mt. Everest. I simply want you to ask a woman to accompany you to your brother's wedding. Any number of ladies would be thrilled to go with you."

Liv's face flashed into my mind. With her sweet green eyes and that mane of curly hair that fell in ringlets nearly to her waist. It was brown on the bottom and dark blonde on top. But just the thought of asking her out made my heart crash against my ribs. I couldn't risk the rejection.

Nona stood from the table. "Evan, as far as I'm concerned, you'd be the best thing to ever happen to any woman. The only thing that could make Gabe and April's wedding better would be to see you having a wonderful time there with your date." Then she walked out of the room, her cowboy boots echoing off the tile floor.

A heavy sigh rushed from my lungs.

How am I supposed to say no to that?

Chapter Four

Liv

BITING the inside of my cheek, I searched through my closet. What was the proper attire for meeting a best man who also happened to be a member of a major leading family? I blew out a nervous sigh. "I only have to interact with the guy for a few hours total. Really just the rehearsals and a dinner or two. Even if he's an ass, I can handle that."

I wasn't sure talking to myself while standing there in my bra and undies was a good sign. Gritting my teeth, I snatched a soft yellow dress with cap sleeves off the hanger and pulled it on. Strappy sandals completed the look. Wardrobe decided, I moved into my bathroom and frowned at my reflection. My hair fell in long, curly ringlets, and I groaned at the thought of April's sheet of flat, glossy hair.

What I wouldn't give to have straight hair!

But I wasn't about to waste money I needed for the bakery on an expensive blowout, so I pulled the hair around the crown of my head back with a silver barrette. After living in Florida for a year now, my hair had developed a two-tone look I rather liked. The effect was enhanced by having the topmost layers contained and cascading down my back. I applied light makeup, then marched out of the bathroom and through my bedroom.

I emerged into a large open room containing my living room and a small, modern kitchen. My apartment was directly above the bakery, accessed by a set of interior stairs at the back of the shop. I loved the convenience.

After tossing my purse over one shoulder, I headed down the stairs. Emerging through the bakery's rear door, I unlocked my Chevy Tahoe and climbed in. The SUV got terrible gas mileage, but its tall, voluminous cargo area was a godsend in my line of work.

All the businesses fronting this side of Main Street shared this same paved alley, with access to Main Street between the buildings. Several stores shared the same layout as Sweet Dreams, of the shop on the bottom floor and a residence above. Others used both stories for their businesses. Pulling out, I made two left turns and was back on Main Street and heading east. I stopped at the only traffic light in town, staring at Island Market to my right and a dive bar named Salty's across the street on the left.

I'd never been in the tavern. It looked seedy to me and not someplace I'd be comfortable in. Dove Key was larger than its cousin Calypso Key and contained many quaint businesses. Sunset Siesta Resort was located on the west end, as well as a fairly substantial residential district. The light changed, and I continued down Main Street. After half a mile, my destination came into view.

Conch Republic Brewpub perched on the edge of a tall bluff. It was housed inside an old cannery, its gray, corrugated metal walls stretching for a considerable length. I opened the heavy wooden door and entered, where the industrial theme continued. The dining section took up half the area, and the bar and lounge the other, with exposed ductwork spanning the voluminous area overhead.

April had told me to look for them in the bar, and my heart fluttered as I stepped across the concrete floor. I paused near the bar until I saw April's face inside a booth against the open window. Two male heads sat across from her. I recognized Gabe's dark hair, and the lighter-haired man next to him had to be Evan. Taking a deep breath, I headed toward them.

As I neared, April glanced up and a smile burst across her face. "Here she is!" She scooched over to make room for me while gesturing across the table. "I'd like to introduce you to Gabe's brother. This is Evan."

I automatically reached my hand out as I started to slide into the booth. I froze halfway, a smile pasted to my face as my pulse soared. There was no mistaking it. He had the same warm blue eyes. The same bushy beard and light-brown hair, and the rugged good looks.

I was staring at Mystery Man.

His mouth hinged open, his face slackening. Our eyes met and held, with mine no doubt reflecting the shock that was clear in his. Then he quickly recovered and flashed the warm smile I knew so well. Reaching out, he shook my hand. His was warm and calloused, the hand of a man used to working with his hands. "Hi, Liv, I'm Evan. Nice to finally introduce myself officially."

I dropped onto the padded seat, bouncing up and down a couple of times as I tried to regain my composure. As the implications of this hit me. "Hi, Evan. Good to finally put a name with the face." Heat flashed over my cheeks.

My sweet schoolteacher/construction foreman crush is

Evan Markham? The man who manages the most prestigious resort in the Lower Keys?

April watched me closely, a line forming between her brows. "Wait a minute. You two already know each other?"

"Not really," I said with a laugh. It came out warbly and nervous, so I cleared my throat quickly. "Evan comes into the bakery, so we recognize each other. We've never formally met."

"Oh? Oh!" April's eyes became round, and her smile reappeared as she put the pieces together. I'd told her about my mystery man. Then she turned her gaze to her fiancé, and her delight became replaced by suspicion, her eyes narrowing. Evan turned to give Gabe the same look.

The elder Markham brother's face was carefully blank. "How about that?" he asked blandly. "You two already know each other. This whole get-together was for nothing."

Several expressions flitted across Evan's face: irritation, embarrassment, and as he dropped his eyes to the beer in front of him, shyness.

Gabe broke into a grin as he turned his attention from his brother to me. "You two should get along great. Evan's a big fan of yours, Liv. He brings your donuts in all the time. Considering the resort has its own pastry chef, that's a serious testament to your skill."

Evan's face was as bright red as mine surely was. At least he had the full, bushy beard to cover some of it. He peeked at me before dropping his eyes again, shifting in his seat. "You're a really good baker. I like your pastries better."

Well, that explained why he visited Sweet Dreams, and I had to admit I felt proud. "Thank you very much. It's hard to start a new business, so I appreciate every donut you buy."

Evan lifted his glass and took a long drink, refusing to meet my eyes. "The beer's on you, Gabe."

April still stared at Gabe pointedly and he gave her a slow wink. Obviously, something was going on here, but I had no idea what. And I got the feeling Evan didn't either. The situation almost felt like a blind date, except that neither Gabe nor April knew that Evan and I had already met.

Right?

April squeezed my knee under the table and turned to Evan. "Liv is a transplant from Boston. Hated the winters there."

He met my gaze, then shot me a fleeting smile. "I can understand that."

I was slowly overcoming my shock and warming up to his shyness. If anything, he was shyer now than in the bakery, hardly able to look at me.

Or maybe he was hoping I'd be someone else?

That was probably it. Well, I could at least be pleasant to the man and not further his disappointment.

Think of something clever to say, dammit!

"Are you not a fan of snow either?" I asked idiotically.

My embarrassment softened slightly when Evan's smile widened. "I wouldn't know. I've never seen the stuff in person."

Apparently, Gabe thought the conversation had veered enough into the ditch and came to our rescue. "Did you have your own bakery in Boston?"

Gabe was darkly handsome, with mysterious dark eyes and a perpetually trimmed, five o'clock shadow. Glancing back and forth between the two brothers, it was hard to see a resemblance except in their shared broad shoulders and muscular build.

I nodded at Gabe. "I did... but it was hard to get a toehold in such a competitive area. I tried to make a go of it, but the time came when I couldn't deny the truth any longer. If I stayed there, I was sunk."

Every word I said was the truth. Just not the whole truth.

Not by a long shot.

"How did you end up here, anyway?" April asked me.

"I watched a travel show about the Keys and was enchanted. In the section about the Lower Keys, they showed Main Street on Dove Key, and it was so pretty! The colorful shops, hanging baskets, and people strolling along." I relaxed, a little more at ease now as I inclined my head at the two men. "And they mentioned Calypso Key Resort, of course. But that street kept running through my mind. I couldn't imagine a more perfect location for my shop. So I did some research and saw there wasn't a bakery on Dove Key."

Evan nodded. "The last one was near Conch Republic. The owner retired several years ago and sold the place. It's a café now." His voice was warm and rich, like melted caramel.

I took a sip of beer, concentrating on my story to get over the shock of meeting Evan. "I packed up my belongings, which weren't much, and drove down here. The premises where Sweet Dreams is located was for sale, so I bought it on the spot and hunted down all the furniture and appliances from a bakery going out of business in Key West."

April patted me on the back. "And you've been a success since day one."

I laughed. "I wouldn't go that far. It's been challenging.

But I imagine you two know all about the difficulties of owning your own business."

Evan straightened, his shoulders relaxing. "Ask big brother here. I just manage the place. He's the one who loves dealing with the money."

"The entire area is doing well," Gabe said. "A rising tide lifts all boats, and all that."

I nodded, not believing Evan's self-deprecating comment for a second. "I've gotten busy enough to hire an employee. Now my biggest obstacle is an oven." I smiled at Evan.

He returned it. "It's still acting up?"

I'd burned a cake the previous day, but after adjusting the oven temperature downward, it was cooperating for the moment. "I wonder if there's a short in a wire somewhere. Or something else—I'm starting to suspect the damn thing might be possessed by a demon, though I'm not sure which one. When it breaks down, I never know whether to call a repairman or a priest."

A round of laughter went around the table, but April was still frowning at her fiancé. "Don't rule out archangels either. They're more devious than people think."

Gabe's grin widened.

As I laughed, Evan met my gaze again. His lips rose in a smile. Then the expression fell just as quickly. He rushed his glass to his mouth once more.

My excitement dimmed. I couldn't tell if his reaction was shyness or dislike. I tried to ignore the heavy disappointment twisting in my stomach.

Oh, well. Even if he doesn't like me, he's still polite. I can live with that.

April poked me in the arm. "I need to go to the ladies' room. Come with?"

"Sure." I bounced my gaze between the two Markham men. "We'll be right back."

We rose, and April manhandled me away from the table, marching me toward the restrooms at the back. As soon as we entered the deserted bathroom, April spun me around. "Evan is your secret crush? Really?"

That hot flush rushed over me again. Getting involved with one of the shining sons might be fine for April, but she didn't have my history. And I couldn't figure out Evan's reaction to me anyway. "Yeah. I had no idea who he was. Did you know about this little meeting?"

April was already shaking her head before my sentence finished. Then she lowered a brow. "I didn't put it together at all, but I'm thinking Gabe might have. I'll need to question him later. But back to you! What do you think? Are sparks flying?"

I needed to backpedal fast. Mystery Man wasn't a schoolteacher. He wasn't a construction foreman. He was *Evan Markham*. "He's very nice, but I've got too much going on with the bakery to get involved with someone. And he doesn't seem interested anyway."

April gave me a long look in the mirror, then brushed several strands of hair with her fingers. "Evan can be hard to read. He's sweet and a little shy, but he keeps his cards pretty close to the vest." Then she met my eyes in the mirror. "Sure you don't want me to try to fix you up? Best man, maid of honor. Sounds perfect to me."

I laughed to cover my embarrassment. No way would I risk that. Evan was a sweet, nice guy, and I needed to count my blessings. "I'm sure. You're the star of the show here, not me. Come on. Let's get back."

Wrapping my arm firmly around her shoulders, I marched us out of the ladies' room.

Chapter Five

Evan

AS SOON AS the two women were out of hearing range, I rounded on Gabe. "Goddammit, you knew all about this, didn't you? You set me up!"

Gabe's grin turned into a full-blown laugh, which only pissed me off more.

"Relax!" he said. "I had my suspicions, but you can thank Maia for this little pow-wow. She's been dying to get you two together for months after she realized you were crushing on Liv. I told her not to bother April with any schemes, and amazingly, I think she listened to me."

I snorted. "Yeah, that sounds like our lovely little sister. And judging from the dark looks April was sending your way, you might have some explaining to do there."

Gabe waggled his brows. "I'm looking forward to it."

I took another long swig, then set my pint glass down with a hard thump. "You made me look like an idiot."

"I did not. And in case you didn't notice, Liv looked a little stunned at first too."

She was probably disappointed.

"I don't need to be set up. I'm perfectly capable of asking out a woman if I'm interested. So just drop it." Of course Liv made me so tongue-tied I could hardly look her in the eye. Why would a woman like that want me?

Gabe held out both hands, palms up. "Okay. I have no interest in turning you into an episode of *The Bachelor*. But you two needed to meet, anyway. You're both in our wedding, remember?"

"No shit, Sherlock. I suppose you expect me to give a speech?"

Gabe's grin returned. "We haven't decided. If you do, that means Liv will have to give a speech also. I'm not sure April wants to put her through that, given how guilty she felt after Hailey backed out. So you might be off the hook."

I gave him a begrudging smile. "I'm really happy for you, Gabe. But lay off the dating pressure, okay? Nona is bad enough."

He swallowed his beer and broke into a wide smile. "Nona's worse than the rest of the family combined."

That made me laugh out loud. "Good thing we love her so much."

I caught sight of Liv and April walking back from the bathroom. Liv's full lips were turned up in a smile, and the dress she wore flattered every one of her curves. I might need to put a lid on my attraction to her, but I was pretty happy we'd be spending some time together.

I elbowed my brother. "Behave. The women are coming back."

"I always behave. You're the troublemaker."

I snorted. "Hardly. Growing up, I never had time to get into trouble."

And when I finally did have the time, it was too late.

THE NEXT MORNING, I ambled down the hill. Passing the Barn, I glanced at Gabe's extensive wood shop deep within, where he made furniture for the resort. Next, the path crossed a broad meadow dominated by several flame trees, all alight with orange blooms. I focused on the building ahead and to my left, a long one-story structure with a red-and-white dive flag flying overhead.

Skirting a canal cut into the eastern edge of the island, I studied the calm waterway. We owned three resort boats. The two main charter boats, one for fishing and the other for diving, were out already. The third, our backup boat, sat tied up. I veered off the cement path and onto a brick walkway that led between the dive shop and equipment building.

Maia's butterfly bush stood on the corner of the dive shop, in a dormant phase. But buds were visible, and it would soon burst into an explosion of lavender and dark-purple blooms. The scuba gear room and tank storage rooms were shut up tight, and I pulled open a glass entry door to my right.

After Gabe moved back, I turned over the managing duties of the dive shop to him. But my eye still panned over the displays of wetsuits, buoyancy compensation devices, and resort T-shirts to ensure all was in order.

A baby's soft coo sounded to my right. A smile rose on my face as I crossed to my sister Maia, who stood in front of the glass counter, rocking her daughter, Skye, in her arms. Carissa, our dive shop employee, stood behind the counter and smiled brightly at me. Twenty-five and with curly brown hair tumbling over her shoulders, she'd worked for us for several years. Despite my irritation at her telling Rea about my fondness for Sweet Dreams, I'd never outed her about Rea's reaction and likely never would. As general manager, I picked my battles, and Carissa hadn't done anything on purpose to cause trouble.

"Good morning, you guys," I said, then glanced at my sister. Like Gabe, she had the traditional Markham features of height coupled with dark hair and eyes. Her long hair was pulled back into a ponytail, probably to keep it away from prying young hands. Skye was now four months old. She had her mother's dark eyes but her father's light-brown hair. Wyatt worked as a divemaster for us. "You're not working today?"

Maia shook her head. "Wyatt and April are. I'm taking his group tomorrow morning, though." She was back to work, leading dives part time. She and Wyatt traded off shifts, so one of them could watch Skye. "I was just talking to Carissa about ordering a new line of UV-resistant shirts. You want to hold your niece?"

Nodding, I took the baby from her. At first, I'd been terrified to hold the tiny infant. But after I'd managed it several times without breaking her, my confidence grew. Now I felt like an old hand. Bouncing Skye gently in my arms, I walked slowly to the other end of the dive shop, where a flat-screen television cycled through a slide show of underwater images.

The baby watched the screen, slowly blinking. I held my index finger next to Skye's hand and she wrapped her tiny fingers around it. When Gabe's daughter Hailey had been born, I hadn't been able to travel to Miami to visit them. So Skye was really the first baby I'd ever been around.

"Look at you," Maia teased as she approached to stop next to me. "You might just get uncle of the year honors."

"Don't tell Gabe that. Though on second thought, he'd

probably rather be father of the year. Skye might have another cousin before too long."

Maia smiled and clapped her hands. "I hope so! April would be a great mom, and we already know Gabe's skills in the dad department." April and Maia were good friends, and Maia had been responsible for April moving to Calypso Key when my sister had become pregnant and couldn't dive.

I shot Maia an assessing look. "Just keep me out of your musings, okay? Gabe told me that little ambush at Conch Republic was your idea."

Maia's eyes became round and filled with angelic innocence. In other words, she was completely guilty. "What do you mean?"

I rolled my eyes. "Cut the crap, Maia. Nothing's going to happen between Liv and me."

Her face fell, her bottom lip poking out. "Why not? Liv's a nice person, and so are you. The two of you needed to meet. That's all there was to it, Evan!"

I arched a brow at her. "Sure. Liv and I will be spending some time together—we have to. But I don't want you meddling in my life. And I sure don't want you making her uncomfortable." I handed my niece back to her. "I'm happy with my life just the way it is. If that changes, I'll act."

Maia reached over and brushed my arm. "I know, and don't worry. I'll be perfectly behaved around Liv. Though I can't promise some comments about how dashing my brother is might not cross my lips."

I groaned, then both of us laughed. "Just try to contain yourself. That's all I ask," I said. "I need to get to the lobby. Unlike you, I actually have work to do."

Maia stuck her tongue out at me as I turned away, and I pretended not to see it.

My office was at the end of a long hallway stretching away from the lobby. *Evan Markham, General Manager* was inscribed on a plaque hanging on the door. The office wasn't fancy, really just a plain white box. But because it was in the corner, I was able to boast of having two windows. As I sat behind my large wooden desk, my eyes fell to the autographed baseball sitting on its stand near the back edge. I picked up the ball with its two scrawled signatures, tossing it from hand to hand before carefully putting it back. I had mixed emotions about that ball—it was both a treasured souvenir and a bitter, painful memory.

But dwelling on the past was never a good idea for me. Waking my computer, I went to work filling out the first of three performance appraisals on my schedule for the morning. All thoughts of the baseball on my desk faded from my mind.

Chapter Six

Liv

THE SAVORY SCENT of popcorn filled my nose, and the evening air was warm, welcoming. A pastel-perfect hue of lavender washed across the western sky and took my breath away. The crowd around me burst into cheering as the batter launched a long fly ball into right field, bringing my attention back to the game. The fielder caught it on a hop and hurled it to first base, but the batter narrowly beat the throw. I rose to my feet with everyone else, my heart taking flight as Dylan stepped to home plate.

"You can do it, Dylan!" I clapped so hard my hands hurt.

The runner at first was the speediest player on the Hammerheads development team and took a healthy lead. The pitcher gave him a long look before throwing a slider toward Dylan. The bottom fell out of it, and he took the pitch. Ball one.

As the pitcher wound up again, the base runner took

off. He slid into second well before the second baseman caught the catcher's throw. The crowd stomped rhythmically. It was the bottom of the ninth inning, and the Hammerheads were tied.

Dylan had pitched a great game before giving up four runs in the fifth inning. But his bat had kept the team in it. He stepped back in the batter's box, swung, and missed a fastball.

"Oh, so close!" I murmured to myself. "He almost had that." I felt a little self-conscious being at the game alone, especially since my sponsorship came with two seats. I glanced at the empty seat next to me.

Maybe I'll ask April to come next time.

Alone or not, nothing could diminish my pride at seeing the large pink banner hanging in left field, and my eyes returned to it.

Sweet Dreams... Where fine confections are always served with a side of paradise! On Main Street, Dove Key.

A sharp crack brought me back to the game as Dylan launched a frozen rope past the shortstop and into center field. The runner at second took off and the third base coach waved him home as Dylan rounded first. He slid into second feet first, but the outfielder was aiming for home plate. He was too late, and the Hammerheads won the game. With the other home-field faithful, I broke into fresh cheering at the happy outcome.

As I filed out of the stadium, I looked forward to discussing the game with Dylan tomorrow at work. He was a solid batter but dreamed of being a pitcher. Hopefully, the instructional season would set him on his way. It was after 9:00 p.m. when I opened the back door of the shop and climbed to my apartment. Much too late for a woman who got up at three most mornings, but worth it.

As I flipped the switch just inside the door, my living room remained dark. I groaned and trudged back down the stairs. Opening the breaker panel, I confirmed my suspicions. The upstairs breaker had tripped again. Second time this week.

"Stupid thing." I reset it and shut the door, pointing a finger at it. "Behave yourself, okay? I can't afford any more repairs."

As I slid into bed, a gentle lassitude swept over me—the happiness of owning a business I loved and starting a new life. A meaningful life. Evan had come into the bakery a couple of days ago, and this time we'd smiled and greeted each other by name.

He was my mystery man no longer. But in all my fantasizing about him, I'd never once seen him as a successful manager of a top resort. Or part of a leading, important family. He might be out of my league romantically, but maybe a friendship could work.

Smiling, I drifted to sleep.

I WAS HAVING one of those weird dreams where I knew it was a dream, yet I couldn't wake myself. I wandered down a series of blank hallways—the floor, ceiling, and walls all a featureless white metal. The hallway was completely silent, absorbing my footsteps. I found it progressively harder to breathe, and my vision dimmed. Panic clawed at my stomach, and I had to resist the urge to run. I waved a hand in front of my face, trying to see through the white haze that obscured my vision. And seared my parched throat.

I dropped to my hands and knees, a vague memory coming back that this would help me breathe. Except it didn't. I reached all around me, but I couldn't find the walls anymore. I was all alone and lost in the white, choking void, and I couldn't even get enough air to scream.

I sat up in bed as a harsh, choking cough ripped from my chest. My bedroom was dark, but there was enough light to see the swirls of nebulous smoke drifting through the room. Except the thick fumes were black, not white.

And they were real.

Fire!

I rolled out of bed and onto the floor. Unlike my dream, this did help me breathe easier, but I continued to cough and hack. Tears slid down my face from the irritating smoke, and my eyes stung as if lemon juice had been poured into them. Fumbling my way to my nightstand, I grabbed my phone and crawled to the window across the room. I took solace that the carpet under my hands was cool.

Glancing toward my shut bedroom door, I couldn't see any flames, just the nauseating, suffocating smoke billowing around the cracks between the door and frame. But I wasn't about to open my door and check. I had only one priority.

Out.

Lifting onto my knees, I heaved open the window. It stuck halfway. I placed my shoulder under the bottom sash and pushed up with my legs, a burst of adrenaline giving me an energetic surge. The window screeched open all the way.

I clambered out onto the fire escape, sending a silent thanks for municipal fire codes, and wiped my eyes to see better. Still coughing, I shuffled down the metal stairs, still barefoot and wearing the oversized T-shirt and terrycloth shorts I'd slept in. Black smoke billowed out the open window above.

Once I safely reached the asphalt ground, I dialed 911. Distant sirens became audible as I reported the fire.

"Yes, ma'am," said the dispatcher, his voice calm and reassuring. "Someone in the neighborhood saw smoke coming from the first-floor windows and already called it in. The fire department is en route as we speak. Please step away from the building and retreat to a safe distance."

I coughed convulsively and spat a wad of gray phlegm on the ground, wincing. "Thank you. I'll do that." Carefully picking my way down the sidewalk, I peeked at the lane between my building and the one next door, which housed a two-story antique store. I couldn't see flames anywhere.

"I'm happy to stay on the line with you until the first responders arrive."

"No, I'm breathing better now. I'll head to Main Street and wait there."

After ending the call, I turned on my camera flashlight and tiptoed down the dark lane toward the street. I still hacked and had to stop once to dry heave, resting with one palm pressed against the wall of the antique store. As soon as I reached Main Street, I craned my head to the left. Dark smoke wafted out both broken windows at the front of Sweet Dreams, billowing into the black sky above.

My breath caught as a whole-body shudder wracked me.

How could my dream be going up in flames?

"Liv! Oh, thank God!"

I turned around to see Brenna Coleridge running toward me. She owned Bookshop in Paradise across the street. She swept up to me and wrapped me in her arms. We were friendly but not close. Brenna was a few years younger than me, but now she took charge as she gathered her long brown hair in one hand and flipped it over her shoulder. "I was up late reading and saw the smoke! I called nine-one-one but had no idea if you were inside or not."

"I was asleep—" I had to stop for a coughing fit. "The smoke woke me, and I got out through the fire escape."

The sound of sirens amplified as a red fire truck turned off Calypso Causeway and onto Main Street, its lights flashing. Brenna wrapped her arm around my shoulders and steered me across Main Street, where we huddled in front of her bookstore. The night was warm, but I shivered, shock rolling through me.

The fire truck stopped in front of Sweet Dreams, and a group of firefighters scurried out. They uncoiled hoses and attached one to a nearby hydrant as an ambulance pulled to a stop near us. A woman with kind brown eyes opened the door as the ambulance came to a stop.

Brenna waved to get her attention. "Liv was inside! She inhaled some smoke."

The paramedic hurried over and took my hand while she placed two fingers of her other one against my wrist. "It's going to be okay, Liv. My name is Linda. Let's just make sure you're doing all right."

Like a child, I allowed Linda to lead me to the back of the ambulance, where her partner had opened the back doors. He was inside, setting up medical equipment on a tray while Linda helped me sit on the back edge. The effort made a new round of coughing come on, deep, booming whoops that felt like my lungs were trying to come out through my mouth.

Linda placed the earpieces of the stethoscope she wore in her ears and pressed the bell against my chest. She listened as I tried to breathe and not cough, then turned to her partner. "Her pulse is rapid, and her breath sounds are a little diminished." She turned back to me. "We need to get you to the emergency room in Marathon and get you looked at."

I shook my head. "No. I'm okay—" I stopped to cough again. "I have to know what's going on with my bakery." I weaved my upper body but couldn't see the shop from this vantage.

Linda placed a calming hand on my shoulder. "They're putting the fire out, so there's nothing you can do. Except take care of yourself. The fire captain over there is a friend of mine. I'll make sure he gives you an update as soon as he knows something, okay?"

Nodding weakly, I waved goodbye to Brenna as I entered the back of the ambulance and lay down on the stretcher. Her forehead was lined, but she waved back as the doors slammed shut.

SEVERAL HOURS LATER, the emergency room doctor entered through a gap in the closed curtain and stopped next to my bed. "Your breathing is much better now, and your lungs are pretty clear. I think it's safe for you to go home. But if your breathing worsens again, call nine-one-one—that can be serious."

Go home.

As if that were some simple thing.

The fire captain had stopped by my curtained bay an hour ago and explained the fire was out. The flames had been contained to the back of the prep area, near the breaker panel, but smoke permeated the entire structure. He suspected the panel was the cause of the fire.

Sweet Dreams was out of business, and I was homeless.

I smiled bravely at the doctor, an older man with gray

hair and a confident, reassuring manner. "Thank you. I'll call someone to come get me."

But who?

I'd texted Dylan just to tell him not to come in to work, and that the shop had to close unexpectedly. He hadn't answered, though I didn't expect him to during the wee hours of the morning.

And I didn't exactly want to call my employee for help now. Brenna's face flashed into my mind. She'd been so kind, and she might have saved my life. But I felt I'd already imposed on her enough. Glancing at my watch, I winced when I saw it was 2:00 a.m. I knew only one person well enough to call in the middle of the night. I had no idea if April would pick up, or if she silenced all calls during the night.

My shoulders sagged when she answered, her voice thick with sleep. "Hello?"

"Hi, April. It's Liv."

Now she was more alert. "Liv? Are you all right?" An indistinct, deep voice came from the phone as Gabe woke up too. She shushed him.

I glanced at my bare feet. "Well, yes and no. The good news is I can speak without coughing or choking. The bad news is I'm sitting in the emergency department in Marathon because Sweet Dreams caught on fire earlier tonight."

"*What?*" Muffled whispering came across the phone as she told Gabe the news.

I laughed, but it was bleak. "Yeah. You heard me. So the upshot is I've been cleared to go home, except I don't have a home to go to."

And just like that, I started crying.

"Oh, sweetie!" April called out soothingly. "You just

hang tight. Gabe and I will be right there. He's already getting dressed."

"Thank you. I'm sorry I'm such a pain in the ass."

"Don't even think that! Do you have any clothes?"

"Just the shorts and shirt I was sleeping in. Shoes would be nice."

April covered the phone, and I couldn't make out her and Gabe's words. Then she spoke to me. "We'll drop Hailey at Maia's. Hopefully, Maia will have some clothes you can wear. I don't think mine will fit you."

Maia was considerably taller than April or me, so that might work. I had no doubt that April's clothes wouldn't fit my curvier figure. "That's perfect. Thank you."

"We'll be there in half an hour."

They didn't even take that long. When they entered my curtained bay, both of them showed the effects of getting ready in a rush. Gabe's normally neat hair stuck up and April's was tousled around her shoulders. I'd never been so glad to see two people in my life.

This time I held it together when April embraced me. "I'm so glad you're not hurt!"

"I had some smoke inhalation. They gave me some nebulizer treatments and other medication, and it cleared me up. Other than the scratchy throat, I'm okay. I've always wished I had a sexy voice, but this isn't what I had in mind."

April handed me a canvas bag of clothes Maia had put together and I went into the bathroom to change. A tight tank top would work as a makeshift bra, and the dive staff shirt wasn't a bad fit at all. The shorts were a little tight over my hips, but I could still breathe in them. I slid my feet into a pair of flip-flops, relieved they were only a little big.

I returned to my room and stuffed my sleeping clothes

back in the bag, still moving slowly and feeling dazed. "The clothes fit great. I'll be sure to thank Maia."

"We have plenty of empty rooms at the Big House," Gabe said. "We'll take you back there."

I spun around at the thought of being ensconced in the huge Markham home. "Oh, no! I couldn't. I'll just... get a hotel or something."

April frowned at me. "Don't be silly. You'll do no such thing. We'd offer you something in our apartment in the Barn, but Gabe's idea is much better than our lumpy couch."

"It's no imposition. I promise." Gabe's voice was warm and put me slightly at ease. "We have a guest suite on the first floor. You can use that until you have a chance to form a plan."

Reluctantly, I agreed. I couldn't exactly afford a hotel stay.

And they did offer...

Less than an hour later, Gabe opened the side door of the three-story stone, cinderblock, and timber structure. He ushered April and me in, and I found myself in a huge, dark kitchen. Gabe padded across it, and we followed, with April behind me. He turned and walked down a long hallway, taking care to keep his footfalls soft.

"We need to be quiet," he whispered over his shoulder. "Evan's room is right next to the guest room, so I don't want to wake him."

My stomach gave a small jolt at that.

Three closed doors lay at the end of the hallway, one in front of us and the others facing each other. Gabe opened the one on the right, flipped on the lights, and ushered us in. After I shuffled inside, he gently closed the door behind us.

The bedroom was large, with a king-sized bed made

from solid wood and a seating area on the other half of the room. The décor was a palm tree motif, done in a sophisticated, upscale way. A large palm tree was screen-printed on the comforter, and others graced the many pillows on the bed.

Gabe pointed to two doors on one end of the room. "There's a walk-in closet and the bathroom through there. The other door by the seating area leads to a private patio."

I turned to give him a shaky smile. "Thank you. It's beautiful."

"Can I get you anything to eat or drink?" April asked.

I shook my head, nausea rolling through me. "No. I just want to sleep for a week."

"I'm sure you do," Gabe said. "Feel free to sleep as long as you want. April and I are both working on *Shark Bait*, so we won't be around in the morning. The kitchen is at the end of the hall on the left. When you get up, a chef can make you breakfast."

My shock must have shown on my face because April smiled. "Don't worry, it's standard operating procedure. Chefs from one of the resort restaurants rotate through the Big House to cook meals for the family. You won't be putting anyone out. I'll text you in the morning, okay?"

After assuring April I didn't need anything else, she and Gabe filed out of the room, leaving me alone. I sat on the bed, listening to the silence around me. Padding to the bathroom, I found double sinks and a large, tiled shower. I opened a door in the vanity and discovered a sealed toiletry kit all ready.

I guess having a resort does have its advantages.

Brushing my teeth was heavenly.

The sheets were cool and very crisp as I slid between

them. I wasn't at all sure I'd be able to sleep, but I finally relaxed. I was safe.

I was under no illusions that I was still in shock, but some of the numbness faded. When I remembered Evan was asleep on the other side of the wall, I relaxed further. My tense-as-iron body unfurled like a sleeping bag, and finally, I slept.

Chapter Seven

Evan

I RESET my alarm clock and skipped my morning weight routine, too tired to get up. My night had been restless, full of uneasy dreams of whispering mice in the walls. A shower woke me up and I changed into khakis and a staff polo with my name embroidered on it. Returning to my room, I sat on an armchair to pull on a pair of boat shoes. My room was fairly utilitarian, containing a king-sized bed and seating area. All the bedrooms in the house had been remodeled to include full en suites. I didn't have much by way of decoration on the wall. Just a watercolor painting of a baseball diamond I'd picked up at a craft fair on Dove Key a few years ago.

But hanging that picture had been a big step forward. To be able to once again look at a baseball diamond, if only in a painting. Marathon now had its own minor league team, the Hammerheads, and I was even feeling the itch to go watch a game.

A smile rose on my face as I ambled down the hall toward the kitchen.

Maybe Nona's right, and it is time to move on.

As I neared, soft female voices reached me, Nona and someone else I didn't recognize. I turned into the kitchen and was surprised to see Nona sitting in the chair at the head of the table. Dad usually sat there. Then I shifted my gaze to the woman next to her and stumbled to a halt.

Liv gave me a tired smile. "Good morning, Evan."

"Liv?" Her name came out as a croak.

She wore a blue Calypso Key Resort dive staff shirt, which was odd, and her eyes were dull and tired. That curly mane of magnificent hair was wet and twisted into a large clip on the back of her head. "I imagine I'm the last person you expected to see in your kitchen, huh?"

After absently nodding at chef Felicia that I wanted my usual breakfast, I took a seat across from Liv. Nona's bowl of oatmeal was gone, but Liv's breakfast was hardly touched.

My grandmother turned to me. "The night has brought us a guest. Liv had a rather unsettling experience last night."

I poured a cup of coffee from the carafe on the table, raising a brow as I did so.

Liv barked a laugh and shook her head. "Remember when you warned me about getting someone to look at the breaker panel?" Her voice was scratchy and rough.

"Yes..."

"I should have listened. It caught fire last night. The whole shop did. I was asleep in my apartment upstairs and was almost overcome by smoke before I got out."

I dropped the carafe and Nona darted out a hand to right it.

Without thinking, I reached across the table and took

Liv's hand. "Are you okay? Do you need to go to the doctor?"

My stomach did a little flopping thing when she squeezed my hand before letting go. "I already have. I was taken by ambulance to the ED in Marathon. I'll be fine." She explained about Gabe and April picking her up and bringing her to the guest room. "But Sweet Dreams might be another story."

"How bad is the damage?"

"I'm not sure. Last night, the fire captain said they put out the flames quickly and most of the destruction was due to smoke. He told me he'd check back this morning and see what it looks like in daylight."

"If it's mostly smoke damage, that might be easier to repair," Nona said, then pushed to stand. "I'd better get going. But know you're welcome here, Liv. We'll do whatever we can to help you get back on your feet."

"Thank you, Nona. That means so much to me."

After she left the room, Liv picked up her fork to move some eggs around on her plate. She set it down again without eating and tapped the cell phone next to her. "I'm waiting for Levi, the fire chief, to text me back about when he plans to inspect the building." She looked up and met my gaze. I swallowed reflexively at the exhaustion in her green eyes. "I've seen a Calypso Key Resort shuttle around town. Can I catch that to get a lift into town? My car is still at the bakery, and hopefully drivable."

Felicia set a plate of eggs and hash browns in front of me, and I smiled in thanks before turning my attention back to Liv. "Don't be ridiculous. I'll take you myself."

"Thanks, but I'm sure you have better things to do. You look like you're dressed for work."

I waved my fork absently as I ate a mouthful of hash

browns, then swallowed. "I'll call the front desk manager and tell her I'm available by phone if necessary. The resort won't crumble if I take off for a while."

Liv's phone pinged on the table. She picked it up.

"That Levi?"

She nodded. "He says he'll be at the shop around ten a.m. That's less than half an hour. Does that give you enough time?"

"Plenty." Though I doubled down on my breakfast. "Did you get any sleep last night?"

She shrugged. "A little. I was exhausted and wired at the same time. But the room is lovely, and I'm very grateful for the help."

I smiled and pushed away my mostly empty plate. "You already said that. And you're welcome. Let's go meet Levi."

After I led her to the other end of the house, we entered the garage. I pressed the opener of one stall, and the door rose behind a Calypso Key Resort pickup truck.

Liv peered around the six-stall garage. "Wow. This is huge. But it's not exactly filled with Ferraris and Lamborghinis."

I laughed as I took in Dad's one-ton pickup, my Explorer, and the resort truck. The other bays sat empty. "Yeah, we're not too fancy here. Gabe has a Mercedes convertible, but now even he's driving a truck more often than not."

I pulled onto Calypso Causeway and headed toward Dove Key. Liv kept fussing with her hair, unclipping and reclipping it. I gripped the wheel harder, trying to concentrate on her state of mind and not the fact that she sat a few feet away from me. As I turned left onto Main Street, she leaned forward in her seat. Her hands were clasped, and the pads under her nails became whiter the closer we got. My gut clenched, but I was tongue-tied again, so I remained quiet.

Sweet Dreams wasn't far down the street and easily recognizable. Except now, black streaks marred the pink façade, running under two broken windows. Yellow caution tape was strung over the sidewalk and wrapped around two *Caution: No Entry* sandwich boards standing in front of the bakery.

Liv's face was pale and the devastation on it made my heart feel heavy in my chest. As I pulled to a stop, I turned to her, determined to speak up. "Hey. It'll be all right. It might not seem that way right now but have faith." She gave me a brave smile that twisted my heart even more.

"I'll try."

Movement in the rearview mirror caught my eye as a Dove Key Fire Department pickup pulled to a stop behind me. A man my age got out as Liv and I exited my truck.

Running a hand over his trimmed blond hair, he sent me a curious look. "Hey, Evan. How are you?"

"Better than Liv, I'm sure." I stepped forward so we could shake hands. "Good to see you again, Levi."

She glanced between us. "You two know each other?"

Levi, wearing a crisp blue uniform shirt and black slacks, smiled. "We went to school together. This is a small town."

"Right. I keep forgetting that." She took a step toward the shop. "Shall we get to this?"

The fire captain stepped forward and held out a palm. "I'll go in alone. You two can look in the door, but you need to stay outside until I check everything out. We clear?" He shifted his gaze to me as Liv and I both nodded.

The firemen had placed a metal hasp across the front door and padlocked it shut. As soon as Levi unlocked it and opened the door, the thick, acrid smell of smoke intensified. Liv swallowed audibly and took a step back.

"You okay?" I asked her quietly. "Should you stay away from the smoke?"

She shook her head and moved forward again. Standing side by side, we peeked through the entry as Levi made his way through the shop. He carried a crowbar, using it to tap and bang on walls and the staircase.

Liv gasped as she stared inside with wide, haunted eyes. The glass display case was shattered, and soot covered every surface. Blackened, misshapen lumps scattered across the floor were all that was left of the pastries that had been inside the case. I moved my gaze to the ceiling, examining it closely. Though discolored, it was fully intact, and so were the walls, except for a large scorched area near the breaker panel. My tense shoulders relaxed slightly.

"Oh my God, it's ruined," Liv said in little more than a whisper.

I wanted to put my arm around her shoulders but was afraid that would be too forward. So I just gave her shoulder a squeeze. "The ceiling looks fully intact, and the walls are in pretty good shape. This is better than I expected."

She whipped her head to me, the desire to believe clear in her eyes.

I shot her a smile I hoped was reassuring. "Really. From here, it looks pretty restorable, but let's wait for Levi's assessment."

"Do you have experience with fire damage?"

"Not in a major way like this. But over the years, I've seen a lot at the resort, including cleaning up after hurricanes. I do a lot of the repairs around the place myself. I love fixing things."

A tiny smile twitched the corner of her mouth. "When

you looked at the oven, I wondered why you kept a screw-driver in your back pocket."

I pulled out the tool I nearly always kept there and shrugged. "It comes in handy more often than you'd think. Your bakery will need more than a few turns of a screwdriver, but I don't think it's beyond saving. Hopefully, Levi says the same."

The fire captain slowly climbed the staircase, tapping the wooden risers with his crowbar. He stopped and kneeled to examine the wall section between the breaker panel and the staircase, reaching with the pry end of the bar to dig into the damaged drywall and studs.

I nodded to him with my chin. "He wouldn't be going up to the second story if he was afraid the floor might collapse."

"This is going to be so much work to clean up."

I tried to be encouraging. "That's why restoration companies exist. Your insurance should pay for them to clear out the debris as well as the construction crew that will make Sweet Dreams as good as new."

After several more minutes, Levi returned to the first level and headed toward us. He moved more quickly now, stepping confidently. Stopping before us at the front door, he turned to Liv. "The building is structurally sound. But you need to get the windows boarded up ASAP and keep the door locked. You never can tell what people will try to steal. I'll give you the key to the padlock we put on last night."

"Is my apartment habitable?"

Levi shook his head and gave her a sympathetic smile. "Structurally sound but not livable. Even if you like the goth look. A county building inspector will have to sign off before anyone lives here or it opens back up for business, and I'm sure your insurance company will have their own requirements too." He ran two fingers around the edge of the shattered window, then wiped the soot on his uniform pants. "Thanks to Brenna's call, we caught the fire early. The entire interior will need to be painted, and the drywall and studs will have to be replaced near the breaker panel. The carpet upstairs will have to be replaced, but as far as fires go, you got off pretty lucky. Let me know when you get the windows boarded up and I'll send one of the guys to take down the caution tape and signs."

"Thanks, Levi," I said as we shook hands. "That's good news, all things considered."

He nodded. "You two take care." After shaking Liv's hand, he drove off in his truck.

I sighed and stared at the two broken display windows. "Let's head to Big Pine Key and get some plywood from the hardware store."

Liv drew her brows down as she studied me. "You don't have to do that. I'll take care of it."

I grinned. She couldn't be more than five-foot-four. "Really? You're going to manhandle and hang full-sized sheets of plywood alone?"

Biting her lip, she turned her attention back to the window and winced.

My stomach did that floppy thing again as I nudged her shoulder with mine. "Liv, I want to help. That's why I drove the truck. I figured we'd be picking up some supplies."

Her eyes became glassy as she met mine. "That's very kind, and I could use a hand. I really can't thank you enough."

Once again, I had a strong urge to take her in my arms and comfort her. But I settled for just giving her a quick touch between her shoulder blades. "Don't mention it. We wedding attendants have to stick together, don't we?"

After a shaky smile, she got in the passenger seat, and we drove to Big Pine Key, which contained the nearest hardware store large enough to have what we needed. I had a moment of hesitation when we checked out with our four-by-eight-foot plywood sheets, wondering if I should reach for my wallet. But Liv still had that dazed, lost look on her face, and I figured she'd feel better knowing she was solidly contributing to the cleanup. She didn't hesitate to reach for her credit card when the cashier recited the total.

The big toolbox in the bed of the truck contained a hammer and nails, and between the two of us, we had the windows boarded up in no time. Just as Liv was pulling out her phone to contact Levi, her text tone sounded.

"Oh, no. It's Dylan. What am I supposed to tell him?"

My heart sank at the word *him*, then I reconsidered. If she was involved with someone, wouldn't she have called him last night? "Who's Dylan?"

She slumped back against the wall of the store. "My employee. Maybe ex-employee now."

"He knows about the fire?"

She nodded and wiped her brow, leaving a smear of soot. I resisted the urge to lick my thumb and wipe it away.

"I called him this morning before you got up. I told him I'd give him an update later." She clenched her eyes shut and sighed. "He helps support his mom and needs his job. Except I don't have any work for him. Hell, I don't have any work for myself!"

I started pacing back and forth along the sidewalk as an idea worked itself out in my head. Liv stared at her phone, her frown deepening. Finally, I stopped and turned to her.

"I might be able to help with that. You need a commercial kitchen, right?"

Brow lined, she nodded.

"Well, we have two. One has an area specifically designated for baking. Our pastry chef works there now by herself. I'm sure she could make room for one more." I firmly pushed away the memory of how mad Rea had been when she discovered I'd been buying donuts from Liv. "I'm sure I could find work for Dylan in the resort somewhere."

Liv stared at me, her face unreadable. "Why are you being so nice to me?"

That made me smile. "This isn't Boston. We help each other around here."

A returning smile stretched her lips. "Thanks. That still doesn't solve the problem of having nowhere to sell my goods."

We were making progress. I could feel it. "Minor detail. How about we set up a pop-up bakery in a corner of our lobby? That will benefit the resort too. People will come in to buy your pastries and see how amazing Calypso Key is. Then they'll think of us when it's time for their next vacation. See? Win-win."

Laughter tumbled out of her mouth, warming my heart. She shook her head. "All right. We'll see what we can figure out. I still don't understand why you're doing it, though."

I shrugged, still smiling. "Because I feel like we've become friends. This is something a friend would do."

And if friends is all we can be, I'll take it. Anything to keep spending time with her.

She held my gaze. "Thank you, Evan."

"You're welcome."

"Is it really all right if I crash in your guest room?"

"Yes! Stop asking. What about Dylan?"

She started pacing, mirroring my movement from a few minutes ago. "Even using your kitchen and opening the pop-up shop, I won't have the income to pay an employee. Do you have a coffee shop? He's a great barista—makes better coffee than I do."

"We do. It's called Local Grind, and it's always popular. A lot of guests don't want a full breakfast, just a coffee and something light. He could help you in the early hours, then move over to the coffee shop for the rest of his shift."

She shot me a measured look. "Again, you're not getting much out of this."

I folded my arms and grinned as I leaned against the sheet of plywood. The rich scent of fresh lumber filled my nose, overcoming the sooty smell. "Oh, yes, I am. A fully trained barista who comes with a glowing reference. People who come into Sweet Dreams could grab their coffee from our coffee shop. Besides, this might be the perfect chance for my pastry chef to learn some of your secrets."

She tipped her head back and laughed. "Not a chance of that, mister." Then she rolled her head to smile at me. "I'll only produce baked goods and will tell patrons they have to get their coffees from Local Grind. You're a good guy, Evan Markham."

"Yeah, well, soon enough you'll meet our chef, Alfonso. He'll be happy to tell you differently."

She pulled out her phone and placed the call. "I'm *fine*, Dylan. Really. And you're not going to believe the news I'm about to give you..."

Chapter Eight

Liv

AFTER ENDING my call to Dylan, I gave Evan a weary smile. "Thanks again for your help, but I can take it from here. I doubt anything in my apartment is wearable, so I need to head to a discount store to do some clothes shopping." I did not want to spend a lot of money on clothes right now.

Evan stared at me evenly. "Where are your car keys?"

"Upstairs, on the table next to my door."

He gestured with his head. "Let's go inside, then. I want to look things over and make sure you get your keys safely."

A mixture of frustration and gratitude swept through me at his concern. I hated feeling dependent and needy, but Evan had proved as stalwart and dependable as men got. "The fire captain said it was."

Evan shrugged and gave me a tiny smile as he stepped through the front door. "I know. But I just want to make sure for myself."

I followed him as he picked his way through the ruins of

my bakery. I couldn't hold back a smile when he warned me about glass on the floor, which was *everywhere*. We peeked out the back momentarily to confirm my Tahoe was undamaged from the fire. It was covered in a fine layer of soot but otherwise undamaged. The stairs were reassuringly solid beneath my feet, though discolored, and the door to my apartment stood ajar at the top.

Evan's neck craned around, never still as he evaluated the staircase. He tapped the walls and entered my apartment. I took a deep breath and followed.

I'd always enjoyed the abundance of natural light my apartment displayed from multiple windows. But now it was a dark, sooty cave. The pungent smell tickled my throat and made me wrinkle my nose. Swallowing hard, I dropped my gaze to the table next to me and picked up my car keys with a jingle. "Here they are. If you'll lock the padlock on your way out the front door, I'll just use the back door from now on."

Evan twisted around. "Are you sure you're okay?"

I stared at my ruined apartment, my insides hollow and twisting. He deserved an honest answer. "I'd say I'm doing as well as can be expected, and I'm sure it hasn't fully hit me yet. I'll see if anything in here is salvageable, then drive to Calypso Key after my shopping trip."

He stared at me for a long moment before answering. "All right. I'll head back and let Rea, our pastry chef, know she's going to have some company tomorrow."

"She won't mind? I'm kind of invading her turf here."

Evan shrugged. "Not really, and it's not permanent. Besides, it isn't her kitchen. I'm the boss, remember?"

"Lucky for me. I'll see you later." He brushed my shoulder as he passed by. "Evan."

He turned back at the top of the stairs.

"Thank you. I really mean that."

"You're welcome. I really mean *that*."

Then he was gone, and I was left with the embers. No windows had broken on the second floor, so I didn't need to deal with broken glass. However, cloying gray soot permeated everything inside my apartment, along with a choking smoky smell. I entered my closet and nearly gagged. My clothes looked gray and dingy, and nothing in here was wearable at the moment. I wasn't sure if professional dry cleaning would be able to get the smell out of my wardrobe.

"Well, that's an experiment, and bill, for another day. Off to the store."

As I passed by my office on the way out, I remembered an unopened box filled with new uniforms. So at least I'd have a clean smock to wear, along with aprons and hats for both Dylan and myself. I placed the box in the back of my SUV and opened the cardboard top, then took a big sniff.

Not too bad. One round through the laundry, and these should be good to go. After slamming the hatch shut, I moved to the driver's seat and headed toward Marathon.

Discount Mart was hardly an upscale shopping mecca, but I had anything but an upscale budget. With my main priorities being price and functionality, I purchased several sets of shorts, pants, shirts, three dresses, and several pairs of shoes. Firmly drawing the line at a six-pack of grannie panties, I found a package of high-cut hipsters that would work. Their bra selection wasn't extensive, but I found two plain bras, one beige and one white, that would do the job.

Armed with shopping bags in both hands, I returned to my SUV and added them to the cargo area. On the way to Calypso Key, I called my insurance agent and reported the fire, thankful I'd gone with a local agency with an office in

Big Pine Key. My agent had already heard about the fire and started the paperwork involved in opening the claim.

"That's great news," I said as I drove across the causeway to Dove Key. "A friend is helping me with a backup kitchen and temporary premises, so I might be back in action sooner than I thought."

I eased off the main road and headed toward the Big House. Ample parking was available without blocking the garage, and I wasn't about to park inside, no matter what Evan or anyone else offered. Grabbing my shopping bags, I hesitated at the path leading to the front door. My guest suite had a private French door leading inside from the patio, and I wasn't at all comfortable using the front door of the massive house. So I edged around the end of the manor and unlocked my door. Soon all my new purchases were laid out on my bed with the tags cut off. I chewed my lip.

I need to wash these before wearing them, but I could search for hours and not find the laundry room in this place.

Squaring my shoulders, I stepped into the hallway. The door to Evan's room was shut, so I headed down the hall-way. The kitchen was empty, and after poking my head into a sunny library, I found a housekeeper dusting an end table. She promptly showed me the laundry room located just off the kitchen, and soon I was feeling a bit more settled as I tossed my new purchases in. Returning to my room, I sat in a padded chair on the patio and stared at the manicured grounds around me. Something was forming deep in my belly. Something that had been missing before Evan joined me to evaluate the shop.

Hope.

I've got clothes to wear, a bed to sleep in, and food to eat. I even have a chance to keep Sweet Dreams going. Things could be a lot worse.

THE NEXT MORNING, Evan and I walked down the concrete path toward Orchid. He opened a solid door on the back of the building and ushered me in ahead of him. The kitchen was typical of most restaurants I'd seen—expansive, bright, and gleaming. To our left, a young woman stood at a stainless-steel counter, smoothing a fruit layer on top of a cheesecake. Finishing, she glanced up at us. "Good morning."

Evan stepped forward. "Hi. Rea, this is Liv."

With a deep breath, I nodded and gave the baker a smile. Evan had told me he'd informed Rea yesterday about my crashing her kitchen, but I still wasn't expecting a warm reception. So I'd be friendly from the start. "Thank you so much for sharing your space, Rea. I promise I'll keep out of your way as much as possible. This arrangement is a real lifesaver for me and my business."

She eyed me steadily for a long moment, then her expression softened. "You're welcome. I was pretty surprised when Evan gave me the news, but if I were in your shoes, I'd be pretty shaken up too."

Evan gave me a quick tour of the kitchen, pointing out the parts that were executive chef Alfonso's private domain and strictly off-limits. Then he informed Rea that I'd be starting bright and early the next morning.

"I'm only planning on making a few varieties of donuts and cookies the first couple of days," I said with a shrug. "No point in going all out if no one buys them."

Rea nodded. "How are you getting the word out about everything that's going on?"

"Social media. I've posted on Facebook and Instagram about the fire and pop-up shop here. My posts have gotten lots of responses and been shared a lot, so tomorrow will tell."

"Speaking of which," Evan said, beckoning me as he headed toward the door. "Let's head to the lobby. I'll show you what I was able to scrabble together."

"See you tomorrow, Rea." My tone was upbeat, but she only nodded in response. Her gaze followed Evan, a curious, slightly puzzled look fixed on her face.

Walking back into the sunshine, we threaded our way between two guest cottages and toward the lobby building. "Dylan showed up this morning?"

"Right on time," Evan replied. "I processed his new-hire paperwork myself and he's in general resort orientation right now."

The fact that Dylan would continue earning a steady paycheck was one less thing I needed to worry about, and I had no qualms he'd be a great hire for Evan. I just hoped he wouldn't be too great. I laughed. "Hopefully, he'll come back to me when I'm able to pay him again. I'd hate to lose him."

Evan shot me a grin as we climbed a short flight of steps and entered the bright, cheery lobby. "I don't think you need to worry about that. I get the feeling he kind of worships you, especially after ensuring he still had a job."

He pointed to the left corner of the lobby, and we headed in that direction. Four glass display cases had been set up to form an L-shape, with ample space behind them to work. "These are some display cases from our buffet restaurant we replaced a few years ago, but we kept them in storage. The compressor to keep the temperature cool doesn't work, but that shouldn't matter for donuts, right?"

I stepped into the area behind the displays. "Not at all. Everything I'll make to start will be room temperature.

Evan, this is amazing!" A small display table next to one case would function as a check-out counter.

"I couldn't find a cash register, though." He pointed at the empty table.

"I'll just use a metal lockbox for cash and an app on my tablet to process credit cards. Most people are cashless these days anyway." I'd paid a printing store extra for a rush job on two Sweet Dreams banners, which would fit perfectly on the front of the glass cases, as well as some other promotional display items. They promised to have it ready by this afternoon.

"Can you think of anything else you need?" he asked.

I shook my head, slightly dazed as I glanced around. Island Market would deliver my baking ingredients to Orchid later this morning, so I wasn't even experiencing a hitch in my supply chain. Finally, my gaze settled on Evan's handsome face and bushy beard. His kind eyes. Small town or not, I could hardly believe he was willing to go to such lengths to help me. "This is perfect. I'll send anyone who wants coffee to Local Grind."

Calypso Key Resort's coffee shop was located around the corner from the lobby, just off Dorado restaurant. The knowledge that the resort was sure to benefit from the additional coffee orders the pop-up shop would hopefully bring made me feel slightly less guilty about all he was doing for me.

Evan glanced at his watch. "I've got a meeting in a few minutes, so I'd better get going. See you at dinner tonight at the Big House?" I paused, and he tilted his head. "Was last night too overwhelming?"

Yesterday, it had been late afternoon by the time I'd finished my laundry and I was starving. April finished work and helped me put away my new clothes, then invited me to dinner, where all the Markhams were in attendance. Including Evan, Gabe, and Maia's father, Warren. He was a handsome older man with a warm nature and had made me feel welcome. The entire family had welcomed me.

But somehow that didn't make me feel any less out of place. Though I couldn't hide out in my room and eat alone, either. I smiled at Evan. "A little more boisterous than I'm used to, but I enjoyed it. As long as you all don't mind, I'd love to eat with you."

"The more, the merrier. Nona loves a big crowd at dinner. Especially since she doesn't have to cook it."

I laughed. Upon meeting me yesterday morning, Evan's grandmother had quickly covered her shock. She'd been funny and gracious, and I got the distinct impression not much got by her. "This afternoon, I have appointments with my insurance agent and with a contractor to tour the building. That should get things rolling on restoration and give me a timeline. Hopefully, I won't be in your hair too long."

"I'll keep my fingers crossed for you."

After a final nod goodbye, he crossed the lobby to the hallway containing his office. I watched his slightly limping retreating form, momentarily curious if his unbalanced step was from an injury, or if he'd been born with a gait impairment. But I didn't want to intrude by asking him about it, and it didn't matter anyway. I'd rather concentrate on how lucky I was that Evan had walked into Sweet Dreams that first day.

And I was even more lucky that he was now my friend instead of my mystery man.

Chapter Nine

Evan

I RUSHED OUT of my office, tearing down the lobby steps and along the path toward Orchid. Moving fast made my limp worse, but I gritted my teeth and soldiered on. Rea's text had been worried, begging me to come quick. And when *Rea* was worried, that demanded action from me. Liv and Rea had worked out a schedule over the previous week, getting along well as Liv settled into her new surroundings. Alfonso had pretty much ignored them both.

Apparently, that had changed.

I opened the kitchen's back door and stopped just inside the threshold. Alfonso leaned back against a stainless-steel counter, his arms crossed and his lip curled as he stared down at Liv. She stood inches away from him, jabbing her finger in his face. Bright red from the neck up, she glowered at the chef.

"We're not hindering you in any way, shape, or form, you idiot!" Liv yelled.

Alfonso saw me enter and raised a brow at me. "You see

what I must put up with? This is harassment. I wish to lodge a formal complaint against this... *verme*."

Liv gasped. "Did you just call me vermin?"

"No. It means worm."

I stepped forward before things escalated further. "Stop it. Both of you. Alfonso, you're too damn old to be insulting people in Italian when you know they don't speak the language."

"I graciously rearranged my schedule for Rea's benefit." He tipped back his head and looked down his long nose at me. "But I will not do it for a second interloper."

"You don't have to!" Rea screeched, standing next to Liv so both were in Alfonso's face. "We're both working the same hours."

"And you are both disturbing my section of the kitchen, despite your promises not to." Alfonso turned to me. "I cannot work like this. Either they go or I do." He threw the towel he'd had tossed over one shoulder onto the counter and stormed out.

Rea narrowed her eyes at me. "Can he really leave? Could we be so lucky?"

"He still has a year left on his contract," I replied. "If he breaks it, it'll cost him a pretty penny."

"What about if you break it?" she asked.

I rubbed the back of my neck. I'd run that scenario through my head countless times over the past year. "Same thing, Rea. That's why they're called contracts. You're supposed to fulfill them. What is going on here? I thought you three were getting along."

Liv slumped and briefly scrunched her eyes shut. "I didn't want to bother you with it. I've handled plenty of difficult coworkers in my time, including primadonna chefs. But that guy takes the smallest little bump and turns it into

Mt. Everest. I used some of his cardamom and forgot to put it back. He threw a fit. I'm sorry, okay?"

Internally, I rolled my eyes at Alfonso. "He's very particular about his kitchen. And he's not going to quit. Give him some time to cool off, and he'll be okay."

"What about us, dammit?" Rea stood in front of me with both hands on her hips.

"You've been getting along with him, Rea, and Liv just needs to figure out the rules."

Liv sighed. "It'll only be for another month or so. I met with the contractor yesterday. They've already got the shop and apartment cleaned out and are starting the remodel. He says it should be done within four weeks. I can keep my cool until then."

Rea scowled. "Evan, your sister is a chef at one of the most famous restaurants in Key West! Why is that idiot here instead of her?"

My sister Stella had been a sous chef at Blue Nirvana for years and now handled all areas of the kitchen, an accomplished and talented chef herself. I'd love for her to take over Orchid. "She likes it in Key West. The last time I brought it up, she wasn't interested." But with Alfonso's contract expiring next year, I planned on putting the thumbscrews to her if necessary.

Rea took off her hat and ruffled her hair. "I'm going to take a break and walk on the beach. If I run into Alfonso, I'll probably push him in. Just so you know."

"Thanks for understanding, Rea," I said as she headed toward the door. "He can be difficult, but we're stuck with him for now."

Sunlight streamed through the door as she opened it. She turned back. "I know you can't just replace him on a whim. But please tell me there's at least a chance you won't renew his contract."

There was more than a chance, but I didn't want to say that out loud. "It might be mutual. He's been talking about another television show."

"Whoop dee do." Rea softly closed the door behind her.

Smiling, I turned back and was surprised to see Liv staring at me with sad eyes. "I'm so sorry, Evan. You've been so great to me, and this is how I repay you. By blowing up at your chef."

I strolled over and leaned back against a workstation, so we faced each other. "Don't worry about Alfonso. It's hard not to blow up at him. At least you and Rea get along."

"We tiptoed around the first couple of days. Maybe that's why I didn't pay much attention to Alfonso's side of the kitchen. I was concentrating on getting along with Rea. You manage staff really well. Everyone gets to have their say, yet you don't take sides."

"Thanks. Most of the time, it's pretty easy. But some days are a bit of a trial."

My heart warmed when she smiled. "I'll apologize to Alfonso when he comes back and promise to take more care. I really don't mean to cause problems, even if he is unreasonable. I'm the guest here."

"You're more than that." I wanted her to be much more but couldn't bring myself to say it out loud. Every day we spent together, I liked her more and more. Noticed little things about her—how she scrunched her nose when she laughed and gathered her hair in one hand and twisted it when she got too warm.

"You Markhams are a big clan. I saw that family portrait in the living room. You looked around ten years old in it. Is Stella older or younger than you?"

"Three years older. She's between Gabe and me in the birth order." I glanced around the spotless kitchen. "Growing up, she always hung out with the chefs. None of us was surprised when she went to culinary school. And she's got a very prestigious position."

Liv nodded. "I've heard of Blue Nirvana. Very difficult to get into."

"She's part of the reason it has the reputation it does."

Liv cocked her head. "There was another boy in the family photo. He was about your age. Is there another Markham brother?"

The air was sucked out of the room. Pain flared in my right knee—completely psychological pain, but that didn't make it hurt any less. I opened my mouth, but nothing came out.

Liv's smooth brow wrinkled. "Oh, dear. Did I do something wrong again? I'm sorry."

Finally, I found my voice. "No, of course not, but it's a difficult subject. That boy is my brother Hunter. He isn't really part of the family anymore. He hasn't been home in years."

She watched me closely, and I had no doubt she could see how stiffly I stood. "I'm sorry to hear that. But at least you have lots of loving family close by, don't you?"

My shoulders felt like they were full of rocks, and I forced them to relax. "Lots of family. I try to remind myself how lucky I am to have them so close, and it helps. Most of the time." I softened my words with a smile. She returned it, though hers was hesitant.

Liv moved to the mixer and picked up a large Mason jar filled with brown pods. "I'd better return this cardamom and get back to the shop. It's time for Dylan's meal break. I hope Alfonso won't actually leave."

I waved at the door absently. "He threatens to quit at least once a week. He'll be fine."

With a final apologetic smile, Liv slid out the doorway. After rubbing my face with both hands, I followed. Squinting from the bright sunlight, I panned my gaze around the area until it stopped on Alfonso. He stood a short distance away, puffing on a cigarette.

Reluctantly, I headed toward him. Seeing me approach, he stepped onto the cement path and stubbed out his smoke, which pleased me. He was well aware of my thoughts about smoking, but since he was well away from the building, I couldn't stop him.

The chef eyed me evenly. "I've kept my end of the bargain. I don't come in before noon. Those bakers are taking too long."

And you don't own the goddamn kitchen, do you? But I bit the words back. "They aren't required to finish at any particular time, and both of them are using this time to prep for tomorrow. When you start at four a.m., having things ready to go is a rather good idea, you know."

"That is none of my concern. Knowing where my supplies are located is."

I nodded. "Liv apologized for that and promised it won't happen again."

He snorted. "If it does, I will not be so easy on her next time."

Oh, goody! I can hardly wait.

He shot me a side-eye. "I will require two days off next week to meet with my agent in Miami. Is this sufficient notice?"

His sous chef and everyone else in the kitchen would probably do cartwheels and throw confetti at the news. "Of course. Any leads on a new series?"

Alfonso gave one of those casual shrugs Europeans seem born to make. "I cannot say. Edward is making inquiries but has said nothing specific. Now I must prepare for tonight's service." With a nod, he marched back to the kitchen like a gargoyle descending upon a cathedral rooftop.

I took a more leisurely pace as I strolled along the path toward the lobby. The ache in my knee had subsided and the stiffness in the leg was barely noticeable. Motion in the nearby meadow caught my eye, causing me to pause.

Dylan, now on his lunch break, stood alone throwing a baseball into a small net target. A few days previously, I'd seen him out here with one of our dishwashers, the two of them playing catch. But he looked more serious today, and I changed course toward him. He was pitching at the target, not tossing the ball casually at it.

I studied his form as I neared. He held the ball in his right hand, adjusting his grip. Then he wound up and launched a circle change at the netted target about sixty feet away. But his grip was wrong, and it slammed into the ground five feet in front of the net and bounced in.

"Shit," he murmured under his breath, then saw me and straightened, his face going carefully blank.

Ignoring his curse, I gave him a friendly smile. "Working on your changeup? A man with a good change is hard to beat."

Dylan couldn't hide his surprise. "You recognized my pitch?"

"I used to dabble in baseball when I was younger."

Yeah. Dabble.

He picked up one of several balls lying at his feet and threw a respectable fastball that fell neatly in the net.

"Nice," I said.

"My fastball is okay, and my curve is coming along, but

my changeup needs work. I'm in the developmental lineup for the Marathon Hammerheads, and I'm trying to get selected for regular season tryouts."

My jealous pang only lasted a moment, which was definite progress. "Congratulations. How are you gripping the ball for your change?"

He showed me, and I adjusted his first two fingers slightly. "You're opening your chest too much and collapsing. Try it with the different grip and keep your stance tighter. Your changeup has to look exactly like a fastball to the hitter."

Dylan nodded and followed my instructions as he threw his next pitch. It made a pleasant whoosh as it landed dead center in the net, noticeably slower than the fast ball that had preceded it. He whipped his head to me. "How did you do that?"

I laughed. "I didn't, remember? You did."

His expression became calculating, his eyes narrowing. "What does dabbled mean, anyway?"

"It means I used to play ball about a thousand years ago. In high school."

Before my life fell apart.

"Were you good?"

I shrugged. "For a teenager, I was okay."

Dylan broke into a sunny smile. "Decided to stay in Calypso Key, huh?"

I pasted a smile on my face as bile rose in my throat. *Nope. Not going there. That was an innocent question, and he's a nice kid.* "It's not such a bad place, is it?"

Dylan laughed as he picked up another ball. "Not bad at all. I can definitely see the appeal of staying here." He threw a curveball, but it didn't break enough and barely made it into the target.

"Keep working on your pitches, and maybe you'll get your chance." I clapped him on the shoulder. "And stop collapsing forward. That will make a big difference."

"Thanks, Evan. If you notice anything else, let me know. Okay?"

"You got it."

I turned around and headed toward my office, surprised to discover working with him on his pitches gave me a warm feeling inside. I could see myself giving him some casual coaching.

Shark Bait had just tied up in the canal. Gabe and April stepped off it together and he draped an arm around her shoulders as they headed toward the dive shop. I heaved a long sigh and murmured, "All I have to do is get through the next month without Nona driving me up the wall any more than she already is."

Because I still hadn't thought of anyone to ask to the wedding. Other than the obvious choice, anyway. Problem was, Liv was already going.

Chapter Ten

Liv

LATE THAT NIGHT, I had trouble sleeping. In many ways, my fortunes were turning around wonderfully. Sweet Dreams Mini was up and running, albeit in a reduced fashion, while the real thing was on the road to reopening. I had a place to stay and was warmly welcomed where no one expected anything in return.

That was the problem.

I felt like a freeloader.

It really hit me this afternoon when I blew up at Alfonso. I hadn't realized Rea had called Evan to intervene until he showed up to defuse the situation. Abashed, I'd swallowed my pride and apologized to the horrible chef, promising to use more care. I got the feeling Evan might have talked to him, because the chef, though not warm to me, wasn't smug and sanctimonious either.

Maybe after I get the bakery up and running again, I'll hold some sort of fundraiser for Calypso Key, offering a weekend stay as a grand prize or something.

I sighed, rolling onto my side but still wide awake. Soft moonlight filtered in through the blinds, throwing slats of pale light on the wooden floor.

I'm not going to get to sleep. Maybe some warm milk?

It was just past 10:00 p.m., which while not late for normal people, was anxiety inducing in me. After throwing back the covers, I put on some leggings and a long-sleeved Henley. As I padded down the hallway, low, tense voices drifted toward me from the kitchen. Evan and Nona.

I flattened myself against the wall just short of the entry, reluctant to disturb them.

"Evan, I have stood by your side and supported you for over a decade now." Tension dripped from Nona's voice. "Your brother's wedding is the perfect opportunity for a new start. For you, not just him."

"I understand that, okay?"

I was frozen in place. I had a strong suspicion this was a conversation I was not supposed to be eavesdropping on, but I couldn't make myself move.

Nona's voice softened. "Dear boy, you have the biggest heart. There's someone who deserves to have you share it with her."

Evan groaned. "Are you speaking in generalities, or do you have the lucky lady picked out already?"

I peeked around the corner, trying to stay invisible. They sat at the table, Evan facing away and Nona on his right. She sat sideways on the chair with most of her face visible. Neither could see me.

She leaned closer. "Are you giving me a choice? The wedding is only a month away! Why is this such a difficult task?"

Evan straightened, his shoulders broadening even more as he folded his arms across his chest. "It's not! Fine, I guess a guy isn't allowed any privacy in this town. I have a date. In fact, I'm in a relationship. Are you happy now?"

My heart twisted, disappointed at his news, though not surprised. Anyone would be lucky to be involved with Evan. My hand pressed harder against the wall.

Nona reared back in her seat. "Really? Who?"

My vision narrowed on Evan's shoulders, which grew tighter with each second. "Liv."

My jaw dropped to the floor. My heart stopped, then took off at double time.

What is he talking about?

Nona cocked her head, studying her grandson. "Really? A romantic relationship between you two is news to me."

Join the club!

My pulse still raced, and my hand bunched closed against the wall. I opened it, pressing my palm against the cool surface. Why was he making up this story about us?

Evan raked a hand through his short hair, leaving furrows in it. "It's new—we haven't told anyone yet. Liv and I have been spending a lot of time together since she moved in, and things just... happened between us."

"Well, I can understand that. You're both attractive people, and you make a handsome couple together." Then Nona's expression changed, becoming thunderous. "Evan Markham! You didn't take advantage of that poor woman, did you? Is that why you've done so much to help her? To put her in a position where she couldn't say no?"

I bit back a gasp, afraid of his answer.

"No!" He practically hissed the word. "Jeez, Nona. I would never do that. Is it so hard to believe she *likes* me?"

I relaxed, a small smile raising my lips. *No, it's not, Evan.*

Nona heaved a deep sigh. "Of course not. That's what

I've been trying to tell you for the last decade. Apparently, you're listening to me at last. This is excellent news. Good work!"

Even though Evan faced away from me, I could practically see him rolling his eyes. "Gee, thanks. I'm so glad I have your approval."

Nona scraped back her chair and stood. I pulled back from the entryway, pressing tight against the wall.

"Now I can sleep with a happy heart. I'm going to turn in now."

"Night, Nona." His voice sounded relieved, yet tinged with worry.

Soft footsteps headed toward me, and I held my breath, afraid to move.

Oh, God! What if she sees me?

But Nona walked out the far side of the wide entry and headed in the opposite direction. She disappeared into the foyer containing the staircase. Now what was I supposed to do? Sleep was the last thing on my mind.

Loud thumping sounded from the kitchen, and I peeked around the entryway again. Evan sat at the table, his head on top of his folded arms. He thudded his face against them repeatedly, hitting the table with his forehead.

Is he okay?

At any rate, I needed to understand what just happened. Taking a deep breath of courage, I stepped into the kitchen. "Evan? Are you all right?"

He froze, then slowly straightened as every muscle in his shoulders tensed. Turning sideways in his chair, he shifted his head toward me. His face was filled with a mixture of horror and guilt.

His expression was so funny I couldn't hold back a smile. A tiny laugh tumbled out, but I got hold of myself quickly. "That's the guiltiest look I've ever seen." I crossed the room to sit in the seat Nona had just vacated.

He briefly squeezed his eyes shut. Moonlight filtered over his face from the windowpane in the door across from him, allowing me to clearly see the flush rising above his beard. "You heard all that, didn't you?"

Now it was my turn to blush. "I did. I'm sorry. I didn't mean to eavesdrop. I was coming for a glass of milk and heard you two talking. Evan, what was that about?"

He rubbed his face fiercely with both hands. "I'm so sorry. Nona backed me into a corner, and it just slipped out. She's been on my case for months about getting involved with someone and let me know in no uncertain terms I'm expected to bring a date to Gabe's wedding."

"So why haven't you asked anyone? You must know lots of people in this town."

He clasped his hands and twiddled his thumbs, watching them circle each other and refusing to meet my eyes. "That's part of the problem. I know just about everyone on both these islands. I didn't feel like getting involved with anyone. Too much... history."

"I can understand that." But being from Boston, where I'd gone to schools with several hundred classmates, I couldn't really.

"I'll straighten this out tomorrow, don't worry. I don't expect you to be my fake date. Or girlfriend."

I pretended to be aghast. "What, I'm not good enough?"

He darted his eyes to me, then dropped them again. "Of course you are. I just don't want to be involved with anyone right now."

I slumped against the back of the seat as a realization hit me—that I felt like a freeloader who wasn't giving Evan anything, after all he'd done for me. Maybe I *could* give him something in return. And if he wasn't interested in me for real? Well, I'd take pretend, then. Even a pretend relationship with Evan sounded like fun.

"And I have more than enough on my plate getting the bakery renovation finished. You've done so much to help me. Pretending to be your girlfriend seems like a pretty small thing to do in return. But I'd be happy to, if you're still interested."

His head whipped up, his face going slack. "Really? You'd do that?"

I laughed. He really was the sweetest man. "Yes."

Then he lowered his brows, peering at me intently. "I want you to understand this has nothing to do with helping you get Sweet Dreams going again. I do *not* expect anything in return. Certainly not this."

"I know that, Evan. I want to help."

"It'll only be through the wedding, okay? Then we can pretend to break up afterward."

I held my hand out, and we shook. His skin was rough and warm. Strong yet comforting. "You have a deal, Evan Markham. We'll have a fake relationship until your brother and my friend get hitched."

At last, the tension in his shoulders dissolved. A smile widened his generous mouth. I smiled back as I stared into those blue eyes, and a pang of regret twisted my stomach. I might wish our relationship weren't fake, but he'd clearly said he didn't want to get involved. And the wedding was only a month away.

What could happen in a month?

Chapter Eleven

Evan

I BENCH-PRESSED THE TWO DUMBBELLS, my arms shaking. Our home gym was a cozy room with motivational posters on the wall and filled with free weights, along with a treadmill, elliptical, and stationary bike. Finally extending fully, I let the weights fall as I sat up on the padded bench. I racked my weights and toweled off my face, breathing heavily. This morning, I was having no problem coming up with the energy for my weight routine.

It was nervous, mortified energy, but whatever.

I'd had some embarrassing moments in my thirty-two years, but hearing Liv ask if I was okay as I pounded my forehead into the table last night might take the cake. At least I didn't have to worry about running into her this morning. I was usually up by five, but she rose much earlier, and the pop-up shop was already open by then.

It felt like every muscle in my upper body was twitching, which meant this was a pretty good time to stop. I ambled back to my bedroom for a shower, still feeling the effects of leg day yesterday. That had been a later workout, though, and Liv had popped in to say hello. Before the fiasco with Nona. I'd never been much of a show-off where my body was concerned, even when I'd had a body worth showing off. But I had to admit I was glad my legs once again looked like they belonged to a healthy human being instead of someone on a hunger strike.

After showering and changing into my work uniform, it was nearly six, so I figured I'd have some company for breakfast. But I wasn't prepared for the full table that greeted me. I pulled out my usual chair to Dad's right and swept my gaze around. "Did everyone decide on a family breakfast and leave me out?"

A few chairs down on my side, Maia laughed. She held baby Skye with one arm, tilted up against her shoulder. "Hardly. We just all showed up at the same time."

"Gabe, Hailey, and I are usually here around now," April said.

"Can I have some more fruit, please?" Hailey called to Martin, who was cooking for us this week.

Gabe smiled at her. "You're shooting up like a weed. I can hardly keep you fed."

She nodded sagely. Her brown hair fell in soft waves over her shoulders, and she had her father's dark eyes. "I am. Soon I'll be taller than April."

"That's not saying much," the divemaster replied with a laugh. "Set your sights a little higher."

"Well, I'm not planning on wearing high heels for the wedding. I don't want to trip on the flower petals."

Gabe's face fell into a frown. "No high heels. Absolutely not."

I couldn't hide a grin. Gabe was having a hard time with

his daughter growing up. Though at nine, she hadn't really discovered boys yet, so he still had some time.

"Speaking of the wedding," Nona drawled from the other end of the table. "Evan has some news about that."

My stomach fell to the floor as all eyes turned to me. I kept my face bland as I shot a glance at Nona, but she just smiled back with a slightly wicked gleam in her eye.

Gabe lifted both brows. "Don't tell me. You want to wear a pink tux with a ruffled shirt?"

"No." A hot flush crept up my neck, and I thought about getting up to strangle Nona. But that might ruin breakfast.

"What, then?" Dad asked over his coffee cup.

I hated being put on the spot like this, well aware of how idiotic I'd sound if I just blurted out, *I have a girlfriend!* like some teenager.

Nona came to my rescue. "Evan informed me last night that he's become involved with someone."

Maia leaned forward to stare at me in front of Wyatt, who was sitting between us. "Really? Who are you seeing?"

I repressed a sigh. I'd have to get used to this. "Um... Liv."

I jumped as April screeched from across the table. "I knew you two were perfect for each other! When did this happen? I can't believe she didn't tell me!"

I raised a hand, my pulse rocketing. "Probably because we haven't been together that long. Take it easy."

"Maybe he doesn't want everyone in his business," Wyatt said.

Gabe snorted. "You don't know this family very well, do you?"

Wyatt answered with a giant grin.

Dad watched me closely, a smile spreading across his

face. He reached over and squeezed my shoulder. "I'm happy for you, Son. I've enjoyed having Liv around."

My heart was heavy in my chest. This was something I hadn't anticipated—the guilt washing over me at deceiving my own family. But now that the ball was in motion, I didn't know how to stop the momentum.

"And the best man and maid of honor also being a couple should make a lovely addition to the wedding. Very poetic." Nona raised her coffee cup to me.

I was saved from any more explanations when Martin slid my breakfast in front of me.

Well, the entire family thinks we're a couple now. Guess Liv and I better go out on a date.

I STEPPED into the lobby and headed toward the corner, which was almost unrecognizable now. An orderly set of stanchions and retractable belts had been placed to form a line. And there was usually a line. Sweet Dreams Mini, as Liv was calling it, was undoubtedly a success. And since she and I had agreed that she'd send anyone who wanted coffee to Local Grind, Calypso Key was seeing direct revenue from it too.

But being the boss had its advantages. I went around the queue and headed behind the counter where both Dylan and Liv were moving about, gathering pastries. Seeing me, Liv grabbed a paper sack and filled it with two mango scones. She handed it to me, brushing her hand down my arm as she did so.

A small thrill tickled down my spine at the contact, and warmth spread through my groin. *This is pretend, remember?* "Morning. Looks like you've been busy."

She nodded. "We have, but it's leveling off now. I was

just about to take a little break. You want to join me for a scone?"

"Absolutely."

We headed out of the lobby and wandered north up the path. I let Liv choose our direction, happy just to be with her. After opening the sack, I handed her a scone, then took a bite of mine. "How do you make these so good? I'll probably gain ten pounds in the next month."

She laughed, a light sound that reminded me of moonbeams on a clear night. "I seriously doubt that. I've seen you work out, remember? But, to answer your question, part of the secret is not overdoing the sugar. Scones are supposed to be only mildly sweet. Plus, the mango pieces add their own sweetness."

I swallowed another bite. "Whatever you do, they're amazing."

We passed Orchid and continued north toward the marsh. The morning was still cool, a light breeze serving as a reminder we were in winter. Reaching the small beach, she pointed to where the path changed to a mixture of gravel and sand before disappearing into the wetlands. "I just discovered this area but haven't followed the path. It's very peaceful here."

"This is my favorite part of the island. That path meanders through the marsh. Depending on the rainfall amounts, it can get flooded, but usually it's pretty manageable. The path goes all the way around the island but skirts around our section. This marsh is a great place to explore by kayak or paddleboard."

A snowy egret glided overhead, and Liv shaded her eyes with one hand to watch its progress. "Me on a paddleboard sounds like a disaster waiting to happen. But kayaking could be fun."

I turned to her with a smile. "Really? You want to join me?" I pointed to where I kept my two kayaks off to the side. "Those are mine. One is much lighter. I'm sure you could paddle it just fine."

"That sounds like fun."

I laughed and shook my head. "The cat is out of the bag about our supposed relationship, by the way. Nona broadcast the news at breakfast this morning."

I watched her reaction carefully, but all she did was laugh. "I can see her doing that. Guess if we're in a relationship, we should be spending some one-on-one time together, right?"

"The bakery is closed tomorrow, isn't it?"

"Yes. I closed every Sunday at the main bakery, so I'll continue that here. Besides, I need a day off, and I make sure Dylan gets a second day off per week."

"How about we kayak down here tomorrow morning? There's usually more animal activity in the early morning." Then I paused. "Oh! You probably want to sleep in tomorrow. We can go whenever is convenient."

She laughed again. "Sleeping in for me is until five."

"That's plenty early for me. Meet in the kitchen at five thirty?"

Liv turned to me, and our eyes held. "It's a date."

THE NEXT MORNING was cool enough that we both wore sweatshirts. And of course, my knee hurt like a son of a bitch. I did my best not to limp as I dragged both kayaks from their shelter.

As I handed Liv a paddle, she frowned at the sleek, light

kayak. "I hope I don't fall out of that thing or roll it. It's cold this morning."

"It's more stable than it looks, and I'll help you launch. You can swim, right?"

She laughed. I liked making her laugh. "Yes, I can swim. I just don't do it much. I can't believe I've lived in the Keys for a year, and my best friend is a divemaster, but I've never been snorkeling!"

We got her kayak set up, and I waded in and steadied it as she carefully climbed in. "There. See? Nothing to it."

I dragged my other, much heavier kayak, to the shore. I considered removing the weights I kept in the bottom, but that was a pain in the ass. I was still sore from yesterday's weight session, so maybe some heavy paddling would help me loosen up. I waded in and slid into the kayak, sighing as I straightened my leg and the ache nearly disappeared.

I gave Liv a quick paddling lesson and we headed into a wide channel. "Diving and snorkeling are like this—they're usually better in the morning. So I'm not surprised you haven't been snorkeling. Your mornings are pretty busy. Have you ever been snorkeling?"

"Never. That needs to change, especially since I'm living here. You guys have a snorkel boat going out most mornings, for God's sake."

"Very true. I'm sure we can arrange a trip for you."

"Plus, we need another activity to do together to keep up our ruse. I imagine you can teach me to snorkel?"

I froze, my paddle stopping mid-stride as tightness filled my gut. I hadn't been in open water since it happened. But there was no reason I couldn't snorkel. I exhaled a long breath through my nose. "Sure. Maybe we'll go next Sunday, when you're off again."

She watched me, noting my change in mood. "Do you

not like snorkeling? I just assumed you were a snorkeler or diver since you grew up here."

"I... used to dive. It's been a long time. But I'd enjoy snorkeling with you." I had let go of my paddle with one hand and was massaging my knee. I hadn't even noticed I was doing it, and I let go with a frown.

"Is your knee hurting? We can turn around and do this some other time."

Giving her a smile I hoped was reassuring, I started paddling again. "No. It just flares up sometimes. I'm used to it, so it doesn't bother me much."

"I've noticed. You certainly keep in good shape."

We turned into a smaller canal with green branches meeting overhead to form a tunnel. The tide was coming in and pushing us forward in a gentle current, so we hardly had to paddle. I set my paddle down, resting it on the shell above my lap, and eased out a sigh.

"I'm sorry, Evan. I didn't mean to make you uncomfortable. It's really none of my business."

This was my least favorite story in the world to tell, but Liv deserved to know. And if we were going to pull off this fake relationship thing, she'd have to know. My family would expect me to tell her. "Don't apologize. It's fine. My limp and the injury that caused it have to do with what we were just talking about. Diving."

"Did you have an accident?"

I smirked, but there was no humor in the expression. "I'm not sure I'd call it an accident, even twelve years later. Accidents are things that can't be prevented. What happened to me should have never occurred. It's also why my brother Hunter isn't part of our family anymore."

Liv raised her paddle out of the water too. She remained silent, watching me and letting me tell the story.

"Have you ever heard of the bends?"

She furrowed her brow. "I've heard of it. Something bad that can happen while diving, right?"

"Yeah. When I was nineteen and Hunter was eighteen, we went diving on a shipwreck near here, the *Benson*. There's always been a rumor about lost gold inside and looking for it was our favorite hobby. We poked into every nook and cranny of that ship, except for one room that was down deep. Too deep. Going to that depth was way too advanced for us, though Hunter thought otherwise. We did it anyway."

I lifted my paddle to push off against an approaching mangrove, then resumed my story. "Hunter was convinced that gold was in the deep room, so down we went. I didn't believe in the gold—that was a stupid old campfire story. But I couldn't let my little brother go alone, and I didn't think anything bad would happen. You never do at that age. When we got into the room, it was empty, of course. So he went into a hallway, which led to another room to explore."

The sun went behind a cloud, throwing shade over us. I shivered, the memory coming back. How my skin had crawled at the thought of all that water between me and the surface. And the deep fear when I realized we were lost. "We were so stupid. *Hunter* was stupid—he was leading. We didn't leave a guideline or anything. I started getting scared and made us turn around. He headed back, searching methodically for a way out."

I had to stop for a moment to settle my pounding heart, not wanting to admit to Liv how terrified I'd been. Lost inside a ship and very deep underwater. "Finally, we found our way back to the original room, and by then I was barely holding it together. We were almost out of air and a hundred fifty feet below the surface."

From that point, the memories became hazy. As soon as I saw that square cut in the side of the ship, I'd panicked and rushed toward it. I'd completely lost my head, something I was still ashamed of. "As soon as we got out of that goddamn ship, I bolted for the surface. Air. Life. Hunter tried to grab me, but I punched him and got away. He followed me and we both surfaced. I lunged for him again, absolutely furious. He tried to calm me down, but all I could see was red. Eventually, he convinced me to get back on the boat."

I rolled my head around on my stiff neck, trying to relax. An osprey flew overhead, but I hardly noticed, locked in the past. "As soon as we boarded the boat, I felt nauseous. At first, I thought it was because of bobbing in the waves. But the sensation broke through my rage, and that was when I noticed my legs were tingling. Hunter started the boat and drove home full throttle. He radioed in on the way what had happened. I started throwing up, and my legs got weaker by the second. An ambulance was waiting when we got back, and I had to be taken off the boat in a stretcher."

Liv raised a hand to her mouth, her eyes round.

"I don't really have a memory of that fight at the surface, but the evidence was obvious when Hunter visited me in the hospital. His eye was swollen shut, his cheek cut and bleeding. I wanted nothing to do with him. I lay there, paralyzed and broken. Because of him. We got in a terrible fight, and that was the last time we spoke. I don't regret a single word I said."

I stared at the thick, green mangroves but only felt the crushing fear and weakness I'd experienced that day. The certainty that my life had been irrevocably changed. "The bends come from rising from depth too quickly. As you dive, nitrogen accumulates in your tissues, so you have to rise slowly so it can leave your body as you exhale. But if you rise too suddenly, it forms bubbles in your tissues, the nervous system and joints especially. The pain causes people to bend over double, which is where the name *the bends* comes from."

I sighed, feeling a thousand years old. "The formal name is decompression sickness, which can be fatal. It wasn't in my case, but it left my legs paralyzed. It took me years to recover. Which I mostly have, except my right leg still gives me problems. I'll never be able to dive again, though."

Along with other things I'll never do again.

"And all because my son-of-a-bitch brother had to go look for a treasure he knew damn well wouldn't be there."

"How awful. Was he injured too?" Liv's voice was soft and hesitant.

I gave a bark of humorless laughter. "Nothing happened to Hunter. Not a goddamn thing. I ended up in a wheelchair and he got off scot-free. The dive was too advanced for *him*, and he was a much better diver than me. But that didn't stop him. I think that's why he loved diving with me so much. It was the one physical activity he was better at than me. I couldn't match his book smarts, but I was a pretty good athlete."

I had to stop and swallow to wet my parched throat. Get myself under control again at that simple phrase I'd uttered so matter-of-factly. "He didn't give a shit about me, and I paid the price. I lost my entire future because of Hunter—everything in my life changed. I hated him for it. I still do."

Chapter Twelve

Liv

I STARED at Evan's angry, tight face. His expression was foreign, out of place compared to his usual empathetic, relaxed countenance. His whole body thrummed with furious energy, as if he wanted Hunter to appear right this moment so he could pummel his brother into the ground. Given that he'd described Hunter as a brainy, non-athletic bookworm, I had no doubt he could.

Then I realized my shoulders were nearly cramping. I forced myself to relax, deeply moved by his story. The last thing I'd expected was to hear that Evan's injury caused a family rift that still caused ripples over a decade later. My heart felt like it was tearing in two.

Letting go of my paddle with one hand, I reached out and softly squeezed his hand. "I'm so sorry you went through that. What a terrible story."

Evan inhaled a giant breath, then let it out in a loud whoosh. "It's not a story I enjoy telling. But my girlfriend should know about it." His lips rose briefly in a smile. "Even my pretend girlfriend. I imagine my family might mention it, and I don't want you caught off guard."

"Thank you," I said quietly, relieved that the tension was draining from his frame. His hand relaxed under mine, and I stroked the back of it.

I wonder if April knows about this?

The odds were she did. We had book club later this afternoon, which would give me a chance to discuss the Markham family dynamics with her. Obviously, Evan didn't want to talk about his brother, and no one else had even mentioned him. Did the entire family blame Hunter for the disaster?

Evan flipped his palm over and squeezed my hand back before letting go and putting his paddle back into the water. "Let's keep going."

We traveled through a narrow channel. Birds sang in the trees, and I smiled as a second white egret flew past, my equilibrium returning. I watched Evan in front of me, the muscles of his shoulders moving with the rhythm of his paddle. I'd seen him lifting weights. He usually wore a tank top and the sculpted muscles in his upper body were evident when he lifted the heavy dumbbells. Now I knew why he'd needed them.

"You've made remarkable progress, considering you were paralyzed."

"Thanks, I have. I spent several days in a recompression chamber in Tavernier, trying to lessen the damage." A brief shudder rippled across his shoulders. "I still don't like tight spaces. That thing was incredibly claustrophobic. But it halted the paralysis, and the doctors told me whatever movement I got back in the first year afterward would be it. So I really threw myself into my recovery."

"You were only nineteen?" Shaking my head, I thought

back to my life at that age. Taking baking classes at the local community college and having fun with my friends.

"Yeah. I got more involved in resort operations, eventually working my way up to general manager. Dad was a huge help. He really supported me, and so did Nona."

"You're lucky to have such a caring family."

Evan didn't reply, moving his paddle in a steady side-to-side rhythm. We emerged from the narrow channel into a much bigger, lagoon-like space. A small island sat in the middle.

The sun bathed my shoulders, making me almost too warm in my sweatshirt. "What a beautiful spot! It's almost hidden."

Evan turned and smiled, his expression back to one I was more used to seeing. "I usually stop here when I kayak. It's peaceful."

We continued, and I slowly moved my paddle, now more comfortable with the motion. And the kayak I sat in was reassuringly stable. Off to one side, a V-shaped ripple appeared in the water, the point headed straight toward us. My breath caught, a chill running through me. "Evan, what is that? Are there alligators in here?"

He paused his motion, resting his paddle on top, and his smile grew. "No gators. Keep watching. You'll see."

I swallowed, trying not to be concerned that the width of the creature's wake indicated it was sizeable. I lifted my paddle out and gripped it with both hands. It would make a handy weapon if necessary. A large gray shape materialized behind the apex of the V, but it was much too broad and round to be an alligator. I looked more closely, then gasped as I recognized a manatee.

Evan reached down and wiggled his fingers in the water. The gray shape moved in his direction and lifted its broad snout to brush against his fingers. "Hey there, big guy. How are you this morning?"

I laughed, delighted, as Evan removed a Thermos I hadn't noticed before from the kayak and unscrewed it. He poured a stream of water into the manatee's mouth, grinning. He raised his eyes to mine. "This is Manny. He's kind of the patriarch of a group who lives in here." He pointed with his chin a distance away where two other gray shapes lay just beneath the surface. "Those two over there are a mated pair. I think she might be pregnant. Betty looks bigger every time I come out here. I keep waiting for a little manatee to show up."

Forgetting all about using my paddle as a club, I returned it to the water and moved closer to the pair. They didn't move away but didn't come closer, either.

Evan joined my side, and we watched them for a few minutes. "Guess they're shy today. Want to head back?"

A small pang ran through me that we were leaving, but seeing the three manatees had been amazing. "Okay." I turned to look at him, feeling much closer to him now. "Evan?"

He raised his brows at me.

"Thank you for confiding in me. I hope you're proud of all you've accomplished. You should be."

His face clouded for a moment, then he squared his shoulders and smiled. "I try to see the positive. That's why I like to kayak here. I always see something that makes me grateful to be alive."

"I'm glad you showed me this. It's a very special place."

He held me with his eyes, neither of us looking away. "It is. Like I said, I always see something special here."

THE WHITE WINE was crisp and refreshing on my tongue. I sat in a chair next to April at a modest bungalow in Dove Key. Brenna Coleridge appeared before me and handed me a paperback book. Swallowing, I smiled at her. "Thanks. It sure is convenient having our next month's book delivered to us."

She grinned, her long, light-brown hair falling forward over her shoulder. Brenna was another one who had hair I'd kill for. She was around my age and very pretty with bright blue eyes. "It's pretty easy for me too, considering I own a bookshop."

Even though January was over half gone, today was the first day Brenna and I had really had a chance to talk about the fire. I'd arrived early to speak to her, bringing a cake and a bottle of wine as a special thank you for calling in the fire.

Once she'd passed out all the books, Brenna took a seat on my other side. A dozen of us sat in a rough circle and had just finished our monthly book club meeting, which was as much an excuse to drink wine as talk books.

At the head of the circle, Pam, who owned the bungalow, held up a paperback in her hands. "Okay, we'll meet again next month to discuss this book. I can't wait—I've been waiting forever for this book!"

The meeting broke up, and I headed toward the front door with April just behind. The heat hit me as soon as I stepped outside, and I pulled my shirt away from my neck. "Man, it was cool this morning, but the afternoon is making up for it."

"You want to get an ice cream?" April asked. "I want to talk some more about you and Evan!"

Nodding enthusiastically, I got in my Tahoe and drove to the opposite end of Main Street. I wanted to talk about Evan and me too. I shifted in my seat, uneasiness washing over me at deceiving my friend that Evan and I were more than we actually were. But his story that morning had shaken me, and I wanted to know more about him.

We found parking a short distance from Brain Freeze and walked in the front door. The shop was blessedly air-conditioned and had a colorful, beachy interior with turquoise shiplap siding and beach balls and blankets attached to the walls. I ordered a scoop of coconut ice cream and April got butter pecan, then we headed toward a quiet table near the front of the shop.

"The townies are going to get jealous all over again when they find out you and Evan are involved," she said, taking a long taste of her ice cream. Like me, she preferred it out of a cup rather than a cone.

Both of us felt welcomed as newcomers to the area. But when April mentioned at one of our book club meetings that she was seeing Gabe, the room had been knocked into stunned silence. It had been a stark reminder that we both lived in a small town now, and dating the local royalty could come with complications.

"Hopefully, they'll be so consumed with your wedding, they won't even care about Evan and me."

"They seem to have accepted that Gabe is off the market permanently." Her warm smile made her eyes crinkle at the corners. "You two make a really cute couple."

"Thanks." I paused, wondering how to bring up the subject I came here to discuss. "Evan and I went kayaking in the wetlands this morning... He told me about his accident. And Hunter." I watched her carefully to judge her reaction.

April's face dropped into a frown, but there was no surprise. She knew. "It's a really sad story. Evan's overcome a lot."

I nodded. "He has. But he's still angry at Hunter. Really angry."

"Yeah, Gabe says he's not sure if they'll ever reconcile. He'd like Hunter to come to our wedding, but he isn't sure it's a good idea."

"Have you ever met Hunter?"

"No. He never comes down here—he lives in South Beach."

I took a bite of ice cream while I gathered my thoughts. The rich, decadent coconut flavor coated the inside of my mouth. "Even all these years later, Evan has a hard time discussing it."

"I'm sure he does. It can't be a fun experience to reminisce about."

I flashed back to how white his knuckles had been on the paddle. "The change in his attitude was so stark. I've never seen him anything but sweet and funny. This morning, he looked like he'd like nothing more than for Hunter to appear so he could beat the hell out of him."

April cocked her head. "Were you afraid of Evan? Did he act threatening to you?"

I sat back in my chair, contemplating the pain and sadness that had been in Evan's eyes—the *betrayal*. That had been as bad as his fury. "No, not at all. I reached out to soothe him, and he calmed down. It was just such a shocking change, you know? Have you ever discussed his accident with him?"

"Yeah, a few times. But talking to a friend about it is a very different thing than discussing the most impactful moment of your life with your girlfriend. Our discussions were more... clinical, I guess. Since I'm a divemaster, I know a lot about DCS."

"DCS?"

"Decompression sickness. The bends."

"You've never gotten it?"

"No, thank God. And I hope I never do. I'm pretty careful when I dive." She studied me. "But I've never gotten even a hint that Evan's got a nasty temper. If that's what's worrying you, I think you can put your mind at ease."

I nodded and took another bite. I wasn't afraid of Evan, but there was a lot more to him than I'd expected. It saddened me that his relationship with Hunter had been irrevocably severed. The fact that our relationship wasn't real gave me some distance to process all this. Satisfied there weren't any more ghosts in Evan's closet, I turned the discussion to something more pleasant. "Has your dress come in?"

"Next week. We need to get you down there too, so you can pick out yours."

"What color and style were you thinking?"

April shrugged. "It's not a formal wedding. Whatever you feel most comfortable in. The guys are going to wear gray tuxes, so that should complement any color you might want."

The image of Evan in a tuxedo flashed through my mind, sending a flutter through my stomach. A very pleasant warmth settled in my abdomen.

Guess I'll see the real thing soon enough. "This morning, Evan and I were talking about going snorkeling. Maybe we could join you and Gabe? I've never been, so I'd like the company of an expert."

April's face lit up. "I love the idea! Don't worry. There's nothing to it. We'll go somewhere easy and protected. Let's shoot for an afternoon in a couple of days. I can get Maia or Wyatt to cover the afternoon dive, and Gabe can drive us in

Indigo Heaven. That boat is better for a small group anyway, since it's easier to handle."

I grinned at her, already excited at the prospect of my first snorkeling adventure. Evan's and my new relationship status would be on public display for the first time. Well, semi-public, only April and Gabe. That warmth in my belly increased at the thought of stroking my hand over his sun-kissed shoulders. Or brushing casually against him and knowing I could get away with it. If we were supposed to be a couple, we'd have to act like one.

A prospect I didn't mind at all.

LATER THAT EVENING, I poured myself a glass of white wine from the refrigerator in the Big House kitchen and stepped out the side door onto the expansive pool area. Nearly hidden from the view of guests, a flagstone patio surrounded a long rectangular pool, and tables were placed at intervals around it. Evan sat at one, twisting a pair of pliers around something he held in his hands.

I approached to see a mysterious object, open with wires and cogs visible. "What are you doing?"

He looked up and smiled. "Repairing part of the motor from an AC unit of one of the cottages. Have a seat."

I sat and watched his hands moving smoothly and with obvious skill over the part. Then I saw something new. "You're left-handed? I never noticed."

He glanced at me from under his brows, a small smile rising. "I am. Hopeless with my right."

I was pleased to learn something new about him. Then I considered what he was doing. "Don't you have repair people on staff? Or someone you can call?"

Without looking up, he shrugged. "Sure, but why

bother when I can fix it myself? I already swapped this one out for a working motor so the guests wouldn't be inconvenienced. I like fixing stuff."

I rested my elbow on the table and propped my chin in my palm. "Which I'm very grateful for. You fixed my oven. Though I wonder if it was the breaker panel all along causing problems."

With a satisfied sigh, Evan closed up the contraption on the table and wiped his hands clean with a nearby rag. "Probably a little of both."

After taking a sip of wine, I raised my glass to him. "The next time you tell me to get something looked at, I'm going to listen."

He grinned, and again I was struck by how good-looking he was. Those soft blue eyes! "It's nice to be listened to. Oh, I talked to Gabe this afternoon. Sounds like we're on for snorkeling the day after tomorrow."

"I'm looking forward to it. Are you okay with this? Snorkeling isn't diving, but if you'd rather not, we can do something else."

He shook his head. "I love being in the water. I've avoided it because of the memories, but it's time to stop that. And I really like the idea of being with you the first time you see a reef."

I felt so comfortable around him. "So do I."

He laughed. "Maia was a little pissed we didn't include her and Wyatt, but I told her no babies were allowed. They're planning on getting Skye into swimming lessons soon."

"They start that so early now! My brother is three years younger than I am, and we took our lessons together. I was eight and he was five."

He settled back in his chair, crossing his feet at the ankles. "Did you have a happy childhood?"

I took another sip of cold wine. "Very. We lived in a small town about an hour from Boston. Parents, two kids, and a dog. Pretty much a Norman Rockwell painting."

Evan reached up to scratch his jaw, then ran his fingers through his beard, making sure it was neat.

I laughed out loud.

"What?"

"Oh, I was just thinking about our new relationship. It's a good thing we're down here with your family and not up in New England with mine. They'd never believe I got involved with a man with a bushy beard like yours. I've always dated men who were clean-shaven. It was actually something of a joke between me and my brother."

Evan's smile faded. "Do you want me to shave?"

I paused, imagining what he'd look like without that luxuriant growth on his face. Then I shook my head. "Of course not. If the beard makes you happy, it makes me happy."

He watched me steadily. "You hesitated when you answered, though."

"You caught me off guard! Evan, I have no right to tell you how to groom yourself. Besides, you keep it very clean and combed." I glanced at my watch. It was nearing 8:00 p.m. "I'd better turn in. See you tomorrow."

"Good night, Liv."

As I strolled back into the kitchen and placed my empty wineglass in the dishwasher, I couldn't help wondering whether he had a strong, defined jaw under that beard. His lips were somewhat hidden behind hair.

I wonder if kissing him would tickle my lips?

Chapter Thirteen

Evan

I PICKED up the brand-new razor, refamiliarizing myself with the feel of it, the ridges on the handle, the weight of it in my hand. My eyes slid to the trash can next to the vanity, which now held most of my beard I'd cut off with scissors. Meeting my reflection, I lifted the razor to my cheek and pulled it down over the shaving foam.

Am I going too far here?

There was no use denying it. Only one thing had led me to this point—Liv's hesitation before she'd told me to keep the beard. I wanted her to think highly of me, even if we weren't really involved. After telling her about the *Benson* and Hunter, I was even more worried that she'd decide I was too much trouble and call the whole thing off. I didn't want that. And not just because Nona would get back on my case.

Because I wanted Liv to find me attractive.

I wanted to see a molten, smoldering stare aimed at me.

Her feelings toward me might not be genuine, but mine

were. And the time we'd spent together since she'd moved into the Big House had only lit my flame more. It had been so long since I'd wanted a woman like this, I hardly remembered how to proceed. So I might as well tip the odds in my favor as much as possible.

Sometimes, I'd catch Liv looking my way, and her cheeks would pink up. But I wasn't sure if it was because she liked what she saw or because of something else. Like maybe she found my beard disgusting but couldn't look away, like a car wreck. I didn't want to be a car wreck to her.

Several minutes later, I tilted my head back and forth as I inspected my newly exposed cheeks and chin. My skin was ghostly pale with a sharp tan line visible. I hardly recognized the face in the mirror and flinched. "Great, I'm trying to impress her, and I look like a two-tone idiot." Oh well, some time in the sun would take care of my pasty skin.

Like during our snorkeling trip this afternoon.

The kitchen was blessedly empty of family when I entered for breakfast. But I got an idea of how different I looked when Martin did a double take upon seeing me, and his eyes became round. Fortunately, after his initial surprise, he treated me the same as always. Hopefully, I'd be as lucky with others.

I headed to the dive shop first thing. Gabe was working in his office there and I wanted to make sure we were still on for this afternoon. I kept my head down as I entered and marched straight toward the hallway, not looking at Carissa. Gabe's office was at the end of the hallway on the right. I knocked on the open doorframe, and he glanced up.

At first, he just stared at me. Then he narrowed his eyes as he focused, his head cocked to the side. Eventually, a broad smile cracked his face. "Holy shit. You actually have a face!"

"Yeah, yeah," I said as I took a seat on the other side of his desk. "Jeez, I don't look *that* different."

Gabe's grin widened. "Nice tan line. You look like you've been four-wheeling with a bandana around your face."

I tried to stare him down, but he wasn't having it. Finally, I rolled my eyes. "That's why I'm here. I wanted to make sure we were still snorkeling today. I need some time in the sun to even out my face."

Gabe didn't laugh often, but he did now. "You sure do. And yes. We're planning on leaving the canal at one. Is this change in appearance due to Liv?"

Yes.

I shifted in my seat, resisting the urge to wipe my hands on my shorts. "No, smart-ass! I thought it would be nice to look clean and presentable for your wedding. And if I'm going to shave, I need enough time to even out my tan line. But if you're just going to give me a hard time about it, I'll grow the damn thing back."

Gabe's expression softened, the smile still playing at his lips. "I'd be proud to stand next to you, with or without the beard. But you look very Markham-like now. I say keep the clean-shaven look."

I nodded, mollified. "Then I will. And thank you. I'm looking forward to your big day."

Gabe's expression changed, his smile fading as his eyes became hooded and assessing. "I am too. This wedding is going to be a real family celebration. Stella wants to do the catering herself. And you should know—I called Hunter and asked if he'd attend."

My blood pressure went through the roof. The walls closed in around me, and my lungs couldn't get enough air. "No way, Gabe. I want to support you any way I can, but I do not want to be anywhere near that asshole." I stopped short of saying, *If Hunter's coming, I'm not.* But it was close.

Disappointment flickered in Gabe's eyes. "You're going to get your wish. Because he said he was out of town that weekend and wouldn't be able to make it."

Relief poured off me in waves. I hadn't seen Hunter since I was in the hospital right after the accident, and I had no desire to change that. "We don't need him to make this a family celebration. He hasn't been a part of the family in over a decade."

"Maybe that should change," Gabe said softly.

"No. You know what he cost me—everything!"

My brother leaned forward and tented his fingers together over the desk. "Yes, I do. But you've made a pretty good life for yourself in spite of that, haven't you?"

I snorted and crossed my arms. "Yeah, nepotism at its best."

"No, it's not. Dad would never have put you in charge if he didn't have full confidence in you. Besides, this place would crumble without you. Can you imagine if I were in charge of all these employees?"

That made me laugh out loud. "Yeah. We'd have a revolving door between you firing everyone and them quitting because you're such a grouchy asshole."

He grinned. "Exactly. Maybe your life didn't work out like you'd planned, but that doesn't mean it's not worthwhile."

"I guess. But I'm glad Hunter's staying away from here. We don't need him. How many people are coming to this shindig, anyway?"

Gabe sat back in his chair and crossed one ankle over the other knee. "Not too many. It'll be pretty small. I invited a few of our cousins, but they haven't confirmed."

I raised my brows. We had three distant cousins who had visited Calypso Key periodically as kids, but we weren't terribly close. Then I reconsidered. "I guess that's what weddings are for, huh? Seeing people you haven't in a long time?"

He met my eyes with a level stare. "Yes, Evan. They are."

I refused to take his bait. "What about April? Who's she inviting?"

"Her family from Ohio. Her mom and dad are divorced but apparently able to handle being in the same room together. Her brother's coming. Oh, and the couple who own the resort in St. Croix where she used to work. Altogether, probably less than thirty people."

I absently reached up to stroke my beard and was surprised to find nothing there. I swiped my hand over my jaw instead as I stood. "Sounds like it's coming together. I'd better get to work. I'll meet you on *Indigo Heaven* at one."

I spent the morning with contractors in one of our garden cottages, discussing the final plans for renovations. Now that the beach cottages were fully updated, the garden ones would begin their remodels right after the wedding. I'd blocked the entire row of beach cottages for wedding guests, and resort guests using the garden cottages would be clearing out within a day after the nuptials, freeing them up.

The garden cottages had the same layout as the beach ones, but the front deck was smaller, as was the bathroom. After remodeling, they would be just as modern, only on a smaller and more affordable scale.

When I ate lunch at the Big House, no one else was there. I hadn't seen Liv all day, and after I changed into a T-shirt and board shorts for our snorkeling trip, I still hadn't come across her. I shrugged as I strolled down the hill.

I'll just meet her on the boat.

I studied the ocean as I neared the canal, grateful the afternoon was calm with a nearly flat sea. I'd thought about snorkeling since getting bent but managed to find excuses not to do it. Although I missed diving and its much more immersive experience, I looked forward to sharing Liv's first snorkeling session. Today was the perfect occasion to get back in open water.

I stepped aboard the thirty-two-foot boat and headed toward the covered bow section. Gabe and April hadn't arrived yet, but a smile rose on my face when I saw Liv under the covered canopy. Facing away from me, she wore a loose green cover-up and was placing a beach bag on the shelf reserved for dry gear.

"Ready to swim with the fishes?" I asked, a big grin splitting my face.

She broke into laughter and turned around to face me. "I hope that's just a euphem—"

Her smile fell as her jaw dropped open. She widened her eyes, the whites clearly visible, and slowly stepped toward me.

"Evan! You shaved." Her voice was soft and breathy.

I resisted the urge to step backward, feeling like a spotlight shined on my face. "Yeah. I decided it was time for a change." My heart raced frantically, and I wondered if she'd be able to see my shirt moving with the force of it. But she was fixated on my face, though I had no idea if that was a good thing or a bad thing. Finally, I asked the question, my heart in my mouth. "Do you like it?"

Stopping right in front of me, Liv raised her hand and

slowly stroked two fingers across my jaw. The contact was light, exploratory.

Her touch seared through me. Every cell on my skin lit up where she touched it, and those she didn't felt cold by comparison. Raising her eyes to mine, we locked gazes.

"Yes."

Her answer was little more than a whisper, and her lips remained parted after speaking the word. I focused on them. They were a lovely shade of rose, plump and delicious. I was almost overwhelmed with a desire to taste them. She took a deep, shaky breath and moved her hand, gently pressing it against the side of my face. The look in her eyes changed. The surprise fled, and desire flooded into her eyes. "I like it very much, Evan."

Inhaling sharply, a hot wave rolled through my abdomen. And lower. I dropped my head. Slowly, giving her time to pull away if that was what she wanted.

I knew what I wanted.

She didn't pull back, and I parted my lips, barely able to keep from licking them in anticipation. Liv increased the pressure against my face, encouraging me. She curled her fingers, slowly drawing the pads of her fingers over my newly exposed skin. Her soft touch sent a live wire through my body, arousal building steadily. We drew closer, our lips inches apart.

"Yo! Anybody here?"

April's happy shout tore us apart. We flew backward, and I blinked repeatedly, not even sure where I was for a moment. Liv shot me a tiny smile, though it was a little shaky.

She's as stunned as I am.

I swallowed, trying to get my blood moving normally through my body again. I definitely didn't imagine her reaction, and elation soared through—the knowledge that she was attracted to me too.

Liv wrenched her eyes from mine to the canal. "We're here, April!"

"Oh, good." April stepped aboard, both arms full of fins, masks, and snorkels. "I think I've got all the equipment here. Gabe's on his way." She dumped the whole lot on a side bench, then brushed her hands together as she turned to face us. She made eye contact with me and froze. "Oh, wow, Evan! That's a change." Breaking into a huge grin, she scampered closer, moving her head from side to side as she inspected me.

A hot flush spread over my face as I resisted the urge to adjust my board shorts. I tried to look casual as she guffawed. "The only problem is now it's really obvious when you blush! Clean-shaven agrees with you, Evan. What do you think, Liv?"

She shot Liv a very pointed look, widening her eyes.

Liv was blushing now too. She smiled at me from beneath her brows as she joined my side. "I agree. It's a very good look for him."

I swore I could feel heat radiating from her body where it was close to mine. That didn't do much to cool my ardor.

April turned her grin back to me. "You Markham men sure won the genetic lottery. Good thing I've already got mine."

Gabe stepped aboard, twirling a ring of keys around his finger.

April parked both hands on her hips and gave him a frown. "You said you talked to Evan this morning. You never said he shaved!"

Gabe was brought up short and sent me a dirty look. "Why would I? Who cares? Let's go snorkeling."

That broke the weird spell and all four of us laughed. I turned back to April. "I just felt like doing something differ-ent. Gabe's right. It's not a big deal."

April gave Liv a long side-eye. "If you say so. The change is rather dramatic."

When I shifted my eyes, Liv was staring at me again, her eyes darting over my face. She blinked, and that hungry look dimmed. Our relationship might be fake, but I had the feeling something had just changed between us. Something I might not mind exploring.

No, I wouldn't mind one bit.

Chapter Fourteen

Liv

AS GABE THROTTLED up and we sped over the ocean, I
tried to concentrate on the water. It shaded from aquama-
rine near the shore to deep indigo as we entered deeper
water.

*I wonder how cool the water is. I could do with a cold
shower right about now.*

Yeah, an ice-cold shower would be a good idea. For the
hundredth time since we left the resort, my eyes slid to
Evan, who stood next to Gabe at the console. Electricity
hummed through my veins.

*My God, I thought he was hot with the beard. Who knew
he had a jaw like that?*

I'd been absolutely stunned when I saw him, literally
weak in the knees. His face was like fine chiseled stone,
newly sculpted. I hadn't meant to reach out and stroke his
chin. My fingers had moved on their own, and I was over-
taken by my desire to feel the texture of that new skin.
Then I'd been fascinated by how it was both rough and soft

at the same time. And wow, that moment between us. I didn't know whether to thank April or throttle her for interrupting us.

A light laugh sounded beside me as she joined me and spoke quietly. "Someone looks a little lusty right now."

I tried to compose myself and stared down my nose at her. "Nonsense. It's the heat making me look like this." I swept my forearm over my sweaty brow.

April just grinned. "You did tell me you prefer your men clean-shaven. Evan did clean up rather well, didn't he?"

This time when I glanced at him, he was staring back. A small smile lifted his lips before he returned his focus to Gabe.

I cleared my dry throat, unable to deny any part of her statement. "Yeah. He looks gorgeous."

"You two should have fun this afternoon, then. While we're snorkeling, I'll do what I can to give you some privacy. Maybe you won't have to wait until we get back to the Key to show your appreciation to him."

That brought reality crashing back down.

This is fake, Liv! Of course he's smiling at you. He's supposed to!

Except no one had been around when we'd almost kissed. That extended moment had been *very* mutual. So what would happen now?

I peaked a brow at April. "Really. We can contain ourselves. Besides, I need to concentrate on learning how to snorkel, so don't wander off too far."

She just laughed and shrugged. A few minutes later, Gabe slowed down just offshore of one of the many small, uninhabited keys dotting the area. April climbed to the bow of the boat and used a long hook to pull a mooring ball out of the water, then attached the boat's line to it. She dropped it back in the water, turned to Gabe, and thumped the top of her head twice with her fist.

"Why did she hit herself on the head?" I asked the world at large.

Evan turned to me with a grin. "That's a diving signal. It means *okay*. We're moored and the boat's secure."

Relieved that he was acting normally again, I nodded to him. "Excellent. I'm learning already."

April returned, and the area became silent when Gabe shut off the engine. The sky was a deep azure, the air stirring my hair with a hint of breeze. The only sound was the waves lapping against the fiberglass hull.

"This site is called Lone Pine," April said and pointed toward shore where a scraggly evergreen valiantly reached toward the sky. "The reef starts only a couple feet below the surface and slopes down to seventy feet, so it's one of our favorite spots for snorkeling and diving. Let's go!" She peeled her board shorts over her swimsuit bottoms but left her long-sleeved rash guard on. I kicked myself.

Why didn't I think of that? A rash guard would have covered me up more.

But it was too late now. I moved to the shady bow and pulled off my cover-up, folding it and placing it in my beach bag. Wearing a one-piece blue-and-green suit, I tried not to be self-conscious. I was a curvy girl and had to wear suits with a built-in bra. No strappy, unsupportive tops for this D-cup. April separated our masks, snorkels, and fins into four piles while the two men peeled their shirts off and joined her.

Oh, holy hell. Here we go again.

I'd seen Evan when he'd been lifting weights. He'd had a shirt on, but it didn't hide the fact that his upper body was toned and muscular. But seeing his glorious chest and shoulders completely exposed was another matter entirely. Light-colored hair covered his pecs and I itched to run my fingers over the strands. To discover whether they were coarse or silky.

Focus! Snorkeling! Concentrate on not drowning.

That was good advice, so I took a deep breath and stomped on my libido. April picked up a web belt with several lead weights attached and wrapped it around her waist. That distracted me from Evan. "What is that?"

"Oh, I wear a weight belt so I can free dive easier. It helps me find critters in the reef better." She handed out the snorkel equipment to each of us.

I gripped mine tightly, swallowing over my dry throat. "Are you kidding? You want me to wear *lead weights?*"

April laughed and cocked her head. "Of course not, silly! I'd never do that to you the first time you snorkeled."

"Okay. Thanks," I said as we shuffled toward the platform at the stern of the boat. I was still flustered, now more at the thought of entering that deep water than the sparks igniting between Evan and me. We were adjusting the fit of our masks when I noticed the torsos around me. "Wait a minute. Aren't we supposed to wear snorkel vests or something?"

Evan turned to me. "Let me get you a life jacket. Sorry, I didn't think about that. Gabe and I are used to not wearing them."

I shifted from foot to foot. "I don't want to be any trouble."

"That's why we have jackets on board," Gabe said. "Lots of snorkelers use them. Don't feel bad."

Moments later, Evan returned with a blue-and-yellow floatation vest that fortunately bore little resemblance to the orange ones I'd seen in disaster movies. He held it for me while I slid my arms through the holes and buckled the straps shut in the front. "Thanks. I feel better wearing this."

"Of course." He winked at me. "Ready?"

Gabe and April already had their fins on. In unison, they jumped off the platform and disappeared with a huge splash. They rose to the surface together, April hanging loosely onto Gabe's shoulder.

Okay, jump into the ocean. Where sharks and barracudas could be lurking just out of sight. Super.

I took another deep breath and stepped forward, determined not to show my uneasiness.

Evan joined me, then sat on the edge of the platform. "Come sit next to me. We'll slide into the water. It's less jarring that way."

I shot him a grateful smile as I sat on the edge and put my fins on. I wasn't sure how he knew what I'd needed, but his idea was perfect. When I slid off the platform, I felt the floatation provided by my vest immediately and relaxed. "Okay, this works. Now let's see if I survive the sharks and sea monsters."

Evan laughed. "Don't worry. We keep the sea monsters locked up, and I'd be amazed if we saw a shark. They're getting rarer and rarer."

His voice was sad, which surprised me. Less sharks had to be a good thing, right? I settled my mask on my face and put my snorkel in my mouth, then we joined April and Gabe.

As soon as I put my face in the water, I forgot all about my nervousness. The reef was a multicolored jewel, shimmering in the bright sunbeams. Tropical fish flitted and swam everywhere. They were all shapes, sizes, and colors. Some were solitary. Others moved in pairs or small groups. I gasped when a school of at least thirty blue fish swooped down to the reef below me. They ranged in hue from the lightest blue to deep indigo, but most were a medium blue shade.

I pointed frantically with my finger and waved at April with my other hand, wanting to make sure she saw the huge group of fish. Laughing, she lifted her head out of the water. "That's a school of blue tang. They're the custodians of the reef. They eat algae off the coral and keep everything clean."

The coral reef was like an underwater city, with everyone doing their jobs and the entire system working in harmony. A bright green, foot-long-fish with a yellow dot behind its pectoral fin swam right in front of me. Evan was next to me, and I grabbed his arm and pointed. We tipped upright.

"That's a parrotfish. I forget which kind." He cupped his hands around his mouth. "April!"

She heard and peered at us.

"What's the name of the green parrotfish with the yellow dot behind its head?"

"Stoplight parrotfish. That's the male. The dot looks like a yellow light. The reddish-white mottled ones are the females."

After she mentioned them, I saw many of the female parrotfish. They moved in loose groups, using the sharp beaks that gave them their names to gnaw on the hard corals.

Eventually, Evan and I separated a small distance from April and Gabe. Evan might not have her encyclopedic knowledge of the underwater world, but he was wonderful company. He always stayed at my side, making sure I was having fun, and his reassuring presence increased my enjoyment by leaps and bounds.

In fact, I was having the time of my life. The vest kept me safe at the surface and the fins helped me speed through the water. Evan dove down ten feet to inspect the reef, but I was happy to float on the surface.

While he was submerged, I glanced in another direction and froze. A fish swam toward me. From its beak, I surmised it must be another parrotfish. But this one was huge, a solid three feet long, and brilliantly colored. Its head was vivid red, and the color transitioned to a bright mint hue on the back half of its body before becoming red again on its tail.

My eyes felt huge as it swam past in a leisurely fashion, then traveled within a foot of Evan. He also halted, becoming motionless as the large fish stopped to gnaw off a huge chunk of coral. The sound of it chewing on the reef came to me clearly through the water. With a dart of its tail, the enormous fish continued on its journey, swimming out of sight.

Evan grinned around his snorkel as we surfaced, then spat the mouthpiece out. "That was pretty cool."

"Amazing! That was also a parrotfish?"

"That one I remember. It was a rainbow parrotfish, one of the biggest kinds. We've been at this almost an hour—you ready to dry out?"

I wanted to continue, but my fingertips were pruny, and I was afraid my sunscreen would wear off. I nodded. "Should we call April and Gabe?"

They had moved a distance away and Evan shook his head. "They'll come back when they're ready."

Evan had dropped the ladder into the water before we slid in, and now we climbed back aboard. I grabbed a towel from my bag and dried myself off, using it to squeeze the saltwater out of my hair. I was grateful no mirrors were around. God only knew what my long, curly hair looked like. I tried to tame it as best as I could with my fingers before grabbing the tube of sunscreen and joining Evan in the sunshine at the back of the boat. I sat next to him on a side bench, rubbing sunscreen into my arms and legs.

"Hope you don't mind being in the sun some more," he said, tipping his head back and closing his eyes. "I need all the sun I can get on my face to even out this color. I look ridiculous."

I barked a laugh. "You look anything but. Why did you hide such a handsome face under that beard?"

A smile widened across his face, but he kept his eyes closed. "It just got to be a habit. But one I'm ready to change."

"Well, don't get too much sun or you'll end up looking like a tomato."

Opening his eyes, he shifted position and our arms pressed against each other. "So you enjoyed your first experience with the underwater world?"

"I loved it! Not sure I'd prefer diving, though. All that equipment—it seems claustrophobic to me."

A faraway look came into Evan's eyes as he stared at the horizon. "No, it's just the opposite. You're completely weightless and don't need to surface to breathe. It's absolute freedom."

I took his hand. "I'm sorry you can't dive anymore."

He lifted a shoulder. "I'm too busy to dive anyway. This is nice, especially with you here."

His eyes were a warm, soft shade of blue that held me captive. He hadn't wiped his face and water beaded over his cheeks and forehead. One slowly trailed down the side of his face. That bolt ran through me again, heat spreading from my abdomen outward.

"Well, look at you two. Staring into each other's eyes!" April called from the water, a short distance behind the platform.

Irritation flashed through Evan's eyes before he quickly covered it. "Does she *try* to have the worst timing in the world?"

I couldn't help laughing as I turned my attention to April. Gabe popped up next to her and swept his arms around her. Wrapping hers around his neck, they settled in for a long kiss. "Hey!" I called. "At least we're not being indecent. Get a room."

April broke the kiss and turned to us with a grin, her arms still looped around Gabe's neck. "So? You're a couple now. Show us how it's done!"

My heart dropped into my stomach.

"Come on," April said, her smile enormous. "I want to see a kiss!"

"Yeah, Evan," Gabe piped in, also grinning. "Consider it practice. I'm sure Nona would love to catch you two making out."

I swallowed hard, my eyes inexorably turning to Evan. He stared at me, and one brow edged upward as he spoke softly. "We are supposed to be a couple, aren't we? I guess a kiss is expected."

A fluttery ripple traveled through my core. This was ridiculous. I was thirty years old and as nervous as a teenager. "Okay." My voice came out nearly a squeak.

Evan brought his hand up and gently cupped the back of my head. Slowly, we moved our faces toward each other. Would his lips be warm from the sun or cool from the water? Closer. My eyes shut, every sensory signal in my brain firing straight to my lips. Closer. The air became warmer between our faces. I could feel his breath tickling my lips and resisted the urge to wet them.

Then our mouths were together. The pressure between us was soft, tentative. I placed my hand against his cheek, mirroring my position from earlier, and his hand closed in my hair. He pushed my face against his, our kiss lengthening.

An enthusiastic whoop came from April in the water.

Still, we didn't stop. I inhaled deeply through my nose, catching a musky, masculine scent from his sun-warmed skin that shot straight through me. I'd meant to keep this first kiss sweet and chaste. After all, it was a fake kiss, right?

Instead, I pushed my tongue into his mouth, probing gently. He answered and we started a wet, hot ballet as our kiss deepened.

"Okay, now who needs to get a room?" Gabe said, his voice much nearer.

Startled, I broke the kiss as he walked to the other side of the boat. Heat flashed over my face, a mixture of desire and embarrassment that I hadn't even noticed Gabe coming back on board. I licked my lips and shot Evan a glance to check his reaction. His bare chest visibly moved in and out, and I couldn't help dropping my eyes to the bulge in his board shorts.

Okay, it's not just me.

Raising my eyes back up, a strong red flush ignited his face, and his eyes said he wanted to rip my swimsuit off right here and now. We stared at each other, trying to process what had just happened.

Gabe tossed his fins onto the side bench, then turned to help April up the ladder. She broke into that bubbly laughter. "Oh my God. You two are just the cutest. I love it.

You're both beet red, like that was your first kiss or something!"

At that, Evan and I both smiled. Small, halting grins at first. But soon our mouths widened. I don't remember who laughed first, but soon both of us were guffawing. April's smile fell, her expression morphing to confusion.

I wasn't about to admit she had been right on the money, so I grinned at her instead. "Don't mind us. We're just giddy."

As I rose to retrieve some drinks from the nearby cooler, I couldn't stop thinking about Evan. How he'd made sure I got the flotation device I wanted. How he'd stayed by my side the whole time we'd been in the water.

His scent. His kiss. That bulge.

A warm, exhilarating shiver tickled from my head down, and my toes curled against the fiberglass deck.

Okay, maybe not such a fake relationship anymore. Maybe more friends with benefits?

Chapter Fifteen

Evan

THE LATE JANUARY evening was cool from a stalled cold front as we walked into the stadium. The town of Marathon had done an admirable job with its minor league field, less than five years old. Rows of seats surrounded the area behind home plate, stretching to first and third base and leaving nothing but a fence and scoreboard in the outfield.

I let Liv walk before me, since technically this was her date. The seats were definitely hers. I let my hand brush up and down her sweater-covered back, enjoying the sensation. Both of us had been a little shaken up by that kiss. I hadn't minded much when April and Gabe kind of steamrolled us into it, but I'd been rather stunned at my intense reaction to it.

To Liv.

I'd barely been able to keep my eyes off her in that amazing swimsuit she'd worn. And, my God, those breasts! It had probably been a good thing she'd worn the lifejacket and covered them up. After returning to the Big House, we'd both been a little shy and had retreated to our separate rooms. By the next morning, I still hadn't figured out what our status was.

Were we still pretending? There was nothing pretend about that kiss.

My biggest concern was her thinking I expected her to get physical. She'd said she wanted to help by posing as my girlfriend, and I'd assured her I never wanted her to feel pressured for anything she didn't want. Now I was afraid to ask what she wanted.

Me? That was easy. I wanted Liv in my bed—and in my life. But I wasn't sure I wanted her in my heart. The success she'd had getting Sweet Dreams Mini off the ground only confirmed how out of my league she was. Plus, she only agreed to be with me until the wedding. As soon as that was over, we were off.

So maybe I should just relax about the future and see where this goes while I still have it.

Yesterday, I'd worked with Dylan again, this time on his fastball. Liv had seen us in the meadow and asked me if I'd like to go to a Hammerheads game. That was a loaded question if I'd ever heard one. But we did need to go out on a real date, and a baseball game was an innocuous choice. Or it would be for anyone but me. Of course, Liv didn't know that, and she was so proud of her team sponsorship, there was no way I was going to refuse her.

So here we were.

She led us to a section between home plate and first base, scooting between the rows to two seats eight rows up. High enough to have a good view of the entire field, but low enough to see well. I took my seat and inhaled a deep breath of freshly cut green grass and popcorn to let the experience roll over me. The murmur of the crowd around us. The sounds of the players as they warmed up, such as the thwack of the ball hitting the catcher's mitt as Dylan warmed up. All of it instantly recognizable. All of it heartbreaking.

I sought to distract myself with conversation and turned to Liv. "I didn't realize you were a big baseball fan."

"Oh, yes. I have been for years. Used to watch every Red Sox game I could." She pointed to the large Sweet Dreams banner in left field. "And I've always wanted to see my own business advertised on the outfield fence."

"You should be proud of yourself. You've done a great job since the fire."

"Thanks. It's worked out better than I expected. My customers are very loyal." She reached out to hold my hand. "They're not the only ones."

"Our arrangement has been good for the resort too. I talked to one of our front desk clerks, and she's had several people come ask about bookings."

"Good. I sure hope you get something out of this."

I nudged her shoulder with mine. "I already am."

Her cheeks turned pink as she smiled. "Apparently, I'm not the only baseball fan. Dylan told me this morning you're really helping him. He said you know a lot."

Rushing filled my ears as my heart raced. Hunter's young face entered my mind and I forced myself to relax. "He's being generous. I'm a fan, like you. I played in high school. Several fields are on Big Pine Key, and there's been talk of starting a local rec league. Do you play sports?"

Liv burst into laughter and hooked her thumbs toward herself. "Do I look like an athlete?"

I cocked my head. She had curves and a voluptuous figure that looked like the perfect female form to me. "Sure you do."

Her expression softened. "You are the sweetest, Evan Markham. I love watching sports but have never been very good at participating. And I was self-conscious about it."

I didn't want her to feel uncomfortable, but I understood what it was like to feel like a spotlight shined everywhere you went. "Well, if you want to make kayaking a regular thing, just let me know. You were great at that."

She leaned against me. "I have a feeling you went easy on me. I went for a walk down there on my lunch break the other day and tried to lift your kayak. You must have it full of rocks!"

I laughed. "Not rocks. Weights. Kayaking was part of my rehab to help me build upper body strength."

Her eyes turned sultry. "Well, you've certainly got plenty of that. I couldn't help noticing when we went snorkeling." She had a smattering of freckles on her cheeks and a dimple that appeared when she smiled. But she wasn't smiling now. A current ran between us—the same one we'd experienced on the boat.

We were interrupted as the crowd broke into cheers. The teams took the field, the Hammerheads playing defense since they were the home team, and I pushed the memories away. I watched Dylan head to the mound, deftly hopping over the baseline. A cold emptiness filled me.

As we had entered the ballpark, I'd bought two score-cards and programs. Now I pulled out one large white card and handed the other to Liv. I needed to stay occupied during this game. "You want to keep score?"

She took the card, her mouth forming an O. "I've never done it before. It looks so complicated!"

"It's not too bad once you get the hang of it. I'll show you."

Dylan threw his first pitch, a fastball for a strike, and I showed her how to note it on the scorecard. His changeup had improved substantially, and he got the first batter out in five pitches. Batter two hit a line drive up the middle for a single, just beating out the throw from the Hammerheads' center fielder. I showed Liv how to record the base hit and found myself relaxing.

By the fourth inning, I was invested in the game and enjoying keeping score. Liv asked smart, interested questions, but I made sure to keep my answers vague enough that she didn't realize just how much I knew.

I couldn't go there.

But tonight was a good beginning, the first time I'd been near a ball field in over thirteen years.

Dylan had a great eye as a batter, hitting the ball sharply while letting those outside the strike zone pass by. But as the game went on, his form deteriorated on the mound, and he started opening up that shoulder again and flopping forward after his pitch. When he went in to pitch the ninth inning, I was starting to worry.

From the crack of the bat, I knew instantly the batter hit a home run. I winced.

"Oh, no!" Liv moaned as the ball sailed over her banner and out of the park. In their last half inning, the Hammerheads came up empty and lost three to two.

We filed out with the rest of the disappointed crowd. "Dylan did a great job until the last two innings," I said but didn't add my surprise that the manager didn't pull him for a relief pitcher. He didn't have the stamina to go nine innings yet.

"Yes, that's true. Last game I went to, he made it seven innings, so he's definitely improving."

The night was downright cold now, probably in the mid-fifties, and Liv rubbed her arm. "I can't believe what a wuss I've turned into. This temperature would be heaven if I were still in Boston."

I put my arm around her shoulders and drew her against me as we walked toward my Explorer. "But you're not, and this is pretty cold for the Keys."

I opened the passenger door and held it for her. Instead of stepping inside, she faced me. "Thanks for coming with me. I really enjoyed this."

"So did I." And with a smile, I realized it was true. Maybe being a spectator wasn't the worst thing in the world after all.

Liv's curly hair was down tonight, and I couldn't resist tracing my hand over it. Soft and wild, I loved her hair. Before I could stop myself, I leaned down and pressed a soft kiss against her lips. Liv met me eagerly, our kiss lengthening until a couple arrived at the car next to us. With a smile, she got in and we started the half hour drive back to Calypso Key. I turned on the heater and headed toward Highway One.

Liv waved her hands in front of the vents. "Ooh, that feels good. When I saw that huge fireplace in the living room, I thought it was nuts for Florida. But now it doesn't seem like such a bad idea."

My heart skidded a few times, my libido at war with my head. I spoke before I had a chance to second-guess myself. "I have a fireplace in my room. I like a fire on nights like this. You want to join me for a glass of wine when we get back?"

She smiled, her face softly glowing from the dashboard

lights as she turned toward me. My body heated up rapidly as her green eyes stared at me. "A warm fire and wine? You do know the way to a girl's heart, don't you?"

"Well, I try." Twitching the corner of my mouth, I tried to project confidence. God, I wanted her. But she'd be moving back to her place on Dove Key soon. Could we keep our hearts out of this? Could I?

Chapter Sixteen

Liv

I SEARCHED through a drawer in my dresser, chewing my lip. I was getting more than a little worried as I tried to decide on undergarments. I'd told Evan I needed a few minutes before joining him. My insurance had made a blanket payment to me, to provide for the remodeling and replacement of any furnishings or clothing that couldn't be salvaged. That first week, I'd gone through my smelly, smoky clothing and saved a few sentimental items and a few nice dresses. The rest of the money was going toward restoring Sweet Dreams and new furniture for my apartment.

So most of the clothes I had with me at Calypso Key were thanks to Discount Mart. They were functional and comfortable, my highest priorities at the moment. Sexy times had never entered my mind. Pinching a utilitarian white bra with wide shoulder straps between my thumb and index finger, I held it up in front of my face.

"They had black," I muttered. "Why didn't I get one in black too?"

I currently wore the same model in an even more utilitarian beige color, but the white was slightly prettier. I quickly changed bras and pulled on a pair of white cotton panties, trying not to cringe at the tiny blue flowers covering them. And tried even harder not to wince at the extra pounds I carried, and the fact that the man I was about to meet had the body of a Greek god. After a brief survey of my clothing choices, I settled on black leggings and a loose green blouse that brought out the color in my eyes. I carefully brushed my hair, wishing for the thousandth time it wasn't curly. Then I stepped back and looked myself over.

Okay, I look nice, but not too nice. Like I'm not expecting anything in particular.

I couldn't do anything about my horrible undergarments, but maybe that wouldn't matter. Maybe Evan really just wanted a glass of wine, then he'd shoo me back to my room.

What did I want?

We'd already crossed over the fake relationship line. But having sex would be in a completely different category. That would leave a chasm we couldn't jump back over. And yeah, it had been a long time since my lady parts had had a workout. I was more than a little tempted.

I frowned at my reflection. "We're both grown adults. We can have a good time without getting the feels for each other. Liv, he's Evan Markham. You need to keep reminding yourself of that." I said the words with conviction. As if I believed them.

Squaring my shoulders, I marched out of the bedroom and knocked on Evan's door. He'd changed too and now wore a dark-red polo shirt and jeans. He looked freshly scrubbed, and a wave of scent hit me, making me flare my nostrils. Not aftershave or cologne. The scent making my insides rearrange themselves was more subtle and fresh. The scent of a man cleaning himself up just for me. A fine growth of stubble covered his firm jaw.

His eyes skated over my hair, taking in the curls that had now worked themselves over my shoulders. He twitched a smile at me, and I had to fight to keep from licking my lips. He tipped his head toward the corner of the room. "I've got a bottle of red open. That okay?"

"Wonderful."

I glanced around the room as we crossed the smooth wooden floor. The layout was very similar to mine, except his bed linens were gray and mint green. A watercolor of a baseball diamond hung on the wall, making me smile. A loud crackling jolted my head toward the corner we neared, where a dark gray couch with a mint-green blanket folded over the top sat in front of a cheery fire. The fireplace was made of stone, the inside black and showing many years of use.

I sat down on the couch, finding the fabric soft and welcoming. With a nod, I accepted the glass of red wine. "Your room is very cozy. I like the décor, plenty masculine and yet cheery too."

He grinned as he sat next to me, our upper arms touching. "Well, I didn't have anything to do with it. When Dad remodeled this end of the house, a professional designer furnished the two bedrooms."

"I still think it suits you." I rubbed my bare feet against the silky floor below. "Though my floor is made of rougher wood."

"We kept the original flooring in that room." He hesitated a moment. "But Dad put in extra smooth wood here, so my wheelchair wouldn't have any issues getting over it. My rehab nurse lived in the room you're using for several months."

Touched he would share that with me, I grazed my fingers over his strong arm and the defined muscles beneath it. I didn't want him to dwell on those times. Especially tonight. "And now it can serve as a reminder of how far you've come."

Evan took a sip of wine and shrugged. "Mostly, I'm just too lazy to move to another bedroom. You can't beat the location."

"I'll second that."

He grasped the section of my hair that had fallen forward over my shoulder and twirled a lock around his index finger. I closed my eyes at the weight of his hand on my chest, just above my breast.

"What made you leave Boston and come here? Just the cold winters?"

A hard jolt ricocheted through my body and my eyes flew open. This was an awful subject for me, a mixture of humiliation and appalling humor. But Evan had shared his terribly painful past. I owed him my story. "The short version is I was run out of town on a shingle. It's a good thing we're not in colonial times any longer, or I'm sure I would have been tarred and feathered first. It was because of the bakery I owned."

His brows flew halfway up his head. "Really? You're an incredible baker. What happened?"

I took a healthy swig of wine, then refilled both of our glasses. "A wedding happened. Not mine," I added when his eyes widened. "I love making wedding cakes, and I had developed quite a reputation in Boston. I was seeing success with my business and finally scored my dream client. She was part of the old-money Boston elite, marrying the son of a similar family. The connections alone could have set me up for life."

"Was she a bridezilla?"

I shook my head. "No, though she had very specific requests. The cake was going to be gigantic. Their reception was for over five hundred people. But the bride requested one thing that was unusual—she wanted a chocolate cake with white buttercream frosting."

"And that was a problem?"

I waved a hand absently. "Not at all. She and her fiancé became engaged in the Swiss alps, and she wanted me to use a very particular Swiss chocolate in the cake batter. The day before the wedding, she brought over a stack of bars of it for me to use."

"Okay..."

I bit my bottom lip, trying not to laugh even as shame caused a red wave to heat my face. "I thanked her and set them on the counter near my mixer, then went out for supplies. I shopped for my business at the local warehouse club—big bags of flour and sugar, other stuff."

"Makes sense." His face was carefully blank as he studied me, trying to understand.

"I was a little... uh, backed up."

His brow wrinkled. "A long line in the store, you mean?"

I groaned. "No. Constipated, okay?"

Evan grinned. "Oh. Sorry. Carry on."

"I figured, as long as I was there, I'd get something for it. I knew I didn't need the industrial-sized pack of laxatives, but it was a warehouse club, you know?"

Evan nodded, his brow becoming lined again.

"I'm getting to the heart of the story. I stood there with

people all around me, and there must have been ten different kinds of laxatives! I was in a hurry and embarrassed, so I just grabbed a block of the ones that are like chocolate candy bars.

"When I got home, I unloaded all my supplies and put them away inside the bakery. I lived several miles away, so I just placed the laxatives on the counter to take home that night. Then I started baking the cake for the wedding the next day. I always let them cool and set up overnight, then frost and finish them the following morning."

I sighed and took another giant gulp of wine. I flopped my head against the back of the couch and stared at the ceiling, pausing until I worked up the courage to stare at Evan once more. "What I failed to notice was that I'd placed the laxatives next to the bride's chocolate bars."

His eyes flew open wide. "No! You're not saying..."

"Yeah. I am. I took the chocolate home and put the laxative in the cake batter."

"Did that make the cake turn out weird?"

"Oh, no. It was spectacular. I needed to add cocoa powder and sugar to get the flavor profile just right, but I thought it was because of the artisan Swiss chocolate. It was one of the most incredible cakes I'd ever designed. The bride practically jumped up and down after I delivered it." I heaved another sigh and rubbed my forehead. "She wasn't quite so happy after all five hundred guests ate their pieces of it. Halfway through the dance part of the reception, the scions of fine Boston society all got a colossal case of the shits."

Evan blinked rapidly, visibly biting the inside of his cheek to avoid insulting me. But he couldn't hold it in and started laughing. "Oh, God. I'm so sorry. I shouldn't be laughing."

Reluctantly, I joined him. "It's okay. Enough time has passed that I can laugh about it too. But I wasn't laughing after the bride's mother called to scream at me. Several of them, including the bride's family, threatened to sue me."

Evan's smile plummeted off his face, replaced by a scowl. "For what?"

"Gross negligence and about a thousand food code violations. Finally, they all agreed to drop everything if I closed up shop and left town. So I did. There was no way I could ever recover without starting over somewhere else."

Evan moved closer and slid his arm around my shoulders. "It was an honest mistake. You're incredible at what you do, and you've proven that here."

"I'm sure trying. And don't worry. Gabe and April want a traditional white cake with cream cheese filling between layers. They're safe."

He started laughing again. "I'm not worried."

My shoulders shook, and I pressed a hand to my belly. "I was amazed how good the laxative tasted when I ate a square that night after baking the layers."

"You didn't look at the label?"

I was howling now. "I was too damn tired. I just opened the bar and bit off some."

We leaned together, both chortling. He was solid and reassuring, and it felt wonderful to share my horrible story with him.

"I imagine you weren't too impressed when it didn't work."

I nodded. "Very disappointed the next morning. But that problem cleared right up after I got the call from the bride's mother that the entire wedding reception had destroyed the toilets at one of Boston's most prestigious hotels."

That was the last sentence I got out for a while—we were both laughing too hard to talk. It felt good to laugh about the disaster. I'd been deeply shaken when I'd arrived in Dove Key and hung out my new shingle. Not at all sure failure wouldn't follow me like some clingy, malignant puppy.

I straightened and took Evan's hand in both of mine, stroking the top of it. "You're the first person I've told that story to here. I was so embarrassed and humiliated, I couldn't tell anyone. I'll let April know all about it eventually, but *after* her wedding."

"Thank you for trusting me." His expression softened, once more becoming the sweet, warm face I knew so well. Except now with that granite jaw and sharp cheekbones on full display, he was also over-the-top gorgeous. And sexy.

The fire had created a warm, luxurious cocoon around us, and he pulled me close again. I rested my head against his shoulder, and he kissed my hair. "You don't have anything to be humiliated about. You put the debacle behind you and forged on. I really admire you."

I tilted my head up to stare at him. "Thank you. I admire what you do too. This place runs like clockwork, and you're amazing at balancing being likable while making sure everyone does what they're supposed to."

He shrugged, shifting in place slightly. "I don't do anything special. This job—"

I silenced him with a finger against his lips. "Don't do that. Your job is damn hard, and you make it look easy. This place would fall apart without you." I placed my hand against his chest, fanning out my fingers. His pec was firm under my touch. Unable to resist, I slowly traced my finger around it and down the middle of his chest. I raised my eyes to stare at him. "I think you're incredible."

Evan grabbed my face with both hands, crushing his lips to mine. The shock of it sent my blood racing through my body. He pressed his tongue between my lips, and I threaded my hands through his thick hair.

"I've wanted to do this since I first saw you in the bakery," he whispered against my mouth.

I nipped his bottom lip, making him grunt. "I used to wonder who you were. I always looked forward to your coming in."

He lowered one hand to caress a finger down the valley of my breasts, and I didn't need the fire to warm up now. I grabbed the hem of his shirt and lifted, rushing one hand below it. His chest hair was soft yet wiry, and his skin was shockingly hot under my fingers. Leaning forward, he ripped the shirt over his head.

I pulled away to stare at him as I slid both hands across those broad shoulders. Letting each finger trace every defined ridge. "I've wanted to do *this* since I first met you."

"Is that all, Liv?"

Chapter Seventeen

Liv

I DARTED my eyes back to Evan's, which now held a hint of challenge. Slowly, I raised my lips into a smile, meeting his gaze steadily. "Not even close, Evan."

Kissing me again, he buried one hand in my hair as he leaned forward, pressing me backward onto the couch. He claimed my mouth, his lips soft and firm. Completely in control. Letting go of my hair, he slid his hand under my shirt, dancing his fingers across my stomach.

I couldn't stop the wrenching moan that escaped me as he slid his hand under the cup of my bra and stroked my breast, rolling the stiff peak between his thumb and finger. Rising onto his elbow, he broke the kiss to lift the bottom of my shirt, coaxing it upward.

That was when I remembered what I had on underneath. "Oh, no."

He froze, the material of my shirt bunched in his fist. "What's wrong?"

"I... I don't have anything sexy here, Evan. You're going

to laugh when you see my bra and underwear. They're from Discount Mart."

At first, he just stared at me, his head slightly cocked. Then he lifted the corner of his mouth. "I don't think you need to worry about that. If this goes how I'm hoping it will, you won't be wearing them very long."

I tried not to squirm or bite my lip. "Okay. Good. I just wanted to warn you in case you've been having fantasies about me wearing something exotic and sexy. I'm not. In fact, I'm really not a very sexy person, period."

Now a genuine smile rose on his face. "Oh yes, you are. Whatever you wear becomes exotic and sexy, Liv." He brushed a soft kiss across my lips. "And I've been having all kinds of fantasies about you. But in every one, you've been naked."

"Oh. Well, I can do that." And at last, I relaxed. Accepted that he wanted me. Me.

He kissed a line over my neck, his tongue making swirling circles across it, and a steady throb radiated out from my core. My concern about my undergarments faded to nothing.

Evan stopped to whisper in my ear, "I don't care what you have on. I'm more interested in what's underneath."

That was all the invitation I needed. I sat up to pull my shirt off and unhooked my bra. I started to pull it off when he placed his hand on my shoulder, over the straps. "Don't. I want to take it off."

I lay back down, and he slowly pulled the strap off, laying a row of kisses on top of my shoulder. He moved downward, kissing the top of my breast as he pulled the strap down my arm, and I maneuvered out of it. With a deep groan, he pulled the cup away and squeezed my breast, taking it into his mouth. A deep, drawing sensation rocketed through me, and I arched my back, reaching with my hands to push against the back of his head.

"Your breasts are incredible," he mumbled against my skin. "When I saw you in that swimsuit, I almost lost it."

I laughed softly. "Believe me, I had the same reaction when I saw you." I stopped speaking and closed my eyes as he drew my bra completely off and explored my other breast, licking and sucking.

His shoulders and upper back were all hard muscle, rippling under my touch. I was more turned on than I had ever been in my life. With one final kiss, he pushed himself up and held out his hand to me. "Come here. My bed is much more comfortable."

I rose to my feet, pulling him down for another kiss, then moved both hands to his chest and pushed him backward. Together, we stumbled across the floor, the wood warm against the soles of my feet. When we reached his bed, we tore the rest of our clothes off, then we came together again in another wet, long kiss. Skating my hand down the center of his chest, I fanned my fingers out and grazed his abs with my fingertips. The muscles danced under my touch, making me smile against his mouth.

Reaching lower, I wrapped my hand around him, softly squeezing the hot, hard length. The air rushed out of his lungs in something that was half exhale and half moan. Hot pulses rocketed through me, and I lifted my thigh and held it against his hip.

"Touch me, Evan."

He traced his fingers over my upper thigh, making me twitch. My breathing grew hurried, every nerve firing in my body. Moving my head, our lips adjusted against each other as he lowered his hand between my legs and slowly stroked me. With a wrenching moan, I pushed hard against his hand, already feeling the waves cycle up, growing stronger, faster.

"Yes, Evan. Like that."

"God, Liv. I want you. Now. Get in that bed."

With a smile, I took a step backward and let my eyes slowly travel down his magnificent body, my core clenching. Spinning around, I pulled back the covers as he opened his nightstand drawer and withdrew a strip of condoms. Tearing one off, he tossed it on top, then became still, just watching me lie on my back. The covers were folded down, leaving my breasts and stomach fully exposed. Instead of feeling self-conscious about my curves, his intense stare caused desire to flame through me. And the other obvious sign of his arousal turned me on even more, its thick length sending another jolt through me.

Evan climbed into the bed and dove for my breasts. I plunged both hands into his hair, letting myself surrender to the sensations flying through me. He rolled his tongue in tight circles lower, circling my navel as he parted my legs with his hands. He lifted his eyes to mine. "I need to taste you."

I wasn't even capable of words at this point, only replying with a breathy moan and a nod. He shimmied downward, settling between my legs. With the first swipe of his tongue, I arched upward and cried out. He settled in, swirling his tongue in a way that made me insane. I slid my knees up the cool sheets, curling my toes as the deep pulsing heat spread through me. Radiating out from my center.

"Oh, God. That's it!" I clenched both of my hands in his hair, pressing against his face as my climax overtook me. I was loud, wanton, and completely uninhibited.

When it finally subsided to volcanic twitches, Evan vaulted to his hands and knees and grabbed for the condom on the nightstand. Ripping the foil package open, he sat on his knees and rolled it on. I felt half-liquid, like my bones had partially melted, and I lazily drew a finger up his thigh, then drew it across his shaft. "Don't take too long with that."

"Not a chance. We're not close to finished yet."

Watching me intensely, he climbed on top of me and settled between my parted legs. My skin was still exquisitely sensitive, and his body on top of me sent twitches and shivers through me. He held me with his gaze, and I couldn't look away as he slid his hand up the length of my inner thigh. I parted my lips with a breathy moan as he slowly stroked me. A shudder wracked me, and a slow smile rose on his face.

"You like that, don't you?"

"Yes, Evan."

"You want more?"

I thrust my hips against him. "Yes, Evan."

He kissed me hard, our mouths smashing together. "So do I." He thrust the words into my mouth.

Reaching between us, I grasped him and maneuvered his shaft to my entrance. Then I raised my hips, slowly pushing him inside. He didn't need any coaxing and thrust sharply. Deeply.

I gasped, pain and pleasure mixing unexpectedly.

He halted, staring at me. "You okay?"

"Yes. I haven't done this in a while, and you're... a lot to take. Go slow."

He raised onto an elbow. "You want me to stop?"

I nipped at his earlobe. "Evan, that is the last thing on earth I want right now."

With a smile, he kissed me again and moved more gently. After a few strokes, my body remembered what to do, and I stretched deliciously. Arching my back, I rubbed my breasts against him and nibbled along his jaw.

"Yes. Like that, only harder now."

I tasted his stubble as my hands skated over his back, reveling in the fact that I—I!—was comfortable asking for what I wanted. He obliged with a deep growl, slowly building speed like a locomotive. He was built like one, all muscle and power. I grabbed his ass and squeezed, pushing him harder into me. We pounded together now, nothing gentle or hesitant in our movement.

"Yes!" he breathed in my ear, gasping in tune with our movements now.

I wrapped my legs around his waist, crossing my ankles, and he gave a deep, shuddering groan. "Oh, God. That feels even better."

I couldn't have agreed more. I was on the cusp of pain and pleasure again, urging him deeper and harder. He grabbed one of my hands and flung my arm out sideways, intertwining our hands. Pinning me. Evan was a big man, but my panting breaths had nothing to do with his weight on me. I'd never been into rough sex, and never really experienced it. But tonight, he brought out something inside me I didn't even know was there. My orgasm mere minutes ago now seemed like years, and my body grew heated once again.

"More, Evan. Give me more."

He did, and from the sounds he was making, it came from the depths of him. I thought of rolling over on top of him but didn't want to break our flow. The pain was still dimly there, but now it had nearly been replaced with hot waves rolling through me. They rose and joined, becoming one long, continuous sensation that swept me away with it. At the same time, Evan froze with one final, guttural cry.

His head was buried in the hollow of my shoulder, his breath hot against my neck. Both of us shuddered.

Slowly, we cycled down, our breath returning from gasps to deep, filling inhalations. Our mouths came together in a soft, tender kiss. My heart filled my chest, and my bones now felt fully liquid.

"Are you okay?" he asked quietly as he lifted onto an elbow. "That got a little rougher than I'd planned."

I giggled, unable to keep it in. "Unless I need to get up and walk somewhere, I'm fine. I hope you don't mind company tonight."

A line formed between his brows. "I'd love it if you stayed here tonight. But are you hurt?"

His sweet concern made me laugh more. "I've never felt better in my life, Evan. That was incredible."

His worry lines disappeared as a smile lit his face. He rubbed his nose against mine. "It was. *We* were. I've never experienced anything quite like that. I'm not generally that... rough."

"Well, now that we got that out of the way, we can try for sweet and passionate next time. Maybe next week, after I can walk again."

Both of us started laughing, and he rolled off me, pulling me tight against his chest. I felt warm and secure in his arms as the remnants of the fire cast flickers over the ceiling above us. I snuggled tighter against him, and our legs scissored together.

And that chasm I'd wondered about earlier? The one I didn't think we could jump back over?

It had just turned into the Grand Canyon.

Chapter Eighteen

Evan

"MUCH BETTER!" I said to Dylan and clapped him on the back. Once again, we stood in the meadow on a warm afternoon as he threw at the net target, and I tweaked his form. Over the weeks since he started working at the resort, we had developed a regular schedule of me giving him pitching tips. Our sessions had grown to three players, adding two teammates who had been impressed by his progress and wanted to ask me for help. Even though I'd tried to explain I was anything but a professional coach.

"But you've got a really good eye and can explain things so we understand," Dylan had said with a shrug. "That's what counts."

What finally convinced me to include the two other kids was that they obviously weren't getting the coaching they needed from the Hammerheads' pitching coach. I didn't want to step on anyone's toes, but impromptu sessions in a field could hardly be considered professional coaching.

Both ball players were bullpen pitchers hoping to make the main Hammerheads team in a few weeks. I was pretty confident Dylan would make the roster, but the other two didn't have his level of talent. But I did the best I could. I pointed at Andre, a tall, lanky nineteen-year-old. "Work on that curveball more. If you only throw fastballs, you're going to get eaten alive once hitters figure out your timing."

He nodded and wound up, throwing a curve with a decent amount of break. I glanced at my watch. "That's more like it. I need to head to Orchid, guys. Keep practicing and I'll see you again on Wednesday."

"You're coming to the game, right?" Dylan asked.

I laughed. "As long as Liv brings me. She's the one with the tickets. I'm just a freeloader."

The young man grinned. "Don't think you need to worry about that. You're all she talks about."

That gave me a little extra spring in my step as I hopped onto the path and strolled toward Orchid. The past week, Liv and I had spent every night together, a couple in her room and most in mine. Despite how good we were together and how comfortable I was around her, I still couldn't bring myself to tell her she was the only woman who had ever spent the night in my first-floor room.

My casual encounters before her had always been in the women's rooms, and I never stayed the night. But from the moment I met Liv, I felt differently around her. Toward her. I found myself looking into any room I entered to see if she was around, and we had developed a regular routine of kayaking on her mornings off. Neither of us had broached the subject of the future, or the fact that we obviously weren't faking anything anymore.

I had plans to tour Sweet Dreams in a couple of days with her and check on the remodeling progress. I was half dreading it, excited to see her dream become something even more impressive than it had been before, but also closer to the point where she would move out of the Big House.

What then?

That was the last thing I wanted to think about. I found myself rubbing my chin, a habit I'd picked up since I started shaving again. At least my jaw had picked up some sun, so my face was all the same shade now. I pushed through the back door and into the Orchid kitchen, where Rea bent over a counter, applying decorative rosettes to a multi-layered dessert before her. As usual, I quickly glanced around the area, but she was alone. "Liv already left for her dress fitting?"

Rea answered without looking up. "Yeah, you just missed her. She and April breezed out, talking about dresses and champagne afterward. Aren't you and Gabe doing something similar today?"

I smirked. "I seriously doubt champagne will be involved. I'm a beer guy, and he likes whisky. But yes, we're going to the tux shop in a little bit." I approached and stood on the other side of the island as she finished the final rosette. "I wanted to say thank you for working so well with Liv. It sounds like you really have your routines hammered out."

Straightening, Rea nodded. "I wish there were a way I could hand over all the morning bakery stuff to her and concentrate only on desserts. I'm much better at them. Any chance that might happen?"

I grinned. "What? You want me to double the pastry chef payroll? Don't think so, Rea. Besides, Liv can't wait to get Sweet Dreams back open again."

She shot me a curious look. "I thought maybe you'd be looking for a reason to keep her around."

Our relationship was now common knowledge, though neither of us had tried to hide anything. "Dove Key isn't far away. I'm sure we can manage the distance just fine."

At least, I hope so.

Rea shot me a devious grin over her shoulder as she cleaned up her station. "And before we know it, you'll be bringing in donuts every morning behind my back again."

I rolled my eyes. "Oh, be quiet. I didn't do anything behind your back." Though I had. A little.

Rea returned with a plastic container to hold her torte until it was ready for serving tonight. "This is all I had left. I'm taking off for the day."

After depositing the dessert in the big walk-in cooler, she was just moving to the exit door when it opened. Alfonso strolled in like a thundercloud, wearing a black chef's coat and white pants.

"Hi there," she said cheerily, throwing him a gigantic smile. "I have the best timing! What a great time to be leaving."

He shot her a dirty look as she slid past him and into the sunshine. As he set his backpack on the counter, the chef saw me standing there and his frown turned to a glower. "You!" he spat. "I have just learned of an intolerable insult."

"Me? What did I do?" I quickly ran through a catalog of our recent interactions but had no idea what could have set him off.

Alfonso drew his hefty frame to full height, though he was still shorter than me. "Your brother and his wedding. Is it true that you are using an outside caterer? You Markhams are too good for my food, is that it?"

I stared at him for a long beat, completely floored. "Alfonso, Stella is doing the catering. Our sister. And it's her wedding gift to Gabe and April. This has nothing to do with you."

Tilting his head up, he stared down his nose at me. "Obviously. If your sister were any good, she would be executive chef here, not me."

Be careful there, asshole. You might get your wish.

"When I recruited you, Stella was too green. But in the years since, she's earned her stripes, learning under one of the best chefs in the Keys."

He sniffed, not mollified. "It is still insulting, Evan, and sends the wrong message."

I took a long, deep breath and kept a handle on my temper. "This wedding is small and intimate. Just family and close friends. It's hardly an affair where we need to worry about image."

"Weddings are always about image."

"Maybe in Italy, but we're more casual around here." He muttered under his breath, but I let it go. "Any word about a new show?"

Alfonso snapped his teeth together with a click, exhaling loudly through his nose as he dropped his eyes to the steel counter. "Yes, my agent is in contact with several producers. But he hasn't received anything concrete yet."

From his reaction, I wondered how true that was. But I'd had enough of my temperamental chef for the moment. "Well, good luck. Speaking of weddings, I'm off to get fitted for my tux. Have a good shift, Alfonso."

Gabe drove the two of us to a men's formalwear store in Marathon. We traveled in his Mercedes with the top down. I had to admit it was pretty fantastic to drive over Seven Mile Bridge with the sun warming me and the wind ruffling my hair.

Our tuxes were a similar charcoal gray with matching bow ties, except Gabe's had tails. He frowned as he looked at himself in the mirror. "This damn thing doesn't make me look like Fred Astaire, does it?"

I laughed. "Hardly. He was much better looking than you. And a better dancer."

"No argument about the dancing." Dad had forced Gabe to endure years of dancing lessons growing up. They'd gotten in such big fights about it, Dad had relented and let the rest of us off the hook. Gabe always had a special place in my heart because of it.

"Planning on dancing at the wedding?"

He broke into a grin, and there was something private about it, like a joke I wasn't in on. "One or two dances for sure. Don't worry, we won't expect anyone else to join in if they don't want to."

Getting up in front of a crowd with my limp on full display was something I wanted to avoid at all costs, so that was good news. The shopkeeper appeared with my jacket and held it for me. Slipping my arms in, I shrugged it all the way on, then froze when I felt my shoulders bind tight. "Uh, this needs to be let out at the shoulders."

Gabe replaced his jacket on the hanger and nodded to the man. "My brother has shoulders like a linebacker. So unless you want him busting out of that coat, you'd better alter it."

"Of course," the man said. "That won't be any problem at all. The pants fit all right?"

Gabe and I both looked down at our gray-clothed legs with our sock-lined feet sticking out and nodded. The shopkeeper carefully removed my jacket and folded it over his arm. "I can have this ready within a few days. Will that work?"

Gabe nodded. "The wedding isn't for a couple of weeks, so that's plenty of time."

We decided to have a beer afterward, and Gabe drove us toward Conch Republic. On the way, we passed Salty's, a dive bar and not one of Gabe's favorite places. Soon, we both nursed IPAs at an outdoor table at the brewpub.

"Wonder if the girls are done with their dress fitting," I said.

Gabe snorted. "If they are, I imagine they're holed up at one of the bars at the resort. I heard April say they're planning on drinking plenty of champagne since neither has to drive."

I laughed and took a long drink. "Easy for her to say. She doesn't have to get up at three a.m."

Gabe eyed me steadily over the rim of his pint glass. "Things are going well between you two?"

Oh, big brother. You have no idea.

Then again, he was the one getting married. Maybe he did. "Yeah. Really well, which is kind of a weird feeling."

"Because you haven't felt like this for a while?"

I hesitated, then decided to come clean. "Yeah, that's part of it. But there's something else. When we first got together"—I used air quotes around the two words—"as a couple, it wasn't real. We were only pretending."

At Gabe's stupefied look, I continued. "One night, Nona was relentless about me getting involved with someone to bring to the wedding, so I blurted out that Liv and I were a couple. Liv overheard the conversation and wanted to help because I'd helped her after the fire. So we posed as a couple to make Nona happy."

"And I'm guessing it's gotten real between you."

"Very."

Gabe sat back in the booth and rested his arm on top of

the upholstered back. "So what? You've liked her for a long time. Sounds like she feels the same about you."

"Our arrangement was that we'd pose as a couple until the wedding, so I don't know what will happen then."

"Why should anything change? You'll still only be a few miles apart."

That wasn't the problem. And I couldn't talk about my insecurities with Gabe. He was the most self-assured, confident man I'd ever known. He'd never understand how baffled I was that Liv would ever be interested in me. "I'm just worried this will all blow up in my face."

"Sounds like there was more of a chance of that when you were pretending. When did you two, uh, really become a couple?"

I laughed, relieved to have the secret out with someone. "When we went snorkeling. That kiss you saw was our first kiss."

Gabe's eyes widened. "Didn't look like it."

My smile faded. "Yeah. I think we both got thrown for a loop. This is really complicated."

Gabe's watched me closely, his eyes crinkling at the corners. "Doesn't mean it's not worth it. April and I had some major things to work out, and at one point I almost lost her. Yet look at us now."

Not that long ago, my brother had been a man who didn't believe in love. And now he was about to get married. I was involved with a woman I could easily fall in love with. Hell, I was halfway there at least. I'd never been happier with someone.

Which was why I was so scared I was going to screw it up.

Chapter Nineteen

Liv

"THERE'S ONE!" I shouted from the passenger seat of April's SUV as we slowly traveled down Main Street. We had been looking for a parking space near Key to my Heart Bridal but had been unsuccessful until I spotted this space a block away.

"Grab it, April," Maia, who came along for moral support, added from the back seat. "You're not going to find a closer one."

The bride-to-be snuck into the spot, and we piled out, April and I walking side by side with Maia trailing slightly behind. We were down and across the street from Sweet Dreams, but as we'd driven by, I had been able to peer through the open front door at the construction crew busy restoring my bakery. I was struck by the odd symmetry of my life. How the first friend I'd made in my new home was now engaged, and I was her maid of honor and involved with her fiancé's brother.

We strolled along the brick sidewalk and under colorful hanging baskets bursting with flowers, each hanging from an ornamental streetlight. Every block featured a different arrangement, and here they were a profusion of pink, purple, and white. As I turned my eyes forward once more, a smile rose on my face at the sight of Brenna Coleridge walking toward us with an iced coffee in one hand.

I pointed at her drink. "I'll have you back in my shop in no time."

"Good! The exercise is probably good for me, but I'd much rather get my java fix right across the street. Afternoon, April." She smiled at the divemaster as we passed, then her smile fell as she spied Maia behind us. The two women gave each other a cool stare and even cooler nod as they crossed, then Brenna was behind us.

I shot Maia a quizzical glance over my shoulder. "What was that look about?"

Maia lifted one shoulder as she closed the distance, resting a hand on our shoulders. "Nothing personal, but we're not friends. She's a Coleridge, after all."

Now I was totally confused. "What's that mean?"

April giggled, the sound matching her personality. "Oh. The Markhams and the Coleridges *do not get along*. Sworn enemies until the end of time."

I raised a brow at Maia. "Really? Why?"

She grinned. "April is exaggerating, and it's a very long story. Plus, we're here. I'll tell you some other time."

Looking up, I saw she was right. I opened the glass door and waved my arm to April. "Brides first. Please."

"Why, thank you," she said and breezed past me.

Maia shook her head and smiled, going second. Key to my Heart Bridal Shop was decorated in white and a soothing shade of soft green. We headed toward the counter, where a twentysomething woman wearing too much makeup stood with her auburn hair slicked into a bun. Looking up from her bridal magazine, she brightened at the sight of us. She brushed a hand over a white plastic garment bag hanging next to her. "April, your dress is all ready to go, and Hailey's is here too. Liv, yours is hanging in the dressing room. The alterations are complete. But is there a third dress I don't know about?"

"Nope," Maia said with a grin. "I've already been through this part, though my wedding gown came off the rack. April's doing things right." Maia's wedding to Wyatt had been a rather rushed affair due to her being pregnant.

"Okay," I said and rubbed my hands together. "I'll go try on my dress."

Several minutes later, I stood in front of a three-way mirror, twisting this way and that as April and Maia exclaimed.

"Do you like it?" April asked.

"Very much," I replied, completely honest. The dress was a muted ice blue and strapless. It hugged my curves nicely, ending just below the knee, and the shape showed my breasts to full advantage.

"Very nice," Maia cooed. "You two will look gorgeous. Can I see your dress again, April?"

"Oh, if you insist." Her grin could have split her face as she grabbed us by the forearm and manhandled us to the hanging garment bag. She unzipped it to reveal a white silk wedding gown with long sleeves and a sweetheart neckline. Sequins flowed in gentle swirls across the bodice.

I hadn't seen the dress yet and gasped as I softly touched the smooth fabric. "It sparkles! Just like you. It's the perfect dress for you, April."

"I just love it." She gave me a quick hug. "I can't believe you and Evan are a couple too! I can't imagine a more perfect wedding."

I hugged her back, squeezing her shoulders. I'd kept silent about the fact that Evan and I had started out as pretend lovers before taking a very sharp turn to real ones. I wasn't about to broach the subject with Maia there. Though she was very down to earth, she was still Evan's sister, and I didn't know how she would react.

Maia had been inspecting a rack of clearance dresses but now returned. "You've been good for Evan, Liv. He's been living in the past for too long. My brother has the biggest heart of anyone I've ever known, and it's high time he shared it with someone."

"Thanks," I said softly. "I really like him."

If I thought he'd been irresistible that first night I spent with him, he had only cemented my opinion in the nights since. Evan was equal measures of sweetness and passion in the bedroom, and I loved every minute of it. He was my idea of the perfect man. Well, as long as no one brought up Hunter. But Evan's little brother was hundreds of miles away and busy with his own life, so that wasn't likely to change. Though it still saddened me that Evan couldn't find a way to forgive him. This hatred was so unlike Evan—he was so even-keeled in everything except his brother.

We'd gone to another Hammerheads game, and I'd kept score again, more assured this time. Evan had watched Dylan raptly, a satisfied smile rising on his face when the young player struck out the side. Evan might not have played for a long time, but he was obviously a sharp student of the game. Something else we had in common.

"I've seen Evan working with a few of the Hammerheads players," April said, then turned to me with a grin. "I can't tell if they come to the resort for the coffee and pastries or the baseball tips."

"Dylan says Evan's got a good eye," I replied. "He knows a lot about the sport and some of his friends wanted help too."

Maia watched me closely, and something in her eyes made me feel I was being evaluated. "It definitely brings some life to that meadow. Does Evan talk to you a lot about baseball?"

That was an odd question. "We've gone to some games together, so I guess it comes up. We're both fans of the sport. Why?"

She smiled and waved me off. "Just being a nosy sister. Never mind. You can satisfy my curiosity about something else, though. I've seen the two of you walking toward the marsh several times. Do you kayak together?"

I nodded. "I've never been athletic, but kayaking is mellow enough to suit me. He's gallant enough to use the heavy boat and I paddle the light, sleek one. There is so much wildlife in there! Ospreys, egrets, even manatees."

A smile raised the corners of Maia's mouth. "That wetland is so peaceful and natural, and we don't plan to ever develop it. The guests enjoy it too. And it's always been one of Evan's favorite places. You're definitely special if he wants to share it with you."

A fuzzy heat spread through my chest at her words, a mixture of happiness and the desire just thinking about Evan brought out in me.

"The other day, Gabe mentioned he might look into fortifying the path more," April said as she studied my dress. "It gets flooded a lot now. He might elevate it with a wooden boardwalk."

"That's a great idea!" I said. "I love walking along that path, but after a good rain, it's pretty impassable."

Evan and I had kayaked after work on many occasions, but last time we took a bottle of wine and shared it on a small islet he called a hammock deep within the marsh. He and I had spent a *lot* of time together lately After a Hammerheads game, and we'd had dinner on Dove Key. We'd spent one afternoon and evening in Key West, watching the sunset at Mallory Square. In the space of one week, everything had changed between us. Yet to everyone else who knew us, nothing had. And the wedding drew ever closer.

I'm really getting in over my head here.

Swallowing back my disquiet, I straightened and smiled at April. "You're going to have a wedding to remember. I can tell already."

"I can't wait to see my cake!"

"It'll be the absolute best cake I can make, promise."

I had no qualms I could do that. Though the disaster in Boston had ended my career there, I was level-headed enough to recognize it had been a simple error. One which should have been prevented, but the debacle ensured nothing like that would ever happen again. I turned my smile to Maia. "If April's the bride, and you and Wyatt are in the audience, who's going to be leading dives that day?"

"We've got backup divemasters we can call. Gabe's already got it arranged."

I nodded, not surprised. Gabe was a man who liked his ducks in a row and his machine well-oiled.

The shopkeeper finished with a customer and strolled over, eyeing me intently. "The dress looks like it fits perfectly."

Lifting my arms out, I twirled in a circle. "It does. I'll take it with me."

Folding her arms, Maia gave me a grin and drawled, "Blue dress this time. Maybe it's your turn for white next."

My stomach lurched, and a confusion of emotions filled me. I didn't know how to feel about all this. I felt like I was within a strong tide that was sweeping me along. Only I had no idea what it was sweeping me toward.

Chapter Twenty

Evan

"YOU LOOK BEAUTIFUL TONIGHT," I said as I trailed a finger over Liv's soft shoulder. She wore a black tank dress, and her long, curly hair fell down her back. I could hardly keep my eyes off her. The night air around us was nearly still as we ambled down the hill toward Orchid, and I took her hand in mine, squeezing softly.

Winking, she looked me up and down. "You clean up rather well yourself."

I looked down at my dress shirt and black slacks and shrugged.

She grinned. "Though I expect this is nothing compared to what I'll see in a few more days."

I winced. "I hate wearing suits. And tuxedos are the worst."

"Oh? Do you wear them often?"

I laughed and swung our clasped hands. "No, thank God. Suits are a very rare occurrence." *And have been for a long time now.* But at least I could laugh about it.

Landscape lights placed at the edge of the concrete path gently lit our way, illuminating the trimmed foliage lining the trail. We passed the break in the landscaping that led to the back door of the restaurant. We'd be walking through the front entrance tonight. The foliage grew taller as we skirted the restaurant, becoming two towering hedges lit with tiny twinkling white lights. Walking through a lit archway, the path ended at a T-intersection with a six-foot bluff in front. A wide vista of ocean lay before us, the western sky still holding a broad stripe of crimson.

We turned right under a trellis that continued the twinkling white lights theme. Colorful and fantastical orchids were placed at even intervals, and Liv walked slowly, inspecting them as we neared the entrance. "These are so beautiful! After spending just about every day in the kitchen of this place, I'm excited to finally eat here."

"I'm sorry. I should have brought you here sooner."

My chagrin turned to warmth when she glanced at me with a shy smile. "Don't apologize. I wasn't criticizing. I had no idea orchids were so varied!"

"These ones are the hardiest of the bunch. They have to be since they're planted out here. But if a storm is brewing, we bring the pots inside so they're protected."

We stepped through the threshold of the open-air restaurant. Warm, tropical hardwood walls lined both sides where more orchids trailed out of pots. These were more exotic, temperamental varieties. I approached the young woman behind the hostess station, who wore a white blouse and knee-length black pencil skirt. She looked up and gave us a warm smile. "Good evening, Liv, Evan. I have your table all ready."

"Thanks, Susan," I said, and we followed her to a table

for two on the outer perimeter of the restaurant, overlooking the ocean. Potted orchids were placed between tables, creating ambiance and privacy.

We ordered a bottle of Chardonnay and Liv decided on Alfonso's seafood pasta special of the evening. Though spending dinner with Liv was something I'd looked forward to all day, I was also on the job somewhat, evaluating my executive chef's skills. He would undoubtedly know we were here. I ordered the fresh catch, figuring his special of the night would be a testament to his skills. And dedication to the job.

When our entrees came, I studied each dish. Both were presented attractively, and I poked at my fish, pleased that it flaked apart easily. Then again, one of our junior chefs could have cooked it, leaving Alfonso to put on the final touches. I scooped up a bite and dipped it in the tropical cream sauce, chewing thoughtfully. It wasn't bad, and as I'd guessed, the fish was cooked perfectly. But Alfonso's sauce was... okay. I could taste a little heat within a coconut milk base, though it was rather bland. Not what I expected from a famous chef headlining one of the best restaurants in the Lower Keys. I frowned at Liv. "How's your pasta?"

She poked at it with her fork. "Good. I like it. I wouldn't say it's the best thing I've ever eaten, but I'm enjoying it."

I exhaled something that was part sigh and part growl. "Exactly. This place is only three-quarters full. I'm almost hoping Alfonso gets a cooking show next year after his contract is up."

Liv smirked. "I wonder if that's even happening, or if he's making it up to sound more important."

"You could be right. But either way, I doubt I'm renewing his contract."

"Why isn't your sister working here?"

"Stella loves Key West. But she's also always loved Orchid, so I'll try to wear her down. She's obsessed with orchids, and many of these are her choices. I'll talk to her about it at the wedding. Speaking of which, did you get your dress figured out?"

"I did, and it's beautiful! I'd actually wear it again. Who knows? Maybe even here sometime." She took a sip of wine, then set her glass down with a thump. "Oh! Maybe talking about your family nudged my memory. Something odd happened when we were walking to the bridal shop, and I've been meaning to ask you about it."

"What was that?"

"We ran into Brenna Coleridge. She's in the book club with April and me and we're friends. We said friendly hellos as we passed, but she and Maia kind of shot daggers at each other. When I asked Maia about it, she said there was some sort of bad blood between the Markhams and the Coleridges, but we didn't have time to talk about it."

I wiped my mouth with my napkin and eased back in my chair, smiling. "Yeah, the enmity between our families goes way back to the mid-1800s."

I grinned as Liv's eyes became round. I loved her enthusiasm and that she was a woman who faced life head-on. She didn't let that awful disaster in Boston stop her. She just pulled herself up by her bootstraps and started over.

"Huh?" she asked. "What on earth was so awful the feud is still going on?"

I barked a reluctant laugh. "I wouldn't say it's an actual feud. Mostly, it's just that the bad feelings have been going on for so long, everyone just perpetuates them. It's kind of silly, really. It's not like we're direct competitors or anything."

"Right. They own Sunset Siesta Resort."

"Yeah. It's smaller and more... rustic than Calypso Key."

"Are they jealous of all the land you have here? Is that what caused the rift?"

I grinned. "You could say that. I don't know about jealousy, but the land definitely caused the feud originally." I took a sip of the rich wine before launching into the story. "The Coleridges used to be the main landholder in this part of the Keys. They were the original owners of Calypso Key and most of Dove Key."

Liv stuck out her bottom lip in a way that made me want to kiss it. "Oh, did they fall on hard times? They had to sell off their holdings?"

"I think they've sold off just about everything on Dove Key except the resort, though we Markhams are the last ones to ask about that. None of us know the details. But Calypso Key was another story altogether."

Leaning forward, I folded my arms on the table. "My great-great-great-grandfather, George, moved here from New York in 1860, when he was only twenty years old. Came here by boat and settled on Big Pine Key. He had designs to start a fishing resort, where people would come from Miami for big game fishing."

"So he was a fisherman? Is that how he made his living?"

I laughed out loud and reached across the table to stroke her hand. Her skin was velvety soft. "On the surface, yes. But the rumor is most of his money came from smuggling. Back then, this was a pretty rough area, filled with rough characters. From what I understand, George Markham fit the mold perfectly. Dashing, courageous, and willing to risk damn near anything."

Liv rested her cheek in her hand, smiling at me as she turned over her other hand to lace her fingers through mine.

"He liked to go to a bar, or maybe it was called a saloon back then, and play cards."

"Oh, a gambler, then?"

"George started out as a small fish, but he was one of those guys who could sell ice to Eskimos. And it didn't take long before he was seated at a high-stakes poker game with three other men. One of them was Archibald Coleridge. Coleridge couldn't stand George. He was older and thought George was shiftless and had grand ideas with no brains to back them up. So he set out to teach George a lesson via poker."

"What happened?"

"They started off with small stakes, but the pot grew as the night progressed. The two other men eventually dropped out, and just George and Archibald were left. The story goes that at almost four in the morning, George proposed one final hand. He'd put up his property on Big Pine Key and every dollar he had in his possession, and Archibald would bet Calypso Key. Winner to take all."

Liv slammed her hand on the table, her mouth dropping open. "He won?"

I nodded, a smug grin washing over my face. "He won. We got Calypso Key in a high-stakes poker game, and the Coleridges have hated us for it ever since."

Laughing, Liv pressed both hands to her face, and I was smiling just watching her reaction. "George trudged all over this Key, locating where to put his home and where the resort would be situated. The Big House dates from a later time, but it's in the same area where George built his home. Originally, the resort was a few ramshackle huts on the beach. He married a girl from Key West a couple of years later and the Markham dynasty was born. The resort's been in the family ever since."

"That's an amazing story!"

I stroked her hand. "Thanks. Over the years, we've had some perilous moments. We almost lost everything during the Great Depression, but my great-grandfather Charles secured financing and kept us in business. He was good friends with Ernest Hemingway, which might have helped. And more recently, Gabe provided financing to dig us out of a hole. He's the majority owner of the Key and resort now."

"You have a devoted family. I'm looking forward to meeting Stella."

"I'm sure you'll like her. And I know she'll get along with you. I can't imagine anyone not liking you."

"I know a few people in Boston who would argue that point."

I burst out laughing. "Touché. But you dusted yourself off and moved on, and that's what counts."

Liv's stare became evaluating, and she opened her mouth but shut it again with a tiny shake of her head. "I've had a great time tonight. Thank you."

"You're welcome, but I'm a pretty cheap date. Free dinner is one of the perks I get from running the joint. So don't be too impressed." She laughed and we clinked our wineglasses together. A hint of a breeze carried the bracing scent of the ocean as it ruffled my hair.

As we neared the Big House, several lights were on, including in Dad's master bedroom at the end of the house on the top floor. Liv studied the structure. "I've never really seen the upper floors—too afraid I'd get lost."

I laughed softly. "I wouldn't worry about that. And the two upper floors are just bedroom suites with some miscellaneous rooms thrown in now and again. My dad uses most of the third floor. And Hailey has a room at the opposite end. It used to be Gabe's, and she loves sleeping in her dad's old room."

"I can see how she'd like that. Which room was yours growing up?"

I pointed to the end, under Dad's room. "Second floor on the end. Nona's room is on the other end and Maia used to live there too. There's a big parlor in the middle that's Nona's domain. She likes to do puzzles there." I snorted. "And play poker with unwary people who underestimate her."

"Ah, she takes after your ancestor, huh?"

"It runs in the family, apparently."

"I'd like to see your old room."

Surprised, I glanced at her as we neared a side door. "Really? The room isn't much. It's been remodeled, and there's nothing left from my childhood."

"Oh, is it a mess? I don't want to poke around in the dust."

I shook my head. "No, it's clean. Our housekeepers clean everything regularly."

"Yeah, I noticed. This is the first time I've had my room cleaned for me several times a week."

We entered the house, and I led her down the hallway and up the grand, sweeping staircase. "Does it bother you? You can ask them not to clean."

Liv grinned. "On the contrary, I could get used to it."

That gave me a happy, contented feeling as I led her by the hand past Nona's parlor and toward the end of the house.

We passed a couple of shut doors. "What's behind those?"

"One is our music room, where Gabe got his dancing lessons." Grinning, I turned and pointed to the one across the hall. "That one is just a storage room now."

"So much history here. I can't imagine what the attic must look like."

A memory flooded me of when Hunter and I used to play explorers up there as kids. She was right—it was full of mysterious, antique artifacts, and we'd spent hours playing. But I didn't want to think about that, and I sure as hell didn't want to think about Hunter. Especially when I was with a beautiful woman I was crazy about.

I opened the door, and we entered the dark room. Moonlight peeked through the sheer drapes, casting a bluish hue to the room. Liv glanced around. "This is the same layout as ours downstairs."

I shrugged. "It works, though. Every room has a king-sized bed, a sitting area, and a patio or balcony. And a private bathroom."

"Oh, I'm not complaining. These suites are incredible, especially in such an old house. And I like how each one is decorated differently. It's hard to tell since it's dark in here, but is this room green?"

I nodded. "The colors are muted and pretty timeless. Stella likes to use this room when she visits."

Liv closed the distance and slid her arms around my neck. "But you were here first. That means you get to call the shots."

Bending my neck, I caught her mouth with mine. Her lips were sweet and absolutely delicious. "I definitely call the shots. Any particular shots you're interested in?"

"Mmm." She unhooked one hand and reached down to

palm me. I pressed against the contact, a grunt escaping, and then my pulse galloped at the smile she sent my way. "I'm sure we can think of something. I feel like an explorer up here. We need to investigate." My breath hitched as she trailed a row of kisses across my jawline.

She pulled back to stare me in the eye. "I suggest we start with the bed. But you call the shots."

I picked her up in my arms and she yelped.

"Shh!" I said, trying not to laugh as I crossed the room. "Dad's just above us."

"Sorry. I wasn't expecting that. I'm not used to being carried. Good thing you're such a broad, strapping man."

I set her on her feet next to the bed and kissed her again, brushing my tongue over her lips. "You're easy to carry." I unzipped her black dress and slid the straps over her shoulders. The black fabric puddled at her feet. Underneath, she wore a black lacy bra, and I grinned. "Upgraded, huh?"

"You deserve better than Discount Mart."

"You're beautiful in the moonlight." I unhooked her bra and swept my hands around to cup both round breasts. They were heaven in my hands, and I kissed her harder. Unzipping my pants, she slid her hand in and took hold of me. I exhaled hard against her mouth, leaning into her touch.

Then I remembered something and froze.

"What's wrong?" she asked.

"Shit. I don't have any condoms with me. Do you?"

"No."

"I can go downstairs and get one." I pushed rhythmically against her hand, timing it to her motions. I pressed my mouth to hers again, craving the feel of her. The taste of her.

She broke the kiss to stare at me, continuing to stroke me. "Why? There are other things we can do."

A slow smile crept across my face. "There are things we can both do." I ran my tongue over my bottom lip, and her eyes followed my every movement.

She squeezed me hard, and a shudder ran through me. "Then what are we waiting for, Evan?" Withdrawing her hand to open my pants fully, she lowered to her knees in front of me.

Chapter Twenty-One

Liv

EVAN WAS WONDERFULLY warm as I snuggled tighter against him. I eased out a blissful sigh as he tightened his arms around me, especially content since I didn't have to tiptoe out of bed hours before dawn. I cracked an eye open. Dim light filtered through the blinds in my bedroom. This was a luxury. We usually slept in his room so I could sneak out and get ready for work without waking him. Raising a hand, Evan slowly stroked my hair, and I could have easily been lulled back to sleep.

"You want to kayak with me this morning?" he murmured in my ear.

I patted his bare chest. "I'd love to, but I need to help out in the kitchen for a couple of hours this morning. Dylan is doing a great job, but he's not up to preparing the entire morning's run. I'll make a second one while he covers the shop. Then I'm meeting April for coffee." I sighed. "I'd better get moving."

I tossed back the covers and scooched to the edge of the

bed. As I tipped upright, Evan lunged toward me, wrapped both arms around my waist, and pulled me back with him. "What if I don't want to let you go? Maybe I'll hold you hostage in here."

I laughed and placed my hands over his. "The bride and groom would probably start to wonder where we were."

He made a dismissive noise. "I can handle Gabe."

"I have no doubt of that, but I don't want my poor apprentice getting overwhelmed. This is the first time he's run solo."

Evan relaxed his hold. "Oh, all right. I guess one of us has to be responsible."

WHEN I DUCKED my head in the lobby, Dylan had things well in hand behind the counter of the pop-up shop. I entered and inspected the glass case, noting what I needed to replace.

Relief filled his eyes at seeing me. "We're selling lots of apple fritters and lemon-filled glazed this morning."

"I'll get to work on replacements then. You're doing great, Dylan."

His chest puffed out as he grinned at me. "Thanks. The baking went pretty well, if I do say so myself."

After pushing out the back door, I strode down the path toward the Orchid kitchen. Since I didn't want Dylan to take on too much and not be able to open on time, he had made a bare minimum of pastries this morning, just our best sellers. Soon I had reinforcements baked, delivering them to the lobby on a rolling cart. My timing was perfect as he'd just run out of apple fritters.

I smiled at a woman in line who'd ordered one. "You're in luck! These are still warm."

I bagged up several pastries and left Sweet Dreams Mini in Dylan's capable hands, heading to Daily Grind next door. I made two chai lattes, then, carrying everything in a cardboard tray, I headed outside to a seating area we'd built on the lawn between the lobby and the coffee shop. It served as a lovely outdoor dining area for patrons of both Sweet Dreams Mini and Daily Grind.

I had just set breakfast on a picnic table when April appeared and sat across from me. I set a chai latte and apple fritter in front of her. She took a big sniff of the pastry and groaned. "This smells amazing! Thank you for breakfast."

"You're welcome. Everything coming together?"

She swallowed a bite and nodded. "The chairs and arch for the ceremony arrived just now up at the Big House, and the tables for the reception are due this afternoon. My parents and brother get here in a few hours, and my friends from St. Croix got in last night." Her text tone sounded, and she brightened while reading it. "Speak of the devil! You mind a little company for breakfast? She just picked up a coffee and wants to join us."

"Of course. I even have extra donuts."

A woman came out of the coffee shop and April waved frantically at her. Smiling, she headed our way. In her mid-thirties, she had reddish-chestnut hair that fell to her shoulders in a glossy sheet. Her cheekbones could have been chiseled from porcelain and her chin tapered to a gentle point. The morning was cool, and she was dressed in leggings and a huge sweatshirt that came to mid-thigh. NAVY was stenciled across the front of it in big block letters.

April rose to her feet and wrapped the woman in a hug. "So great to see you! Liv, I'd like you to meet Hope Monroe."

With a warm smile, Hope held out her hand for me to shake. "Nice to meet you, Liv."

"Same here. I've got extra pastries here. You want one?"

Hope sat next to April across from me. "The correct answer is yes," April said to her. "Liv owns her own bakery."

"I can't turn that down! Hit me."

I passed over a chocolate glazed. "Are you staying here at the resort?"

"Yes. My husband and I stayed here on our honeymoon. Which reminds me," she said, turning back to April. "The beach cottage we're in is amazing! Huge upgrade from last time."

April nodded. "We finished them just after Christmas. You're in one with a private pool, right?"

"Yes! I love it. I thought about adding some private pools at Half Moon Bay but couldn't justify the expense at the time."

"We only have two cottages with pools, and they're both two-bedroom."

"April worked at your resort in St. Croix, didn't she?" I asked.

Hope nodded. "And we miss her. I hope Calypso Key knows how lucky they are."

I arched a brow. "Well, one particular member of the family certainly does."

Hope wrapped an arm around April's shoulders and squeezed. "I am so happy for you! I can't wait to meet your fiancé."

"If you go diving, you definitely will. His office is in the dive shop, and he drives the boat a couple times a week. Speaking of diving, where's Alex?"

Hope shaded her eyes with her hand and peered at the

distant ocean off the beach. "He went for a swim, then we'll have breakfast together. But I wanted to catch up with you first."

"You two diving today?" April asked.

"Yes, and I managed to talk Alex out of bringing our own equipment with us. It's hardly worth the hassle of packing it for only one day of diving, but you'd have thought I was asking him to walk blindfolded over a tightrope."

April laughed. "We dive pros like our own gear, don't we?"

"You and me, yes. Alex is in another category."

"Why is that?" I asked.

Hope had taken a bite of her donut and closed her eyes. "Oh my God, Liv. This is incredible. No wonder you have your own business—you'll probably have a franchise soon."

I laughed. "I don't know about that."

"I'm sure you're successful with your bakery. But to answer your question, Alex is ex-military, so he's... rather particular about how he does things."

April laughed and shot me a sardonic look. "He used to be a Navy SEAL."

"Oh. I can see how that would do it." I smiled back, the pieces finally falling into place at who Hope was. April had mentioned carrying a torch for a former SEAL for a long time, though he hadn't felt the same. She'd finally given up when he fell in love with someone else. Hope. And April had found her own happy ending with Gabe.

I glanced at my watch. "I'd better get going. I'm meeting Evan at the main bakery with my contractor to get the latest update." I gave Hope a quick rundown of my fire fiasco.

"Oh wow! That's terrible. Sounds like things are going great here with your temporary shop, though."

"Evan is Gabe's brother," April piped in. "In addition to

being resort general manager, he's one of those guys who can fix anything. So Liv likes him to come along on her remodeling updates."

I shrugged but couldn't bite back a grin. "And maybe because he's very easy on the eyes too." We all broke into laughter as I rose and left the two friends to catch up.

A NERVOUS FLUTTER ran through me as I parked next to Evan's Explorer behind Sweet Dreams. He was still behind the wheel, and we exchanged smiles before stepping out of our SUVs. I was desperately anxious to get my bakery back up and running. Though the pop-up shop had fared better than I ever hoped, the building in front of me was what I'd sunk everything into. It was my dream.

And I was almost in the home stretch now. Work had progressed without delays, and the contractor was close to finishing up. After securing the final necessary permits, I'd be able to move home. Except would it feel like home? My apartment was brand-new, sterile. I'd grown accustomed to my suite at Calypso Key and to ambling down the hill to the kitchen each morning. Used to having lunch and dinner with various family members and strolling along the path that encircled the Key. And Evan was a big part of the reason why.

Evan. The man who'd said at the very start of this that he didn't want to be in a relationship.

And sex wasn't a relationship. Sex was... sex. Wasn't it?

No matter how I felt about him—and I was falling hard for him—I wasn't about to give up my independence to live like a kept woman in that huge house. Even if that was what Evan wanted. Which he'd never even hinted at. Neither of us had brought up the future. But the building in front of us would force us to. Soon.

We met in front of my Tahoe, and Evan bent down to brush a kiss over my lips. "Dylan do all right this morning? When I went into my office, he looked as cool as a cucumber."

"He did great. I helped by making a second batch of donuts, but he handled the shop all by himself."

"Guess if his baseball career doesn't work out, he's got a future as a baker."

"With you giving him pointers, I'm sure he'll have teams knocking down his door to sign him."

Evan shot me a crooked grin. "I doubt I'd have anything to do with it."

As I opened the door, the sharp scent of fresh paint and drywall tickled my nose. I peeked into my office. It was still tiny, but now sported pure white walls and a fresh gray-and-white tile floor. I went around the corner and looked at the beating heart of my bakery, a chill running down my spine.

It was magnificent.

A brand-new cooktop and multi-drawer commercial oven anchored one entire wall, with several rows of stainless-steel counter islands in front. A prep area with multiple sinks lay adjacent to the ovens with rows of cabinets stretching above. A long row of glass display cases stretched along the front, separating the kitchen from the dining area, which was still bare. The new tables and chairs were due in several days.

"Wow," Evan breathed, sticking both hands in the back pockets of his jeans. "This looks fantastic."

"Yeah." I wasn't capable of more than one-word answers.

Jason, the construction supervisor, saw us and

approached. "Well, what do you think? We're just putting on the final touches. The faucets for the apartment upstairs got delayed a little, but I should have them installed tomorrow or the next day. Then you'll be all set to get your permit and move back in. You'll be open again in no time."

A smile widened my lips, but it felt forced. I almost wished Evan weren't here to see this. "You did a fantastic job, Jason. It's everything I've ever dreamed of."

Evan panned his gaze around the room, eyeing everything intently. "You really did nice work here. I'll keep you in mind the next time we do a major project at Calypso Key."

The contractor's face lit up. "Thanks! That would be great."

My smile became more genuine, sheer happiness that I could facilitate this. Though my project wasn't minor, Calypso Key would be in a completely different league. A fact that brought that tight, hard feeling in my stomach back.

"Come on!" Jason said, beckoning us. "I'll show you upstairs."

The same gray-and-white tile stretched through the entire building, and he'd used a slightly textured version on the stairs to keep them from getting slippery. Opening the door at the top, Jason stepped through and stood to the side to let me enter.

The smell of new carpet and paint was even stronger up here, making me rub my nose. The apartment was painted a modern white with a gray carpet stretching across the great room. A living room set had already been delivered, and I was relieved to see my choice looked great. Light gray, the couch and love seat matched the tile perfectly, and yellow throw pillows placed at the ends provided a cheery contrast.

Two white-and-yellow striped armchairs sat across from the couches. In a daze, I floated to the kitchen, which now contained a modern suite of stainless-steel appliances. Though the sink was still without a faucet and the white shaker cabinets didn't have pull handles yet.

"This looks so much better now!" I said.

Jason beamed while I shot a glance at Evan. He was bent over, inspecting the quartz counters, but the muscles in his clean-shaven jaw were tight. Maybe he was thinking about the future too.

My bedroom, containing the same wall and carpet colors, was still empty, the new bedroom set to be delivered the following week. I gasped when I saw the modern rectangular tile lining the huge walk-in shower, the one major upgrade I'd made to the apartment. The bathroom had originally contained a tub-shower combination, but the walk-in was much more functional.

"It's gorgeous! I love all of it, Jason." I turned to the contractor with a smile, less forced this time. "Thank you."

"I should be completely out of your hair by the end of the week, but call me right away if anything needs tweaking. Something always does."

We followed Jason down the stairs, then said our goodbyes to him. Evan and I stood alone in the bright sunlight. We were both quiet, undoubtedly thinking the same thing.

Sweet Dreams would be open for business soon. Maybe by the end of next week.

Then what would happen between Evan and me? Our pretend relationship had become something more. Soon we'd have to decide how much more.

Chapter Twenty-Two

Evan

OUR FOUR PINT glasses made a satisfying clink as they met in the center of the table. The toast was to celebrate Gabe's so-called bachelor party, which was really just us four siblings getting together for a beer at Conch Republic. The groom-to-be sat across the table next to Maia, and Stella sat next to me. Between Gabe and me in the birth order, Stella was a classic Markham, with dark eyes and long, almost-black hair, currently plaited into a side braid that lay over one shoulder.

The late-afternoon sun lay behind us and our outdoor table had a wide-open ocean view to the east. Several other tables were occupied, but patrons had chosen to sit away from us, as if the sight of four Markham kids together needed to be kept a safe distance from.

But as long as the fifth Markham kid was nowhere near —which Hunter wasn't—they needn't have worried.

Stella grinned at Gabe across the table. "Look at you. All relaxed the night before your impending doom. I have to say, this is a big change from the night before your first wedding."

Gabe winced. "Because my first marriage was a disaster, except for Hailey. I look relaxed because I *am* relaxed." He shrugged. "I can't wait until tomorrow."

I hadn't been to Gabe's first wedding because I'd been too messed up from being in a wheelchair to appear at a big public event. So I was looking forward to tomorrow too. And not least because I couldn't wait to see Liv dressed up as maid of honor. I had no doubt she'd be spectacular.

But touring her shop and apartment yesterday had hit me like a punch to the gut. She'd be back home within a week at most. And we were going to have to decide what to do about us. Glancing around the table, I knew my siblings wouldn't understand why I agonized over this. I'd been attracted to Liv at first sight, but when we were faking our relationship, I'd felt safe. I didn't need to worry that she was only with me because she was attracted to the Markham name. I'd had a few of those over the years. Or worse, that she was with me out of pity. And she didn't even know how far I'd fallen. I just couldn't open up about it to her. Maybe someday, I'd tell her the full story, but not yet.

"Penny for your thoughts, Evan," Maia said. "You look serious as a heart attack. This is supposed to be a bachelor party."

I snapped my head up. "Sorry. Got lost in my thoughts for a minute there."

Gabe tilted his head to the side and regarded me steadily. He was the only one who knew that Liv and I had started out pretend and were now... whatever we were. And that his wedding signaled the end of that. "Is Liv moving back home soon?"

I nodded, the motion stiff and slow. "Probably next week."

Stella wrapped an arm around my shoulders. "I think what you did to help her was incredibly sweet, and now the two of you are together. Her moving back home doesn't need to change that."

Maia raised a manicured brow. "Dove Key is only a few miles away."

"I know," I said, staring at the golden liquid in my glass. "We've never really discussed the future, and I'm still trying to figure out how I feel about her."

Maia barked out a laugh. "Are you kidding? You can't take your eyes off her. You two are a great couple, Evan."

"Fessing up to your feelings can be pretty terrifying," Gabe added. "But it can also change your life."

I glanced up at him. "I'm not sure I want it to change."

Stella squeezed my shoulder, her arm still draped over my shoulders. "Well, maybe seeing big brother over there get all misty-eyed tomorrow will change your mind."

That made us all smile. Maia took a drink. "What's Liv up to right now?"

"Baking the layers for the wedding cake," I said. "Sweet Dreams Mini is closed tomorrow so she can spend the morning decorating it."

Stella breathed a long, exaggerated sigh. "What a lucky couple you two are, Gabe. You have a professional baker *and* a chef donating their services."

Gabe broke into a giant smile. "Luck has nothing to do with it. We're just that good."

After the laughter died down, Stella pointed to Gabe. "Are all the guests here?"

Swallowing his beer, Gabe nodded. "Everyone made it.

Not that it's a lot of people. And Maia even got a chance to catch up with April's old bosses from St. Croix."

"I did! And this time I didn't get sick. God, that was embarrassing."

Stella's brows lowered. "What are you talking about?"

"They came here on their honeymoon a few years ago. They own a dive resort in St. Croix and Alex is a dive instructor. I came down with the flu and he led dives for us for a couple of days."

"Yeah, that was a little dicey, liability-wise," I added. "I wasn't about to put him officially on the payroll. But he didn't care about the money anyway, so we just comped their stay. And I gave them a hell of an upgrade this trip."

"And you left the two cottages next to the one April and I will be using tomorrow night unoccupied?" Gabe asked.

"God, yes! No one wants to be near a couple on their wedding night."

"I toured that one this afternoon," Stella said after I ducked Gabe's mock punch and the laughter faded. "The pool is fantastic. You guys did a great job with the remodel. I can't wait to see the resort when everything's redone."

"Phase two starts next week." Gabe relaxed in his chair. "The garden cottages, the lobby building, and Dorado."

I poked Stella in the side as Maia and Gabe got into a conversation about the dive trip tomorrow. "I think there is a very strong possibility Orchid is going to have an opening for an executive chef in less than a year."

Stella smiled, but her eyes were clouded. "The prodigal son returned, so now it's my turn? It's tempting, Evan. I've always loved Orchid. But I also love Key West. I haven't said anything about this, but I've been approached by a restaurant there, also for an executive chef position."

I groaned. "Don't take it! You belong here. With us."

"It's not that easy. Here, I'd just be another Markham working in the family business. There, I'd be making a success of a restaurant completely on my own."

I frowned and set my beer down with a clunk. "You'd have complete autonomy here too. I don't micromanage anyone, not even that strutting asshole peacock-of-a-chef we have now."

Stella laughed. "The new job might not even materialize. I'll keep it in mind, okay? That's the most I can promise."

"Think of all you could do with the orchids. I'd give you a line item in the budget just for orchids." Stella's apartment in Key West was full of colorful, fragile, and temperamental flowers. And all thrived under her lavish care.

"Oh, now you're sweetening the pot."

"I'm not the general manager for nothing, you know." Tipping her a wink, I turned my attention across the table. "So does it feel good to hang out with grownups, Maia?"

She picked at a light-colored stain on her T-shirt. "Skye managed to give me a parting gift before I left and threw up milk all over me. But yes, this is nice. When was the last time we all got together like this?"

None of us could remember, but I didn't miss the shadows that flitted through their eyes at the fact that we weren't all together.

Yeah, well, that's not my fault, is it?

But the wedding marked a momentous day for our family. All of us felt it. Not only were two critical members of Calypso Key Resort marrying each other, they were having the wedding here. At the Big House.

After tomorrow, nothing would ever be the same.

Chapter Twenty-Three

Liv

I BENT down and squeezed my piping bag, easing out a ribbon of dark-blue frosting and fluting it to form a flower. The sun had barely been up when I'd started, but the job was nearly done. Fortunately, Rea had given me room and remained quiet as she worked, providing a distraction-free environment for me. To top it off, even Alfonso stayed away.

April's wedding cake was four layers, much more than was necessary for the intimate wedding. But this cake was important. For one thing, it was my wedding gift to her and Gabe. But it also represented me triumphing over that disastrous cake in Boston.

Finished with the flower, I swapped my piping bag for another filled with ice-blue frosting. I was using the two colors, plus white, to make a cascade of flowers in shades that matched my ice-blue dress as well as Hailey's darker blue one. The decoration started at the bottom layer, swirling its way up the sides of each layer to where I was now putting the finishing touches on the top. Knowing the cake would sit outside in the Florida air for several hours, I'd gone with a white fondant frosting, which would hold up to the heat. Each of the four layers was rimmed at the bottom in a dark blue highlight that faded to ice blue a quarter of the way up, then became white. The color then transitioned to white. I was very pleased with how it suggested the ocean, a perfect image for the bride and groom.

April had been a very low-key client with her request, just shrugging when I'd asked her what she wanted. "I just want a classic white cake. You can decide the rest."

I'd given her a classic cake with modern touches. Each of the four main layers was composed of four thin layers, separated by cream cheese filling. With the fondant frosting around the main layers, the cake was perfectly smooth and crisp. The contrasting blue-hued flowers gave it enough contrast to really highlight the design.

I loved it.

I trotted to the walk-in refrigerator and retrieved the larger, very elaborate edible flowers I'd made yesterday, and placed them on top of the cake. I added a few finishing touches, then stood back and spun the cake on its turntable.

"Oh, this is gorgeous!" I took out my phone and snapped several photos to memorialize it.

But now that it was done, I needed to complete the most dangerous maneuver of all—transporting the cake from the Orchid kitchen to the pool deck behind the Big House. I'd considered transporting the four layers separately and finishing it on the patio, but I didn't want the cake outside that long. Fortunately, Rea was there to assist. She helped me transfer the cake to a decorative serving plate and we carefully, *carefully*, carried it to the back of my Tahoe, which was parked just outside the back door.

Once we reached the Big House, I drove as close as I could get, and we repeated the maneuver in reverse. A table was set up against a shady wall of the house and draped in a white cloth. A runner of the two blue colors lay on top and we set the cake down with huge sighs.

"Thank God that's over," Rea said, wiping a bead of sweat from her brow.

"Thanks for the help. Having someone experienced really makes a difference."

She nodded, then turned her head this way and that as she inspected the display. "I could never make a cake this beautiful in a million years. Great job, Liv."

"You have plenty of talents I can't match, but thank you. And the cake will be out of direct sunlight the whole time, which should keep it from melting." Just in case, we filled several plastic totes with ice and hid them under the table and behind the cloth.

We took a moment to appreciate the patio, now trans-formed from its usual state. In the long rectangular pool, three fountains floated on displays of white-and-blue flow-ers, sending up cheerful, watery plumes. Stella's caterers were setting up long tables at the far end of the flagstone patio under a wooden lattice-covered shade structure, and a dance area was being constructed on the other side of the pool. Several workers strung party lights overhead.

"Looks like everything's on schedule here," I said.

"Are Gabe and Evan together?"

I nodded. "They're getting ready in Gabe and April's apartment. I haven't even seen Evan since yesterday morn-ing. April and Hailey are dressing in my guestroom."

A pang twisted my heart. I missed him. But yesterday, both Gabe and April had needed some last-minute errands, so Evan and I had jumped in to help, our only communication via text. I couldn't wait to see him in his tux, thoughts of which had kept me awake last night. I brushed the front of my apron, streaks of blue frosting dusting my fingers, and forced my mind back to the wedding. "Speaking of my room, guess it's time for me to get ready."

"Hopefully, they've got some champagne in there for you to drink. Your day might be busier than April's."

Laughing, I brushed my hands together. "I doubt that, but the morning sure flew by. Dylan will be in to open the shop tomorrow. He's making a skeleton batch of donuts and manning the store himself so I can have the morning off."

"I'll give him a hand if he needs it, don't worry. But he's great in the kitchen. He told me he finds baking calming."

I nodded. "I'll almost be sorry if he makes the Hammerheads. He still wants to work part-time, but he'll be away on road trips often enough I'll have to hire a second employee."

After we said our goodbyes, I entered the house and headed toward my room. Hearing muffled voices, I opened the door to find April wearing a white silk robe and Hailey getting her hair done by a stylist who had made a house call for the bridal party. Hailey's and my dresses hung on hangers on the closet doors, while April's dress was inside the closet in an empty section I'd created for it.

Gabe's daughter sat in the chair in front of my desk as the stylist, Candace, curled her brown hair into ringlets. Gabe's daughter wore only a touch of makeup, just enough to accent what a beautiful girl she was. "You're going to look so grown up when you're all ready!"

Hailey smiled at me in the mirror. "Yeah. This is a lot of fun. But I'm glad I'm only the flower girl. I just have to sprinkle some flowers, then stand behind Dad."

April shot her a long, assessing look. "You might need to catch him if he faints. He's not going to recognize you."

We all laughed, then I held out both of April's arms as I studied her. Her hair was up in a twist and accented with white flowers and pearls. Candace had artfully applied her makeup and she looked breathtaking. "Nope. I think he might just faint when he sees *you*. Let's get you married!"

THE PRIVATE GARDEN adjacent to the pool deck was surrounded by an eight-foot hedge of red-and-yellow hibiscus. The riot of color created a lovely backdrop for the ceremony. It was late afternoon, and the sun had descended past the upper edge of the hedge, bathing the wedding assemblage in cooling shade. April and I shared a smile as she handed me her bouquet before turning to grasp both of Gabe's hands.

Evan stood behind the groom, and I had to remember how to breathe every time I glanced his way. The dark-gray tuxedo jacket emphasized his shoulders, and his clean-shaven, firm jaw made him stunningly handsome. He gave me a slow wink and I formed a tiny smile in return. Just behind him, Hailey stood watching the bride and groom with a somewhat bewildered look on her face.

My eyes became misty as April and Gabe recited their vows. To distract myself, I let my eyes wander to the guests. Warren sat in the front row, dressed in a blue suit and tie as he rested one arm around his mother's shoulders. Nona had dispensed with the western wear, instead dressed in a dress a shade of blue between Hailey's and mine. Stella, now in a dress, sat nearby, as did Maia and Wyatt. Skye slept in her mother's arms. Gabe's former business partner was attending from Miami, as well as a few key resort employees and friends. April's mother, a plump woman with the same shade of blond hair, dabbed her eyes with a tissue as her husband gripped her hand. April's younger brother panned his gaze around the area, looking bored.

Behind them, April's friends from St. Croix sat. Hope's hair was now styled in an intricate updo, her dress a lovely shade of pink. Before the ceremony, I'd briefly met her husband, Alex. Tall, handsome, and with brilliant blue eyes and sandy hair, I'd expected a former SEAL to be stand-offish and brusque. But he'd been friendly and affable, telling me he couldn't wait for the cake. That alone made me like the guy. Dressed in slacks and a white Cuban shirt, he draped an arm over Hope's shoulders, and they shared a private smile.

My attention turned back to the couple before me when the pastor told Gabe he could kiss his bride. Stepping forward, he softly cupped April's cheek, and they pressed their lips together.

And kept them together.

April mirrored his position, raising her hand to brush his trimmed scruff, and a low ripple of laughter went through the crowd. Still their kiss continued.

"Dad!" Hailey hissed, *sotto voce*. "Stop it!"

I had to bite my cheek to keep from laughing, but her words had the desired effect. The bridal couple ended their kiss with a soft brushing of noses. Smiling, I moved my gaze to Evan, expecting to see him watching them too.

He wasn't.

He stared straight at me. His look was one of deep yearning and something else, a look that made warmth spread through me. He was so gorgeous, pride straightening his shoulders at standing beside his brother. As I stared back at him, helpless to look away, the rest of the crowd faded away. He parted his lips slightly, and I leaned toward him, stymied by the distance between us.

Both of us jumped slightly as the pastor announced in a loud voice, "Ladies and gentlemen, I present Gabriel and April Markham!"

Laughing, April turned to take her bouquet back from me, and I remembered why I was there. Like the flowers I held, hers was an arrangement of white roses and blue carnations but more ornate. I handed it to her. "Congrats, Mrs. Markham."

"Thank you!"

I couldn't help laughing at the absolute elation etched all over her face, the gigantic smile, the sparkle in her clear blue eyes. Gabe took her free hand, and they strolled down the aisle together as the crowd applauded. Evan pressed a hand to Hailey's shoulder and steered her between us as we followed. Once the girl was situated in front of us, he moved his hand to the small of my back, a comforting weight as we headed toward the reception. I caught his eye and both of us smiled—the worst was over and now we could relax.

Chapter Twenty-Four

Liv

AFTER EXPERIENCING DINNER, I understood why
Evan wanted to steal Stella away for Orchid. Her meal beat
the entrée Alfonso had prepared for me by a mile. My
chicken was perfectly spicy and sweet, topped with a salsa
of mango and chiles. Pineapple rice and perfectly steamed
vegetables only added to the meal. Evan and I were separated by the bridal couple between us, and my back still felt
warm where he'd pressed his hand against it. I couldn't wait
until the formalities were over so I could spend some time
with him. Both during the reception and after.

Especially after.

Most gratifying of all, my cake was a stunning success. I
secreted away the top layer for staff to wrap up in case April
and Gabe wanted to eat it on their anniversary. When they
cut the first piece, the bride and groom behaved themselves,
with Gabe wiping a bit of frosting on the tip of April's nose
and kissing it off.

Even I had to admit the cake tasted incredible. I'd added

a touch of almond flavoring, which elevated the flavor considerably, and the fondant frosting held in the luxurious creaminess of the cake layers. Several people went back for seconds, including Alex, who gave me an enthusiastic thumbs-up. I smiled back, immensely proud of myself, and took a healthy swig of champagne.

And of course, no one had a bathroom emergency.

The bride and groom took to the dance floor. I expected Gabe to move well, but April's dance acumen came as a surprise. They moved in an intricate arrangement, their feet moving and swooshing around each other like they were born knowing how to move together.

After the first dance, others joined them as the music transitioned into a sultry Latin rhythm. Nona and Warren danced together, as did Hope and Alex. Evan slid across to sit next to me. I would have loved to dance, but I knew he would feel his limp was on display, and I'd never want him to be uncomfortable.

I leaned against his solid warmth, then squinted as I watched the newlyweds striding across the dance floor. "Wait a minute. Are they doing the *tango*?"

Evan laughed. "Looks like it. I think Gabe truly met his match."

I shivered as he slowly brushed his fingers across my shoulder. "I'd say you more than made up for that Boston wedding. I hope you're proud of yourself."

"I am," I said softly and pushed my empty cake plate away. "I worked really hard on this cake. And I'm confident there won't be any, er, untoward effects." I hadn't said anything to April about my Boston fiasco since I didn't want her to worry on her big day, but I'd be sure to tell her soon.

On my other side, Hailey let out a jaw-cracking yawn, even though it was only early evening. Nona saw it. "Why don't we head indoors, young lady? I got a new puzzle in, and we can work on it until you're ready to turn in."

I smiled at the girl, who was already blinking like an owl. "You like sleeping in your dad's old room?"

She nodded and shot me a sweet smile. "It's fun. He carved his name in the back of his closet and it's still there."

"He did what?" Nona asked, pressing her lips together. "I never knew that."

On my other side, Evan laughed. "Yeah, he did that when he was around ten, I think."

Nona gave him a long, evaluating look. "And what other secrets did you kids get up to that I don't know about?"

With an angelic smile, Evan pinched his thumb and index finger together and drew them across his lips to zip them shut. A round of laughter broke out.

Nona shook her head and stood. "I guess some things are better left a mystery. Come on, young lady. At least I can depend on you."

As Nona and Hailey walked away, Evan took my hand under the table and squeezed. I returned the pressure and held tight. We would have to make some decisions about our future, but I was determined to live in the moment for now. This perfect moment, holding hands with a man I cared deeply about, and maybe more than that, while watching my dear friend happier than I'd ever seen her.

An hour later, I stood on the patio with Hope, a glass of champagne in one hand. April floated over to join us, and I wasn't sure her feet touched the ground. Her hair and makeup were still perfect.

"Nice dance moves," I said. "Where have you been hiding those?"

Hope laughed. "Yeah! I had no idea, either."

"I haven't danced in ages, but I used to be on the dance team in school. It's something Gabe and I enjoy."

"I can see that," I said, grinning as I squeezed her arm.

Hope stared at the bottom of her empty wineglass, then peered around the pool patio. "I'm going to get a refill and try to find my husband. I know he's around here somewhere."

I pointed to one side, near the bar. "He's talking to Evan over there." Evan saw me point and gave me a wink. I blew him a kiss back. As Hope moved off, I turned back to April. "Are you happy with how everything went?"

"Oh, yes. The ceremony itself was what mattered the most to me. As amazing as your cake was, this part is just for fun and celebration."

"I guess the ceremony is the part that makes the whole thing legal, huh? Well, that and signing the certificates, which we already did. But what if someone gets drunk and makes an idiot of themselves dancing?"

She grinned. "Even then. I am a very happy woman. Besides, a little extra excitement would make our wedding all the more memorable."

I reached forward to hug her. "You deserve every happiness."

As we embraced, a tickle ran down my spine, a hint of uneasiness. I pulled away and took a sip of champagne, casting my eyes around the area to determine what caused my sense of disquiet. Everything on the patio was the same, people standing in small groups talking. I panned my gaze farther, then my eyes stilled.

A man stood in the shadows, near the hibiscus hedge. He took a halting step forward, the overhead party lights illuminating him. He was towering, a solid six and a half feet, and with a face that could have been carved by

Michelangelo. His dark hair was cut short, and his jaw was covered in a neatly trimmed, short beard. Dressed neatly if oddly for a wedding celebration, he wore black slacks and a black button-down shirt that did nothing to hide the bulging muscles in his arms and shoulders. His shirt was short-sleeved, and the tapering points of tattoos on both arms reached down toward his elbows. I caught a hint of ink in the V of his shirt too. The man slowly looked around the patio, searching with eyes that were expressionless and gave nothing away.

A dim, detached part of me noted that he might be the most gorgeous male specimen I'd ever seen, but the way he stood at the periphery, just watching, made me uneasy. Wanting reassurance, I glanced at Evan, who was talking with Alex and Hope at the other end of the patio. I relaxed at seeing his handsome, comforting face.

But that tickling sensation didn't go away. It traveled across my shoulders, and I looked back at the stranger. He hadn't moved. He studied the scene before him while remaining unnoticed. The man's eyes hadn't moved in several moments, and I followed his gaze to where Gabe stood, laughing on the other side of the patio.

Turning back, I elbowed April. "Who's the latecomer by the hedge?"

She squinted at the mystery guest and shrugged. "Never seen him before. Gabe said something about inviting some relatives from Atlanta. Maybe he's one of them and got delayed."

Maia was walking by, and April grabbed her arm. "Hey, who's the Hulk over there?"

Maia grinned at her words, but as she turned in the direction April indicated, her smile plummeted. Her feet froze on the spot, and the blood drained from her face. Her eyes became enormous. "Oh, dear God. Not now!" She spun back and grabbed my upper arms, gripping so hard it hurt. "Liv, get Evan out of here! Now."

"What? Why?" I darted my eyes to Evan, who was concentrating on something Alex had said. He looked completely normal to me.

"Hurry!" she hissed, an edge of panic in her voice. "That's Hunter. He said he wasn't coming. Get Evan out of here! This isn't the time for a reunion between them. Go back to the house, go kayaking—anything! Just get him out of here before he sees Hunter. Oh my God!"

My stomach felt hollow, and my feet were rooted to the spot as my gaze slowly turned back toward the man. Hunter had always been described as a bookish, intellectual type, so I'd pictured him as a frail, nerdy-looking guy. The man standing near the hibiscus hedge looked like he could knock over a tree with one finger.

"Liv—move! Now." Maia let go of my arms and pushed me toward Evan.

That stirred me into motion, stumbling to catch my balance as a swirling, confused mass of emotions took flight within me. These two men hadn't seen each other in thirteen years. Evan couldn't even discuss Hunter without becoming furious and bitter.

His words came back to me, when he'd told me his story. *"I hated him for it. I still do."*

I hurried around the corner of the pool, desperate to intercept Evan before something awful happened.

Chapter Twenty-Five

Evan

I STARED at the former SEAL, then gave him a quick once-over, still processing the story he'd just told me. "Wow, that sounds horrible. You look like you're moving fine." I'd seen Alex swimming just offshore yesterday.

He stuck out his lower leg. "A year later, I'm pretty much recovered, though I've got a pretty impressive scar. Thanks for letting April stay those extra weeks. We'd have been sunk without her."

April's arrival in Calypso Key had been delayed by several weeks due to a disaster in St. Croix. "We got someone to cover," I said, now even more grateful I hadn't made a fuss over the delay. "I'm glad you're better. That was quite a story."

"Yes, it was." Hope melded against Alex's side and rested her head in the hollow of his shoulder. "And not one either of us ever wants to repeat. But the resort is doing great and so is Alex."

He kissed the top of her head, and I couldn't help but

smile. Catching up with returning guests was one of the best parts of my job, and I had been looking forward to seeing these two again.

In fact, the entire afternoon had been fantastic, and I floated on a cloud of elation. The ceremony had gone off without any hitches, the bride and groom blissfully happy. Liv looked amazing, every bit as beautiful as I thought she'd be. Every time I glimpsed her, I wanted to grab her and run back to my room on the spot, though I got hold of myself before the desire became reality. But more than simple desire, I was proud to be with her. The cake Liv had made was an inspiration, and everyone had oohed and aahed over it.

I swept my gaze over the patio. Gabe was entering the Big House with Stella, while April and Maia stood together, apparently having an intense discussion. That was kind of weird, but nothing could disturb my composure tonight. I was getting ready to ask Hope another question when I felt a strong grip on my upper arm. I turned to find Liv next to me, a tight set to her shoulders and her mouth a firm slash on her face.

"Evan, can you help me with something?" she asked. "I just realized I forgot something with the cake."

I laughed. "What are you talking about? We demolished the cake already, remember?"

"Yeah," Alex added with a broad grin. "I had three pieces. It was fantastic."

She bit her lip, then gave us a tight, fleeting smile. "Thanks. I know the cake part is over, but I really need to grab the... thing, and I can't get it alone." She tugged on my arm, trying to nudge me into motion.

"Uh... sure." I nodded to Alex and Hope. "See you

later." I turned my attention to Liv as we turned away from the pool area. "What's the rush?"

"I feel so silly for forgetting. Thanks for helping. It won't take long." She tightened her hold.

As we stepped away, a curious murmuring started up behind me. Dad breathed, "I can't believe it," in the strangest voice.

Liv tightened her death grip on my arm, marching faster as she led me to the edge of the patio. As the song ended on the PA system behind us, the reception definitely took on an odd tone, a curious mixture of hushed whispering and loud silence. My curiosity got the best of me, and I tossed a glance over my shoulder. It took me a moment to process the image, my mind not wanting to admit what I was seeing.

My feet became lead bricks, rooted to the flagstones beneath them. My vision tunneled down, my focus laser sharp as I tried to make sense of what was happening.

"No, Evan! Come on. We've got to go." Liv tugged on my arm with both hands, but I hardly felt it.

Across the flagstones and near the hedge, Hunter stepped onto the patio. *Hunter.* Though I barely recognized him. Hardly any vestige of the eighteen-year-old who had left home remained in the man moving forward now.

No!

This couldn't be happening. I went numb all over, like my body was flashing back to the last time we'd been together. But now I stood on my own legs, both strong and firm. The breath exploded from my lungs.

Dad wore an enormous smile on his face as he moved toward Hunter, who approached more slowly, almost diffidently. His lips twitched in a hesitant smile, and I lost it.

Tonight isn't about you, you bastard. You—of all people—

don't get to have the happy homecoming. Not if I have anything to say about it.

Shaking Liv off, I stormed forward, and the tunnel vision disappeared. I saw with stunning clarity as Hunter hesitated again, watching our father. Dad was on the other side of the pool, still walking toward him.

Hunter turned his head and saw me. I didn't hesitate, hardly limping as I flew around the pool toward him. His eyes widened momentarily, then a mask flew over his face. He held out a hand, palm out, as I neared.

"Take it easy, Evan."

Even his deep, measured voice was different now. The last time I'd seen him, Hunter had been on the gangly verge of manhood as he tried to adjust to his towering frame. Now he couldn't be more different. He was chiseled, radiating controlled strength and power, which only pissed me off more.

But not as much as the fact that he had a good five inches on me, and I had to stare up at him. Stopping right in front of him, I jabbed my finger in his face. "Who the hell do you think you are? To show up now!"

"I'm here because Gabe asked me, all right?" His voice was even but held an iron edge.

"After thirteen years, you think you can just walk on in, and everything will be forgiven?" My raised voice echoed off the water, but I didn't care.

"I'm only here for the evening, Evan. Can't we get along for a couple of hours for Gabe's sake?"

I sneered, balling one hand into a fist. "No one wants you here, Hunter. You tore this family apart."

A wounded look flashed through his eyes, but he quickly covered it. "Maybe it's time I started making up for that."

I barked a laugh, but it was utterly humorless. "You. Can't! Get out of here before I kill you."

An angry glint rose over his eyes, and he folded his massive arms across his chest. Tattoos peeked out from under his short sleeves, and his upper chest visible under the neck of his black shirt was covered in ink too. "Yeah, I'd like to see you try, tough guy."

A red haze descended, and I swung as hard as I could at his stomach. It was like hitting a concrete wall. The son of a bitch didn't even move. He didn't stagger. He didn't fight back. Hunter just stood there and took my punch, his arms folded.

With an inarticulate roar that felt like it was ripping my lungs out, I grabbed him by both shoulders and pushed. He lost his balance as I surged forward, windmilling his arms as we tumbled together.

Right into the pool.

The water was shockingly cold as I fell under the surface. We'd landed in the middle section of the pool, and my back softly hit the bottom. Pushing with both feet, I rose to the surface where I treaded water.

Shock replaced my fury. The crowd on the patio all stared at us with slack-jawed expressions.

Hunter rose next to me and whipped his head to clear the water from his face, his eyes also wide and stunned. "Oh, shit."

"Yeah," I replied. "Great idea to show up, huh?"

I breast-stroked to the side of the pool and pushed myself onto the deck, Hunter next to me. We both rose to our feet, dripping all over the patio.

Dad stood a good ten feet away, his face ashen. "Evan..."

Guilt filled me at his horrified expression, but it

morphed back to fury as I turned to stare at my brother. "Just leave, dammit. Get out of here."

Before Hunter could answer, movement distracted us. Gabe marched toward us, both hands clenched at his sides and with murder in his eyes. Sensing his fury, the crowd parted around him as he crossed the patio from the kitchen.

Alarm clenched my gut tight as he grabbed us both, bunching our sodden shirts in his fists. He shoved us backward, moving forward as we had no choice but to back up to keep from falling over. Gabe shoved us across the patio and slammed us repeatedly against the wall of the Big House. He was shorter than Hunter and taller than me, though he was so livid his size didn't matter. He was our big brother and mad as hell.

"What. In God's name. Is wrong with. You. Two?"

I bit my tongue as he slammed me against the wall, but I hardly felt it. Gabe's eyes looked black against the night backdrop, which fit his current mood. I was speechless.

"I'm...s-sorry, Gabe!" Hunter stammered between collisions.

Then Gabe dropped his hands and took a step back. He stood there in his tuxedo with tails, breathing like a locomotive as he glowered at me.

Me. Not Hunter.

"I couldn't stop thinking about what you told me last week." Staring at Gabe, Hunter rushed the words out now. "That you wanted me to come. So I changed my plans. It was a mistake. I'm sorry. I'll leave now." He started to move, but Gabe's hand snaked out again and pinned him in place.

"You invited him? Again?" I asked, answering Gabe's glare with one of my own.

"Yeah, Evan. Because I wanted my brother at my

wedding. Like an idiot. I should have known better. Just get out of here. Now."

"Me?" I snarled indignantly. "Why me?"

Still holding Hunter in place, Gabe clicked his teeth together, his jaw bulging. "In case you haven't noticed, Evan, you're standing in a tuxedo dripping all over the ground. After you rammed into Hunter and crashed into the pool. At my wedding reception. I think we'd all be better off if you cooled off." Lifting his hand from Hunter's chest, Gabe stared daggers at me. He pumped both fists open and closed twice, then spun around and stalked off. For the first time, I noticed both of my hands were shaking wildly.

I jerked my head toward Hunter, who stared at me. At first, his eyes were wide, then they narrowed, becoming angry. "Are you happy now? You can't blame me for this, Evan. I was going to avoid you all night."

I spun to face him, closing my shaking hands into fists and itching to throw a punch. "Like hell I can't blame you!"

"You heard Gabe. I'm here because I'm part of this family too. Whether you like it or not, asshole." He took an aggressive step forward, and I was reminded that the gigantic man before me was a far cry from the brother who had left my life. He had spent the decade since in the Marines. Special Forces, no less. If I attacked him, I'd only make a fool of myself.

And that only made me more furious.

I stepped forward so we were nearly nose to nose, my neck craned up. "I don't like it, you prick."

Hunter inhaled sharply, then let the breath out in a long, tight sigh. "Tonight is supposed to be about Gabe and April. I've tried really hard to keep it together and not let you push my buttons. I'd say your finger is on the last one right now." Anger poured off Hunter in waves, and you could bounce a quarter off his shoulders. I swore he was growing larger by the second, his eyes flashing. And all directed at me. "Evan, I'm two seconds from—"

A large hand pressed against his chest. I blinked, distracted, when I felt the pressure of another hand firm against mine. Alex, the former SEAL, stepped between us. He faced Hunter, pressing me behind him so he stood between us. "Stand down, soldier. That's enough."

Fury flashed in Hunter's eyes. I stepped to the side, forgotten as the two men engaged in a staring contest. Neither one moved. The patio was completely silent as the battle of wills went on. Their eyes locked together, neither man gave an inch, and I waited for my dick brother to throw his first punch.

Chapter Twenty-Six

Evan

TIME STILLED as everyone on the patio watched the two military men locked in silent combat. No one moved. No one breathed. Tension flowed off them in waves, and for the first time, I started to wonder if Hunter might be dangerous. But the former SEAL wasn't intimidated in the slightest, meeting my brother head-on.

Should I step in? How the hell does Alex even know Hunter was in the military?

Finally, Alex tilted his head and leaned slightly forward. Hunter was several inches taller, but Alex's authority in the situation was palpable. "Now, soldier. That's an order." His voice was soft, yet carried a clear, steel edge.

Hunter blinked, and just like that, he stepped back and lowered his eyes. "Yes, sir."

Alex relaxed his posture and nodded. "Good man."

A murmuring exhale went through the crowd as the tension dissipated into the warm night. Even my own shoulders relaxed a little. With a small smile, Alex clapped Hunter on the shoulder. "Come on. I'll buy you a beer." And sliding his arm around Hunter's shoulders, he steered him away from me and toward the bar area. Alex nodded at me as the two men passed by.

Then I was alone, looking at a group of people who all stared at me with varying expressions. Some were openly horrified, while Dad's face was lined, and he looked physically in pain as he followed Hunter's progress with his eyes. Liv stood next to Dad, trying to cover an expression of what looked like grief.

All because Hunter crashed the wedding. He and Alex were now huddled together by the bar, no one near them. I ground my teeth together, anger ratcheting up again. Then I remembered Gabe asking me to go cool off. The bride and groom were nowhere to be seen.

Without another word, I whirled and stomped toward the kitchen door. The crowd moved aside as I passed, as if no one wanted to be near me. My pace quickened, even though that made my limp worse. I didn't care. I just needed to get away now.

"Evan. Wait."

That was Liv, and I could hear her rapid steps behind me. I didn't slow. "Everyone made it pretty clear I'm not welcome."

"Not me."

I slammed open the door and crossed the kitchen, ignoring everyone inside cleaning up. Including Stella, whose gigantic eyes followed me as her mouth hung open. "I'm really not in a good mood, Liv."

"I'm not leaving you alone right now, dammit!"

She was hot on my heels as I turned and strode down the hall. "Suit yourself, but don't say I didn't warn you."

I thrust open the door to my bedroom, and she entered behind me, then softly latched it shut. I paced back and forth across the wooden floor while Liv quietly walked to the couch and sat perched on the edge of it. Still dressed in her blue bridesmaid gown, her hair was artfully pinned up with a few long locks spiraling around her shoulders. "Talk to me, Evan. What's going through your mind?"

A dim part of me was grateful that Alex had stepped in and potentially defused what could have become a very ugly situation, but mostly I was just too shocked and furious to sort out my thoughts.

She sighed. "I know Hunter was the last person you wanted to see tonight, but did you have to behave like that?"

Her words brought me to a halt, and I whipped my head to her. "Like what? He's the one who showed up unannounced and ambushed everyone."

Liv took a deep breath and spoke quietly and evenly, like she was trying not to get upset. "Evan, that was April and Gabe's *wedding reception*. You couldn't have just ignored him for the sake of family harmony?"

My mind circled back to Gabe's furious glare, which had been aimed mostly at me. "No! Goddammit, this isn't my fault."

"Of course it's not. Just like every other thing that's happened to you since you were nineteen isn't. Evan, Hunter asked you point blank to try to get along tonight! I don't understand your hatred toward him."

Her words stung like hell, and my anger rose like a volcano. "Of course you don't understand. How could you? You have no clue what he took from me."

She threw both hands in the air. "What? What did he take that you refuse to even consider forgiving him?"

Nostrils flaring with each breath, I stared at her for a

long moment. Then I spun on my heel and stalked to my closet, going right to the spot in the back. I rifled through the clothes hanging there, some of them falling to the floor.

There it was. Right where it always hung.

I ripped the garment from its hanger and returned, tossing it to her without a word. She caught it deftly. Her forehead deeply lined, she held it in front of her and inspected the large letters embroidered on the front of the gray jersey. "Rangers?" She turned it around and saw the number three and my last name across the top. Slowly, she lifted her gaze to meet mine. "You played for the Texas Rangers?"

"No!" I spat the word like brittle shards of ice. "I never suited up for them, even once. Because. Of. Hunter." I resumed pacing, trying to rein in my fury. My anguish. "I was a first-round draft pick out of high school. Number six overall. The Rangers traded up to get me, and you're holding the jersey from my signing. I was a double threat—I could pitch and hit."

I pressed the heels of both hands against my closed eyes. I'd spent so much time in this room, I didn't need to see to know when to turn around. "My first year with the farm teams, I advanced from A-Ball all the way to Triple-A. The Rangers signed me with the intent for me to be a pitcher. But in the minors, I was a designated hitter on the days I didn't pitch. My batting average was just under four hundred."

Gripping my jersey on her lap, Liv watched me closely. Her eyes tracked my back-and-forth movements, but she didn't interrupt.

"When I came home to visit, I was due to start the new season in a couple weeks. They were going to start me at Triple-A, and the plan was to call me up within a month to pitch out of the bullpen." I halted and removed my hands from my eyes. Immediately, they filled with tears. I didn't care and let them fall as I turned to face her. "The Major Leagues, Liv. Texas Rangers. What I'd worked for my entire life. My *dream.* You know that baseball I keep on the desk in my office?"

She nodded but remained silent.

"It's signed by Nolan Ryan and Randy Johnson. I got that ball when I was ten, at a prospect camp hosted by the team. I vowed then that I would play for the Rangers someday. That I would someday rival those two pitchers, two of the greatest of all time. And during my senior year in high school, I got drafted by Texas—my dream came true. I was being prepped to pitch to my first big league hitters. And I lost it all."

Liv squeezed her eyes shut and clutched my jersey against her chest. "I'm so sorry, Evan. That's awful."

I wiped my angry tears away. Hunter wasn't worth my tears. "Instead, I ended up broken and paralyzed. Now you know what he took from me. *Everything.*"

Regarding me evenly, she gave me a tiny smile. "He didn't take everything, did he? I'm sure your work ethic and physical condition were a big factor in your recovery."

I snorted and started pacing again, not interested in platitudes. Even Liv's.

"So what happens now?"

I shot a glance at her. "What do you mean?"

She stared at me, then flung an arm toward the patio. "Evan, you pretty much ruined April and Gabe's wedding. You're still sopping wet, for God's sake!"

Surprised, I glanced down. My tuxedo wasn't dripping anymore, but all of a sudden, I could feel the clammy coolness of it. I peeled off the jacket and ripped the tie off. I returned to the closet and pulled the shirt over my head, flinging it and the tux pants on the floor before quickly changing into sweats. My heart hammered in my chest, and a fine tremor still ran through my hands. Returning to the bedroom, I held out both arms and glared at her.

"There. Better now?" I was being a dick, but I didn't care.

She pressed her lips firmly together and exhaled through her nose. "I'm simply trying to point out a more... impartial perspective."

Halting midstride, I stared at her. "Wait a minute. Are you saying this is *my* fault?"

She folded my jersey neatly and set it on the coffee table. "I'm saying that you've been through a tremendous tragedy and that maybe you aren't seeing clearly. But it seems to me like your family has been tiptoeing around this situation for years, hoping you and Hunter would resolve it yourselves. I'm pretty sure tonight brought everything to a head."

I made a rude noise and waved her off. "Nothing's changed. Hunter's still a bastard, and I still hate him."

"Evan. Stop this. Your anger isn't solving anything."

I rounded on her, finally breaking. "My anger is all I have left! I have nothing. No one. Even what you and I had was fake, wasn't it?" I was a black, swirling mess inside, and words tumbled out of my mouth without thought. "Just get out! I don't need you either. Leave me alone."

Liv's face was pale as she rose stiffly and padded to the door. She opened it, then stopped to look at me. "Maybe when you wake up tomorrow, you'll be able to comprehend the damage you did tonight. How can you say you've got no one? You are literally surrounded by people who love you. You even had me. And you know as well as I do that what we had was much more than pretend. You wear your hatred and fury like a suit of armor, Evan. But it's not protecting you. It's destroying you. Hunter may have instigated the event that started all this. But he's not the one ruining your life. You're doing a fine job of that all by yourself." Without waiting for an answer, she turned around and shut the door softly behind her.

With fury, shame, and inescapable loss all threatening to overtake me, I whipped my gaze around the room. My eyes settled on my jersey, lying on the coffee table where Liv had set it down. Stomping across the room, I snapped it up and rammed it in the trash can. A glass manatee sculpture lay on the coffee table, and I stalked over to it. I picked up the hefty item and hurled it at the closed door. It shattered into pieces and scattered over the floor.

Finally, I fell to my knees on the wooden floor, slumping as hot, furious tears poured down my face.

Chapter Twenty-Seven

Liv

I HUDDLED outside the door I'd just closed, undecided whether I should go back in. I hated to leave Evan alone in this frame of mind, despite his hurtful words. Then I jumped, gasping as something slammed against the shut door and broke.

Okay, not going back in there tonight.

Tears pricked the corners of my eyes, but I refused to give in to them. I was devastated that my sweet, generous Evan had this other, tortured side to him. A side that would eat him alive if he didn't face it. As much as I wanted to help, he'd made his feelings very clear. He didn't want my help. And dammit, his words had stung like hell.

I entered my bedroom, and after flipping on the light, stood inside the threshold. I swept my gaze around the lovely room that had been my home for the last month. It was still messy from the afternoon when April, Hailey, and I had gotten ready for the wedding.

Which now seemed like a lifetime ago.

My arms felt like they weighed a hundred pounds each as the exhaustion of the long day followed by the turmoil of tonight hit me in full force. I was numb all over, probably a defense to avoid the pain that was surely coming.

Trudging into the bathroom, I removed the beautiful dress, then draped it carefully on top of my bed. I took a long, hot shower, trying to wash my feelings away. Or the numbness. I couldn't decide which was worse. I dressed in comfy clothes and twisted my hair up in a clip. When I came out, Pilar was curled up on the foot of my bed. I padded over and scratched under her chin, her soft purr soothing me slightly. Very slightly.

There was only one answer right now and I knew it.

With a sigh, I crossed to the closet and pulled down my suitcase. Sweet Dreams's final inspection was tomorrow, and though my new bed hadn't been delivered yet, I couldn't stay here anymore. The couch in my apartment would work just fine.

Packing my meager belongings didn't take long. Everything fit into a suitcase and an overnight bag. I set the two bags next to the door, still numb.

Evan's words rolled through my skull on repeat. *"Even what you and I had was fake, wasn't it? Just get out! I don't need you either."*

Were they just the words of a man who had been through a terrible shock? Or did he really mean them? "Does it even matter?" I asked the empty room. "His motives don't change the basic facts."

But I couldn't walk out of the Big House without a word of thanks for the warm hospitality I'd received. Crossing the room, I sat at the desk and pulled out two pieces of stationery with Calypso Key Resort letterhead. I wrote my two letters, choosing my sincere and heartfelt words carefully, then placed them inside two envelopes.

Returning to the bed, I gave Pilar's beautiful gray coat a final, long swipe with my hand. A twisting hollowness filled me as I stood and padded across the floor, slipping the strap of the overnight bag over my shoulder. The handle of my suitcase felt cold as I grasped it and opened the door. After one final, sweeping glance at my room, I exited and softly shut the door behind me. I carried the suitcase to avoid noise, tiptoeing down the hall. The kitchen was dark when I entered. I blinked at the dim room, surprised everyone had disappeared so quickly. Then again, time had lost all meaning for a while. Glancing at my watch, I got another surprise. It was nearly 11:00 p.m.

No wonder everyone's gone.

Even before the fireworks between Evan and Hunter, I was sure April had better things to do than hang out all evening at the reception. Wincing, I remembered her words from earlier that nothing could dampen her mood after their perfect ceremony.

"I wonder if she feels that way now. I sure hope so," I whispered to the empty room. Crossing to the mammoth dining table, I rested my two envelopes, one addressed to Nona and the other to Warren, against the salt and pepper grinders.

Then I stiffened my spine and walked out the door.

THE STREETLIGHT OUT front cast a ghostly hue over the inside of Sweet Dreams as I entered through the back door. I thought about flipping on the bank of lights but reconsidered. All I could think about was how different I felt from the last time I'd been here.

When I'd toured it with Evan.

Everything was different now, and I wasn't ready to face that in bright light. I still needed the cover of darkness to grapple with my feelings. With the fact that I'd fallen in love with him. With the fact that the tortured soul who had screamed at me to get out was a man I didn't know. Where Hunter was concerned, he wasn't capable of reason, and I couldn't change that for him. But after tonight, I understood Evan wouldn't ever be able to move on with his life until he found a way to deal with the tragedy. And I couldn't help him if he didn't want to listen.

Heaving a giant sigh, I stepped through the kitchen, trailing my fingers along the cool surface of a stainless-steel island. On the far side of the glass display cases, tables and chairs were neatly lined up against the walls, ready for hungry visitors. That was new. In fact, as I cast a more focused look around the bakery, everything looked ready for the final inspection tomorrow.

All the ladders and construction equipment were gone, and the tile floors were clean. The walls were still bare, but I had been able to salvage my framed prints of pastries, and Dylan had gotten me a new Hammerheads poster to hang.

After picking up my suitcase and overnight bag, I crept up the stairs and opened the door to my apartment, inhaling the sharp scent of fresh paint. All traces of the fire were completely gone. I dumped the two bags unceremoniously by the door. They could wait until tomorrow. A neat stack of cardboard boxes sat near the kitchen—all my personal kitchen supplies that the restoration company had boxed up for me.

Similar boxes were in the bedroom, containing the items they'd been able to salvage and clean. Opening a box at random, I discovered a blanket I'd kept tucked away at the back of the closet. I folded it over my arm and headed back to the living room and the couch. Slipping out of my shoes, I stretched out and tossed the blanket over me, fluffing it until it was just right. With nothing left to do, I laced my fingers together over the soft fabric and stared at the ceiling.

And the crush of emotion I'd been holding back could no longer be denied. It started with a single tear slipping from my eye. Then a deep, wracking sob wrenched from my throat, and I was crying in earnest.

Letting out the grief at finally understanding why Evan despised his brother so much. Tears for what he'd lost in that diving accident. I knew from being around Dylan how difficult the road to the Major Leagues was. Yet Evan had been so talented he'd been on the cusp of his dream after only one season in the minors. I rolled onto my side and curled into a ball, deep cries wrenching my lungs.

I knew firsthand what a warm, generous heart lay alongside all that bitterness. But I couldn't fix him. Only Evan could work his way through the swamp of his misery to forgiveness. And right now, he didn't seem to even understand what a toll his hatred was taking on his soul. But tomorrow would bring a reckoning.

I thought of my dear friend and hoped she was happy tonight. I was worried about her, but now was not the time to check on the bride and groom. They had each other. Eventually, the tears and sobs diminished, and my sore, scratchy eyes grew heavy.

I woke to muted light filtering through the window and a text from Dylan.

Dylan: Are you okay? Call me as soon as you get this.

From his worried tone, I got the feeling his concern had to do with the debacle last night rather than any problems with the pop-up shop this morning. Still, I had to be sure, so I called him back.

Dylan picked up right away and I heard his muffled voice as he talked to someone nearby. "This is Liv. I'll be right back, okay?"

"Who are you talking to?"

"Natalie," he replied, his voice now loud and clear. "She's giving me a hand during the rush. She was a server at the wedding last night, Liv. Is what she said true? Evan met his brother, and they got in a huge fight?"

I sighed, desperately needing a cup of coffee, yet knowing there was zero in my brand-new apartment and shop. "Yes, it's true, and rather threw a damper on the whole occasion."

"Where are you? Are you with Evan?"

"Definitely not. I spent the night on the couch in my apartment after he threw me out."

"*What?*"

I ran a hand through my tangled curls, frowning when it got stuck. I carefully rearranged the strands and smoothed my hair. "We broke up and things are a mess right now. The final inspection is today, so my plan is to open the bakery tomorrow."

"Whoa. You can get ready that fast?"

Damn right I can. Because the only other alternative is to go back to Calypso Key, and that's not happening.

"Yeah," I said, sitting up straighter on the couch. "I can get baking supplies delivered today, and we'll start tomorrow just like we used to. Only with that wonderful, new-shop smell."

"Holy shit. Are you doing all right, Liv?"

I smiled, and the expression felt good. He was such a sweet kid. "If I could survive a fire, I can survive a breakup. I'll be fine. I just don't feel like showing my face at Calypso Key."

"Don't blame you. What was the fight about? This all sounds so unlike Evan."

I wasn't about to get into it. "It's a long-running feud between them." Then I sighed again, trying to be objective. "Evan's a good man, Dylan. And believe me, if he wants to coach you to make the Hammerheads, listen to him. Just because I don't want to see him anymore doesn't mean you have to keep away from him."

"Thanks. I was wondering about that. I don't want to be disloyal to you, but Evan's helped me more than the pitching coach has, for God's sake."

Yeah, and now I know why.

But if Evan had never shared his background with Dylan, I wasn't going to out him. "Don't worry about that. Though you don't exactly have a reason to hang around the island either, do you?"

"That's true. Should I give my two weeks' notice? Or quit immediately? He only hired me while the pop-up shop was open. This is so confusing."

"I'm sorry about that. Tell whoever's in charge today, and I imagine it's Jenna, the assistant manager, that I don't want you working there anymore. I don't think it will be an issue given the circumstances, but put the heat on me."

Dylan hesitated. "Are things that bad between you two?"

The starch left my spine, and I tipped over sideways on

the couch, staring at the bare wall. "I have no idea. Last night, Evan wasn't exactly in the frame of mind to have a calm, rational conversation. And the bottom line is I have a business to run. You were my guy first, so I'm claiming you back." I laughed, trying to inject a little humor. "How's the mood there?"

"A little quieter than usual. I don't hang out in the other parts of the resort except the coffee shop."

"Well, the inner workings of the Markham family aren't anything you or I have to be concerned about. I think it's time we just moved back to Dove Key where we belong. You'd better get back and give Natalie a hand."

"Okay. Call me if you need any help setting up the shop. I have practice this afternoon, but I'm free this evening."

After assuring him I'd contact him if I needed help, I tossed my phone on the couch next to me and rubbed my eyes. Right now, the task of getting Sweet Dreams up and running in less than twenty-four hours seemed Herculean.

But it would only get more impossible the longer I waited. By sheer force of will, I rose and padded to my suitcase, still sitting by the door. I dragged it to my empty bedroom to face the day. Ready or not.

Chapter Twenty-Eight

Evan

MY EYELIDS FELT LIKE DRY, scratchy sandpaper as I blinked my eyes open. I quickly shut them again as bright light stabbed a thousand daggers into my brain. After the throbbing diminished slightly, I tried again, slowly cracking one eye open before the other.

I lay on top of my bed, still in my sweats and with an empty bottle of scotch whisky next to me. I didn't have Dad's or Gabe's appreciation for the drink, but I kept a bottle in my room for the occasional nightcap. Fortunately, it had been less than half full or my hangover would be even worse. I glanced at my clock. It was after 9:oo a.m.

Groaning, I rolled up to a sitting position. I looked blearily around my room until my gaze settled on the shattered remains of the figurine I'd launched against the door last night. And my head pounded anew, my heart racing as it all came back to me.

The shock of seeing Hunter, getting in his face, falling in the pool, Gabe's fury.

And finally, Liv.

Who had followed me to try to talk some sense into me. Instead, I'd told her to get lost. The cold light of morning brought home some of what Liv had tried to tell me last night. That I was the one who had caused us to fall in the pool.

"It never would have happened if he hadn't shown up, though," I spat out.

That was the bottom line. As long as Hunter stayed out of my life, I functioned just fine. I scowled, thinking about Liv's parting words. That was bullshit. My feelings toward Hunter weren't ruining my life.

Hunter ruined my life.

I needed to know if he was still around, and I needed to talk to Liv.

I carefully rose to my feet and shuffled across the room in my bare feet. My leg ached like a son of a bitch, and my limp was worse than usual. After deciding my sweatshirt and pants were presentable enough, I winced at my reflection. My hair stuck up all over the place, so I wet it and smoothed it as much as I could. But I didn't have the energy to shave. I downed three ibuprofens, sending a silent prayer that it would dull the thumping pain in both my head and my leg quickly. Limping across my room, I left to check the status of life on Calypso Key this morning.

Liv wasn't working today, and her door was wide open. Then again, the morning was half over, so that was no surprise. But I needed to mend things with her, so I crossed the hall.

I entered her room and stopped, the corners of my lips drawing down. Flowers and hair supplies lay on top of the made bed, like it hadn't been touched since the women had prepared before the wedding yesterday. Half empty bottles of champagne and sparkling cider sat on the coffee table. I took a tentative step forward, surprised Liv hadn't cleaned up. Her blue maid of honor dress lay draped across the comforter, cementing my impression that she hadn't slept in the bed last night. My frown deepened as I crossed to the closet. My shoulders slumped. It was empty. Her clothes were gone, as was her suitcase.

Liv was gone.

A tendril of fear began winding its way through my stomach. I'd figured I owed a few apologies and might need to grovel some, then things would be back to normal. But something about this empty room gave me chills. And not just about Liv. My heart hammered in my chest, but I hardly noticed the accompanying knocking of my headache. Gabe's furious face and his snarling words flashed before me again, then Dad's shattered expression when he'd stared at me on the pool deck. Ice poured into my veins and a shiver rolled over my shoulders.

"God, what have I done?"

Because it wasn't just Liv. Gabe and April might never speak to me again.

I'd ruined their wedding.

I turned around and shuffled to the kitchen, where I poured myself a cup of black coffee. The chef was only on duty until eight, but my stomach was already unsettled. Food would only make it worse. I sat in my customary place at the table and rubbed my temples. I needed to get hold of both Liv and Gabe. He would be easier, but I had no idea how long he and April were planning on spending in the beach pool cottage.

Maybe he's already texted me to tell me what an asshole I am.

Rising to my feet, I headed to the kitchen counter,

where I'd deposited my phone before the ceremony. Which was a good thing, or it would be a waterlogged paperweight right now. I opened it, but there weren't any messages from Gabe or Liv.

With a groan, I pocketed my phone and returned to my coffee, cradling it with both hands. Footsteps sounded behind me in the hallway, then slowed. They became louder when the person changed direction and headed toward me. I closed my eyes and rested the warm side of the mug against my forehead as the person neared.

"How are you feeling this morning?" Dad asked softly.

"Horrible."

He poured himself a cup of coffee and sat on his usual seat at the head of the table adjacent to me. "I've been trying to think of some fatherly advice to give you, but I keep coming up blank, Evan. I can hardly comprehend what you did last night."

I lowered my mug and opened my eyes. Dad hadn't shaved and his eyes were bloodshot. "I didn't mean to fly off the handle like that. I saw Hunter and just... lost it. What happened after I left?"

"Hunter left right after you did, and Stella followed him."

I grunted. Stella and Hunter had remained close, and she tried to walk a tightrope of maintaining a relationship with both of us.

Dad continued, "Last I heard, they were back in South Beach."

That made me relax a little. At least I didn't have to worry about coming face to face with the bastard. "What about Gabe and April?"

Dad eyed me, his expression level and not giving anything away. "Last night, the rest of the family, along with some of the wedding guests, banded together and salvaged the situation. We grabbed some booze and headed to the beach barbeque area, where we danced for another hour or so, then gave the bride and groom their alone time. You might be interested in knowing they were both smiling again by the end. Then again, maybe you don't care."

The wrenching disappointment in his eyes was worse than anger. "I care, believe me. I'll touch base with them soon. And Liv too. She's gone, by the way."

"I know."

I snapped my head up, making me wince as the pounding returned. "You do?"

"She left both your grandmother and me a lovely note thanking us for our hospitality and help during her time of need. But now her bakery was ready to open, so she was ready to move back home. The timing was... rather coincidental."

"She tried to talk me down last night. I told her to get out and leave me alone."

"Sounds like she listened to you."

I dropped my face into both hands. "God, I've really screwed things up, haven't I?"

This time Dad's voice was softer. "Yes, Son, you have. I think you need help. Maybe talking to someone would help you deal with your feelings toward Hunter."

I lifted my face to scowl at him. "A shrink? I did that a long time ago."

"Evan, this hatred you carry for Hunter isn't healthy."

I glared, my anger rising. "So I'm just supposed to throw my arms around him and forgive? Is that it? While he went off and had a successful military career and became... whatever the hell he is. Good God. He looked like G.I. Joe or something. And here I am, with legs that hurt so much I can barely walk sometimes."

Dad reached out and placed his large, weathered hand over mine. "Drowning in self-pity isn't going to solve anything. If you're not interested in seeing a professional counselor, I suggest you try to patch things up with Liv. I could see you two really cared about each other, and right now you need someone."

I thought about telling him our relationship wasn't real, but that wasn't true. Which she'd had the courage to admit last night. A new emotion slithered through me, the one that had been lurking since I'd seen all those shocked faces after climbing out of the pool last night. And the hurt look on Liv's face afterward. And the disappointed expression in Dad's eyes now.

Shame.

I didn't know if I could make this right, but I had to try. My gut told me I needed to let the situation with Liv cool off a little. I'd contact her tomorrow.

Today, I'd try to set things right with my brother.

My legs loosened up as I limped down the hill and toward the beach. When I reached the cottage where Gabe and April had spent their wedding night, I peeked around the edge, not wanting to interrupt anything newlywed-ish. They were both in the pool with their arms draped loosely around each other. At least they both wore swimsuits. Gabe murmured something in April's ear, and she tipped her head back, laughing. Pushing off against his chest, she sent a wave of water toward him, and he joined her laughter as she swam a few feet away.

Deciding this was as good a sign as I'd ever get, I

stepped onto the artificial deck that surrounded the pool. "Morning, guys." My voice came out low and worried, but I couldn't help it.

Both of them whirled toward me. April's happy expression morphed into one of concern, but Gabe just glared at me, water beading on his trimmed, dark hair.

"You back to see what other shit you can stir up?" he asked me. "There are lots of windows in the cottage that need breaking."

April swam to her husband and squeezed his shoulder. "Take it easy, honey."

Gabe just snorted as I approached the edge of the pool. I took off my flip-flops and sat, pulling up the legs of my sweats to let my legs dangle in the cool water. "I'm here to apologize. That doesn't make up for what I did, but it's a start. I'm really sorry."

His eyes softened a fraction, but he remained quiet. April gave me a sympathetic smile. "It wasn't a boring reception, that's for sure. And after the, uh, fireworks, we moved down here and hung out for a while. We ended up having a really great time."

April had a sunny, sweet personality, so her reaction didn't surprise me, though it made me feel even more guilty. I stared at her, a hollow emptiness inside me. "I'm really glad to hear that. The last thing I wanted was to ruin your wedding."

"Oh?" Gabe asked, his voice hard. "What were you trying to accomplish by grabbing Hunter and toppling into the pool, then?"

"It was stupid, Gabe. I'm sorry."

April stroked Gabe's arm, but his entire body remained rigid, his face thunderous. "Yeah, Evan. The entire thing is stupid—the whole situation between you and Hunter. I'm sick and tired of tiptoeing around it all the time. He didn't hurt you on purpose. It was an *accident*. What's it going to take for you to finally forgive him?"

I stared at the horizon, still seeing the ocean as it had been that day thirteen years ago. "I'm not sure, Gabe. Dad said the same thing to me this morning, though he was a bit more diplomatic about it."

Gabe took a breath to speak, but April squeezed his shoulder. "We both want the best for you, Evan. For Hunter too, but especially you."

Her kind words made me feel even worse. "Thanks, April. Does that mean you'll forgive me?"

"Of course. I don't believe in holding grudges. They weigh you down more than the other person."

That comment was obviously aimed at me, but I just smiled at her and said, "Thanks." Then I shifted my gaze to Gabe. "And what about you? I'm really sorry, Gabe. I wish I could take it back, but I can't."

Finally, his tight, angry look diminished. He shook his head and exhaled a long sigh. "Yeah, I forgive you, asshole." That made me smile, though it fell as his expression became serious again. "But, Evan, you should spend some time thinking about that last sentence you just said, okay?"

Chapter Twenty-Nine

Liv

WITH MY BEST PROFESSIONAL SMILE, I handed a box of donuts to the man across the counter. He accepted with a laugh. "So, does it feel good to be back home again?"

"It's wonderful," I replied.

Though the truth was that I was so freaking exhausted I could hardly stand up. The inspection yesterday had been a non-issue, and I'd received my permit on the spot. After taping it to the wall, I was officially open for business. Except for the minor detail that I had no supplies or any inventory to sell.

But Island Market had been happy to fill a special order for me and delivered it straight away. I'd scheduled a series of posts all over social media advertising the main shop was opening before placing sandwich boards on the sidewalk outside. Dylan had come by after practice and we'd unpacked everything, getting ready for the big day. Then, after he left, I'd cleaned the entire bakery one last time from top to bottom.

At midnight, I'd forced myself to go upstairs for a two-hour nap on my couch, but my sleep had been fitful and full of bad dreams I couldn't remember. At one-thirty, I'd given up and gone back downstairs where I started baking in earnest. And I hadn't stopped, still adding to my inventory at 10 a.m.

A few people came in grumbling that they'd gone to Calypso Key for nothing, but most were thrilled to see Sweet Dreams back in business. Maybe I should have planned the transition a little more deliberately, but I couldn't face going back there. At least the frenetic pace kept me from thinking about things too much. About Evan too much. I'd texted April yesterday afternoon asking if she was okay, and she'd answered right away that everything was fine. That Evan had come over to apologize first thing in the morning and felt awful. Which had sent a knife through my gut. He never contacted me at all yesterday. Radio silence.

Which made me feel like an idiot for falling in love with him. And I had no one to blame but myself. The whole reason he'd wanted the pretend relationship was because he wasn't interested in a real one. He'd been honest about that.

Sex, yes. Strings, no.

But I couldn't help feeling hurt that he didn't think I was worth apologizing to.

I pushed the useless, miserable thoughts aside as Dylan handed me two lattes for the next customer in line. I added their glazed raised donuts, then ran back and got more that were cooling on the counter. We stayed busy all morning, and I took several orders for cakes and pies.

I didn't have a set closing time for the bakery, staying open until the trickle of people died off or inventory was mostly gone, which was usually around noon. For our grand reopening, I was pleased that the traffic didn't die off until after 1:00 p.m. I sent Dylan home at 12:30 and kept the front door open as I cleaned up.

After marking everything left to fifty percent off, I got a few stragglers as I prepared to close. I was on my knees with my head inside the glass display case, wiping the shelf clean, when a large pair of feet in brown loafers appeared in front of me.

"Hi, Liv."

My arm paused its sweeping motion at Evan's voice, and I thumped my head on the shelf above. Crawling backward out of the cabinet, I rose to my feet as gracefully as I could. Which was to say, I did it like an arthritic hippopotamus rising from the watering hole.

Evan stood in front of me. He was dressed in a button-down shirt and slacks, clean-shaven and his hair neatly combed. Which was a drastic change from the waterlogged, wild-eyed man who had thrown me out the other night.

I nodded coolly at him. "I'm afraid you've missed the fresh stuff. I'm getting ready to close."

"I don't need a donut. I'm here to apologize, Liv."

I paused, twisting the rag in my hands. "Thank you."

He pointed with his chin toward my office in the back. "Can we talk for a minute?"

He was so gorgeous, and I ached to touch him. To console him and to help him with his pain. Then I remembered that crash as he threw something against the door after I left. Nope, I wasn't giving in so easily. "I don't really think there's anything to talk about. You said it all the other night. You told me to get out, so I did."

Surprise flickered through his eyes. He'd expected me to agree to talk. "I did a lot of things and said a lot of things I shouldn't have. I want to make up for it."

Sighing, I threw the rag on the counter. "Why? We had an arrangement, remember? This was all going to end after the wedding anyway. So let's end it. Shut the front door on your way out." I spun on my heel and held my head high as I walked away. Without looking back, I climbed the stairs and entered my apartment.

Because if I looked back and saw his face, I'd crumble. Because I wanted more than anything to throw my arms around his neck and tell him I wanted to help him deal with his pain.

And that was the problem. I couldn't force Evan to deal with anything. He had to make that decision himself. There was no point in torturing myself with what might have been. I had to look at what was.

A man who'd pushed me away and told me to get out rather than face his feelings.

I sat down on my couch, moving a paperback onto the coffee table. Brenna Coleridge had dropped it off earlier as a sort of welcome home gift. She'd been sweet, friendly, and obviously curious, but I hadn't had time to really talk to her. Instead, I'd accepted the book and promised to read it by our book club meeting in a week.

I opened my laptop to several new emails requesting quotes for wedding cakes. Before the whole debacle, I'd posted a picture of April and Gabe's cake on Sweet Dreams's Facebook page, and the post had really taken off. So at least it looked like I'd fully exorcised the demons that drove me out of Boston.

I had plenty to occupy me this afternoon and to keep me from thinking about Evan. And how good he'd looked standing in my bakery. And the hurt that had flashed through his eyes when I'd refused to speak with him.

Nope. Don't go there. Stay busy.

And as I lost myself to the familiar motions and rhythms of the activity that had always brought me peace, Evan slowly slipped to the back of my mind.

THE FOLLOWING MORNING WAS A REPEAT, with people lined up outside as soon as I opened my doors at five thirty. But I didn't care how busy it got, I was going to make sure Dylan was out the door by ten. "I want you to rest this afternoon. Meditate or listen to nature sounds or something. And get a good night's sleep tonight."

He grinned at me as he expertly prepared a customer's ridiculously complicated coffee. "I will, except for the good night's sleep part. I figure I've done all I can to prepare."

"Tryouts are at nine tomorrow morning?"

He nodded and rang up the customer. "They might spill over into afternoon."

"Is it like the movie *Major League*? Will they hang a big red tag in your locker?"

He burst into laughter. "I'm pretty sure the Hammerheads don't do that."

After the customer left, we had a brief lull. Dylan shot me a worried glance. "I'm not taking it totally easy this afternoon. Evan said he'd work with me on my pitching one last time. I hope that's okay with you."

I crossed the floor and squeezed his arm. "Don't feel put in the middle, because you're not. Take all the pointers you can get from Evan. But you won't need them. You'll make the team—I can feel it in my bones."

I expected him to flash me that smile that had most of the young women on Dove Key swooning, but he didn't.

Instead, he fidgeted, looking at me from under his brows. "I talked to the Hammerheads' manager yesterday and told him I'd been getting some extra coaching on the side. When I told him it was from Evan Markham, he almost fell over, Liv. Did you know Evan was one of the top prospects in the country in high school?"

So much for not thinking about him...

But of course Dylan would be curious. "Yes, but I have a feeling that getting involved with the game again is a recent development. I think you had something to do with that."

"I'm sure it was more you than me."

"Either way, I think it's a good thing. For you and for him." I hesitated a moment. "Have you talked to Evan about this?"

"No. I figured he had plenty of time to bring up his history if he'd wanted to. I'm curious, but I don't want to make him uncomfortable. Bill, the manager, told me about his diving accident and that it ended his career."

"It's a long, complicated story. But that accident has to do with the animosity between him and his brother too."

"It makes me even more determined to chase my dream."

I reached out to pat the back of his hand. "You should, Dylan. You never know when your life might change in an instant. Don't let opportunities pass you by." I glanced at the clock. "Go on and get out of here. And best of luck. The next time I go to a game, I expect to see you on the mound of the main team. Or in the lineup—I'd be happy with either."

He laughed and took off his apron. "So would I! Thanks for your help, Liv. I'll let you know how it goes."

As Dylan walked out the back door, I had to smile. Despite my life feeling like a dumpster fire lately, at least someone was headed in the right direction.

246

Chapter Thirty

Evan

I DRAGGED my kayak to the shore, got in, and pushed off. A gentle wake trailed behind me in the placid water as I headed into the quiet mangroves, the morning growing lighter around me. As I started paddling, my arms felt the extra weight of this kayak. Now two weeks after Liv had moved out, I couldn't bring myself to use the lighter craft, even though it was much easier to paddle. A mixture of penance and stubbornness, I supposed. It had been her kayak.

I'd texted her a couple of times since she shot me down in the shop, just asking how she was doing. I got polite, yet curt, responses back, letting me know loud and clear her feelings toward me hadn't thawed.

Why should she feel differently?

I flinched as my mind circled around to what I'd said to her that night. Again. I'd known even as those words poured bitterly from my mouth that they were lies. As an adult, I'd never been in love, and I wasn't sure puppy love affairs during high school counted. And now that I'd solidly wrecked the ship on the rocks, I had no idea how to pry it off and put it back together.

I only knew I was miserable.

My family wasn't helping. Their attitude change was subtle but definitive. Before Gabe's wedding, they'd always treated my attitude toward Hunter with supportive forbearance. Now I felt waves of impatience and irritation coming off just about everyone. They all thought it was time for me to get over myself and forgive Hunter. Even I was starting to wonder if I should.

Except I had no idea how to do that. The idea of calling him on the phone and apologizing made me physically nauseous.

I shifted position in the kayak, trying to stretch out my sore knee. The pain in my legs ebbed and flowed, and lately it had been flaring. Which hadn't helped my mood any. In a few hours, I would have my annual appointment with Dr. Nelson, who had been my physician my entire life. I doubted my increased pain presaged anything ominous, but I never missed my checkups.

A chorus of *cheep, cheep, cheep* came from the trees, and I glanced up, cracking a smile. A huge osprey slowly lowered to its nest as its hungry babies cried out for their share of fish. Liv and I had watched the pair build their nest, but the young ospreys hatched after she'd left. I continued paddling and without conscious thought, found myself entering the private lagoon.

Insects buzzed in the trees, but otherwise the area was still and silent. I stopped paddling, resting my paddle across the kayak's top as I glided to a stop. Soon enough, Gray approached for a drink, and I dug the Thermos out to pour water into his mouth. He would always take as much water as I was willing to spare. After a healthy pour, I screwed the lid back on and paddled a distance away to see if he had any company this morning.

Rising like a long gray wraith, Betty glided toward me. I was lifting my Thermos when I froze. A second, smaller shape swam at her side, and the tiny manatee lifted its snout out of the water to inspect me more closely. Betty edged in front of her baby, keeping herself between me and it.

"You're a good mom, aren't you? I knew you were pregnant!" Unbidden, a smile stretched my lips at being able to witness this.

But it quickly fell, my blood becoming cool and thin as it traveled through my body. Liv and I had always meant to witness this together. Even more so than the ospreys. Except she was on Dove Key, moving on with her life.

Without me.

I pulled out my phone to send her a picture, knowing she'd love to see the youngster. Then I hesitated. Why? I didn't want to send her a picture. I wanted her here with me now. I wanted to experience this moment *with* her.

Life had become monochromatic. But how could I win Liv back when she wouldn't even speak to me? A few days ago, I'd gone into Sweet Dreams, and she'd waited on me like I was any other customer. Polite and friendly, with no hint of flirting or of the hunger that used to enter her eyes when she touched my chest and shoulders.

I needed to tell her I loved her, and that I'd made a terrible mistake. But I didn't know how. And I had a feeling time was growing thin to do anything about it.

Dr. Clarence Nelson's office had been located on the same block of Main Street as long as I could remember. It was near the western edge of Dove Key, where the commercial district transitioned to residential structures. The Coleridges' Sunset Siesta Resort was at the far western edge of the Key. Dr. Nelson's building had been thoroughly remodeled several years ago, and was now fully modern.

I sat on a vinyl exam table, the paper crinkling beneath me as the doctor listened to my heart and lungs. He'd already completed a thorough exam on both legs. Wrapping his stethoscope over his neck, he sat on a portable stool across from me. He'd had brown hair once, but now it was snowy white, and his craggy face was lined. But he always had a smile for me.

"You're healthy as a horse, Evan. Your blood work is reassuringly boring. Not a thing out of line."

"That's good. My leg pain has been flaring lately. I was worried maybe something was going wrong."

His brow wrinkled. "Let's increase your dose of gabapentin. That should help, but I can put you at ease that your strength and reflexes are the same as last year. That you recovered from such a devastating injury and then maintained your fitness is a testament to your athleticism. And your work ethic. I've rarely seen such happy outcomes."

I smiled, though it felt forced. I didn't feel very happy lately. "Thanks. Physically, I'm really grateful and proud of what I've achieved. Mentally, I still struggle sometimes."

He leaned forward and rested his elbows on his thighs. "I heard there were some fireworks between you and Hunter at Gabe's wedding."

I winced, rubbing a hand over my jaw. "I imagine everyone on both Calypso and Dove Keys knows about that by now."

"I remember you didn't feel counseling was very beneficial when you tried it before, but new people are practicing in the area now. I could give you some referrals, and your experience might be different this time."

"Thanks. I'll keep it in mind, but I'll hold off for now." I didn't see how talking about my problems with a stranger would help. I'd rather confide in someone close who knew me.

"Of course. Just call if you change your mind." Then he straightened, his face brightening. "But this will likely be our last visit together. I'm retiring, and Jane and I are moving to Boulder."

I smiled, unable to resist his eagerness. "Congratulations. So is someone else taking over?"

"Yes. I sold my practice and a new doctor is arriving next month. He grew up around here, so you might even know him. He's not that much older than you. Aiden Mitchell?"

I mouthed the name silently, knowing it was familiar. "I've heard of him, but I can't place the face. Aiden..." In a flash, it came to me. "You know, I think Stella might have dated him in high school. I remember a kid named Aiden, but I'm not sure of the last name. If it's him, I'm sure I'll recognize him. Enjoy your retirement. Won't be the same place without you."

Dr. Nelson nodded at me. "I certainly will, thanks. Evan, your life certainly hasn't gone the way you thought it would. But that doesn't make it... less. Or you. I know you've had a hard time overcoming your accident. Before I left, I wanted you to know that I think what you've accomplished is remarkable."

A smile tugged at my lips as I tried to assimilate his words and take them in. But as I drove back to Calypso Key, my mood dimmed again. I thought about stopping by Sweet Dreams, just to see Liv, but I chickened out.

And my mood didn't improve any as I faced my next task. After parking at the Big House, I strolled down the hill and toward Orchid. We had a large family group staying at the resort, and tonight they had the private room at Orchid booked for a family reunion celebration. I opened the back door of the kitchen, steeling myself as I prepared to make sure all the preparations were in order.

"These potatoes are awful!" Alfonso loomed over his sous chef Luis, holding a cube of chopped potato between his thumb and forefinger. "Half are smashed, and the other half are ten different sizes."

"They're the same as I always cut them, Alfonso," the young man replied, wiping a hand on his white apron. Several inches shorter and ten years younger than the Italian, Luis's black hair was slicked back. He had been excited to learn under such an illustrious chef. Of course, that had been a year ago. Luis's sunny attitude and brilliant smile made him a hit with the wait staff, but he was also a quick learner and had thrived at the resort. In spite of Alfonso's overbearing attitude. I repressed a sigh.

Oh, great. Here we go.

Chapter Thirty-One

Evan

A DEEP FLUSH spread over Luis's face as he stared at the stainless-steel counter. The executive chef loomed over him, his posture aggressive and both hands parked on his hips. My irritation at Alfonso inched even higher. I walked over to where the two men stood and peered at the giant bowl of cut-up potatoes. All looked the same size.

"They look good to me," I said to Alfonso. "What's the problem?"

His face blooming with heat and his brows pinched together, the chef threw his hands up and stalked away to the other end of the kitchen. "Standards! No one here has any standards. I am surrounded by idiots." The last word came out *eeediottts*.

After my depressing kayak trip and the news that my doctor of thirty-plus years was retiring, I wasn't in the mood to put up with Alfonso's shit. "Everyone here has standards, including Luis. So cut the crap."

He deflated slightly, watching me evenly. "If you insist.

I am trying to ensure a successful dinner tonight for the heel-billies."

I didn't bother to correct his pronunciation. "The Buckleys have paid us handsomely for a special family reunion. And we're going to give it to them, Alfonso. They're no different than any other guests here. I don't care if the person is the President or a janitor, we treat them the same." While quietly assuring that the extra needs of our VIPs were always met, of course.

He snorted. "I have things well in hand. Though I wasn't able to procure any opossum to cook." He pronounced opossum carefully.

I rolled my eyes. "Can you be nice for once in your life? Or is that completely impossible?"

He folded his arms and pinched his brows together. "I am nice. I am also talented. At least I can cook in peace now that I have my kitchen back."

I stiffened. I was not in the mood to put up with any barbs thrown toward Liv or Rea. Especially Liv. "Rea was done hours ago, and she's been meticulous in her area. So was Liv."

The chef shrugged. "At least that one is gone. I suppose rooting in the slop comes naturally to one like her."

I inhaled sharply and balled my hand into a fist, itching to punch him. But the asshole wasn't worth the paperwork. I moved forward, closing the distance between us. "Don't talk about Liv like that. Don't speak of anyone like that, Alfonso. I've had it with how you talk to people *and* how you treat them."

He sniffed, rearing back. "I give credit where credit is due. Last night, I complimented Rea on a dessert she made. The other one never earned any accolades. When people are stupid, I simply let them know."

I spoke through gritted teeth. "And you need to stop that. Now."

Luis watched the two of us like a tennis match, his head going back and forth.

Malice sparkled in Alfonso's eyes. "Protecting your girlfriend? How noble. Though I heard she is no longer your girlfriend."

My blood was very near boiling now. "That has nothing to do with it."

"It is all irrelevant. She is gone, and that is the important thing. I should not have to work alongside common bakers." He flicked his wrist at me. "I act as is my right. It is my kitchen, after all."

A grim smile rose on my face. I had him right where I wanted him. I was done putting up with his insults, no matter who they were aimed at. But most of all, I was finished with his superior, condescending attitude toward Liv, who outshined him in every way possible. No one was going to insult her in my presence and get away with it.

I raised both arms and rested my hands on my hips, facing him squarely. "Wrong, Alfonso, and that's your big mistake. It's not your kitchen. It's mine. You strut around here like you're God, but you're not. You're a B-list celebrity has-been who's been resting on his laurels since he arrived here. You're not God around here. I am. You're fired, Alfonso. Get out."

Luis had been listening to my diatribe with his mouth open. Now he spun around and hurried out of the kitchen.

Alfonso laughed out loud. "You can't fire me! I have almost a year left on my contract."

I stepped forward until he had to crane his head to look at me. "Don't worry. You'll get your money. Unlike you, we Markhams hold up our end of bargains. And I've never been more serious in my life. Collect your shit and get the hell out of my kitchen right now." The money was definitely a problem, but I didn't care at the moment. I just wanted the sanctimonious bastard gone.

Alfonso stepped back, the smug smile replaced with uncertainty now. His eyes flickered around the kitchen before settling back on me. "But I don't have anything else lined up yet."

"I guess you should have thought of that before you opened your big, fat mouth, huh? I should have fired you a long time ago. If you're not out of here in five minutes, I'm calling the police to have you forcibly removed."

Without waiting for a response, I turned and pushed through double doors into the service prep area. Half a dozen employees were listening round-eyed to Luis as he gesticulated wildly. Spinning around, he dropped his hands, his face carefully blank.

I nodded at him. "Congratulations, Luis. You just got promoted to temporary executive chef. You're in charge of dinner tonight."

His eyes widened with horror. "Me?"

My anger at Alfonso finally fading, I laughed and clapped him on the shoulder. "Relax. The family didn't pick a single dish you couldn't make blindfolded. And this is only temporary. We'll get an experienced chef in ASAP, and I promise I'll do a better job hiring this time. You'll do great, especially without Alfonso breathing down your neck."

"You really fired him?" he squeaked.

"I did."

It took several more minutes of convincing, but in the end, Luis was so happy I got rid of Alfonso that it overshadowed his fear over his sudden promotion. By the time I returned to the kitchen, it was empty. The back door stood wide open. I glanced at where Alfonso kept his personal knives. They were gone, along with his other prized items.

But now I had a major problem to solve. Closing the back door behind me, I rushed across the Key to the dive shop. Gabe and I had mostly made up, with only a slight residual tension about Hunter between us. Nodding at Carissa behind the counter, I headed down the hall and knocked on Gabe's open door. "Got a second?"

He looked up from his computer screen and nodded. A framed picture of him and April on their wedding day stood next to his computer. "Sure. I could use a break from financial spreadsheets."

I laughed, but it came out a little shaky. "You might change your mind about that in a minute."

He cocked his head. "Is something wrong?"

I dropped into an armchair facing him and curled my fingers around the wooden arms. "Yes and no. I just solved one big problem, but I created another one. I fired Alfonso."

At first, Gabe didn't react. Then he narrowed his eyes, trying to tell if I was joking.

"I'm dead serious."

"That's a lot of money we'll have to pay him in one lump sum, Evan."

"I know. I'll pay it out of my own pocket if I have to. I've been saving for years."

Gabe tipped forward and grabbed a pencil, bouncing it by the eraser on his blotter as he thought about what I'd just said. "He had about nine months left, I think. I can scrape that up, so don't worry about dipping into your piggy bank." Closing his hand on the pencil, he raised his eyes to mine. "What the hell happened?"

I told him, and his eyes became calculating when I

mentioned that Alfonso insulting Liv had been the final straw. I ran a hand through my hair. "Anyway, we need to lean on Stella. We both know she wants to work here—she just needs to be talked into it. And this is an emergency. I'm sure we can convince her."

Sitting back in his chair again, Gabe nodded. "Yeah, she's the obvious choice, and it would be great to have her around again. Maybe she can give notice at Blue Nirvana and swing both jobs for two weeks."

"I got tonight covered at Orchid. I promoted Luis to temporary head chef. Should I drive down to Key West and talk to her now?"

Gabe's eyes got steadily larger during my last sentence. He paused, just staring at me. "You? Beg Stella to drop everything and run home? Evan, I hate to tell you this, but you're not exactly Mr. Popular in the family right now. Especially with Stella. She went after Hunter that night, remember?" He sighed, running both hands through his hair. "Shit. I'll go. Alone."

His words stung. Not because he'd said them in a nasty tone of voice. He hadn't. They hurt because of the simple truth of them. The echoes of my actions that night continued to ripple out.

Gabe rose to his feet and grabbed his phone. "April's on the afternoon dive now. I'll text her and let her know I'll be home late. Hailey's at softball practice, so she's taken care of."

Guilt rolled through me like a noxious cloud. "I'm sorry, Gabe. I didn't mean to cause you any more problems. You want me to call Alfonso and apologize? See if he'll come back?"

He snapped his head up, a wide smile forming. "Hell no! This isn't exactly how I would have planned it, but at least we're rid of the ugly son of a bitch now. We'll figure it out. I won't give Stella a heads-up that I'm coming. That way she can't think up any reasons to say no." He breezed by me and clapped me on the shoulder, still smiling. "Nice work, asshole."

I couldn't help a reluctant laugh as he walked out the door, then I was alone. My smile faded. How had I made such a colossal mess of everything? Gabe and April had forgiven me, but they never should have had to. Dad suggested I needed help. So had Dr. Nelson. But I still didn't want to bare my soul to a stranger. I could only see myself doing that for one person.

I knew what I wanted.

Liv. Us. Together.

Slowly, I stood and rubbed my cheek as I walked down the hall, deep in thought. For this, I couldn't go in half-cocked. I needed to think over my actions carefully, but I knew one thing without doubt.

I was going to get Liv back.

Chapter Thirty-Two

Evan

I HUNG out at the Big House all evening, keeping an eye out for Gabe's return. Key West was nearly an hour drive, so I wasn't sure when to expect him back. It was almost 11:00 p.m. when I saw his headlights heading down the hill toward the Barn. I rushed out of the house and ran down the path after him.

When I reached the Barn, Gabe was just exiting his Mercedes. I got a second surprise when I took in the dark-blue suit he wore. "Wow. When was the last time you wore a suit?"

He turned toward me, loosening his yellow tie. He pulled it over his head and stuffed it in his jacket pocket. "Lately, they haven't signaled pleasant occasions. But I was pitching a business proposition, after all. Shouldn't I look the part?"

"Of course. I was just surprised, is all. You've always pulled off the serious businessman look better than any of the rest of us." Anxiety was eating a hole in my stomach. "So? What did she say?"

"Let's go sit on the patio. I don't want to wake up April or Hailey."

He grabbed a couple of beers, and we sat on the covered back deck. The moon streaked from behind a cloud, lighting the ocean before us in pale light. Gabe took a drink, then rolled the cold bottle over his forehead. "Stella was working tonight, but I talked her into an extended break. I explained that Alfonso mouthed off yet again and you had no choice but to fire him."

"That's pretty much how it went."

"She didn't exactly fall over in delight at being offered the job. She was really torn at the thought of leaving a successful career in Key West."

"She said as much when I talked to her at Conch Republic during your bachelor party."

Gabe turned slightly on the couch to look at me squarely. "In the end, she agreed to take the position, and for the next several weeks, she's going to do her best to be in two places at once. Though mostly at Blue Nirvana. She'll leave instructions for Luis to implement at Orchid."

The breath in my lungs exploded out, tension flooding out of my body. "That's great news! Thanks, Gabe. You did a fantastic job."

He watched me steadily, not reacting to my words. "She had one non-negotiable stipulation. I accepted on your behalf."

My stomach flopped over. This sounded ominous. "What?"

"That you find a way to bury the hatchet with Hunter. And I agree. You don't have to be best friends with the guy, Evan, but it's high time you two found a way to coexist."

Slowly, I leaned forward and placed my half-full bottle on the coffee table. "Gabe, I'm sorry about what happened at your wedding. I shouldn't have blown up like that, but he caught me off guard. I realize I caused a lot of damage that night, and now Stella is affected too. But look, I can't help how I feel."

"I know. But you can control how you react."

How? How the hell do I do that?

But I didn't voice that question out loud. "I'll try, okay? That's the best I can promise."

Gabe still had his poker face on, staring at me steadily. "All of us want Hunter to come home for a real visit, including Dad and Nona. Evan, he hasn't just been joyriding around the world since your accident. I know you don't want to hear this, but you're not the only victim here. His life hasn't been easy, either."

I snorted and sat back. "And I'm supposed to feel sorry for him? I was the one in the wheelchair, remember?"

"Yes, I remember. And I'm not saying you don't have a right to feel the way you do. But you need to start moving beyond it." He paused for a moment, picking at the label on his beer. "I'd hoped you were starting to turn the corner when you and Liv were together. You seemed really happy."

"I was happy," I said miserably.

"Are things between you two... beyond repair?"

I sighed and rubbed my face with both hands. "I don't know. She won't talk to me."

"How hard have you tried?"

"I was just thinking about that earlier today. Finding a way to make her listen. I've never really told her how I feel about her, and now I'm scared shitless to."

He smiled. "I know the feeling."

I gaped at him. Gabe was the last person I'd expect to have confidence issues. "You? When have you ever been insecure about a woman?"

He nodded with his head toward the master bedroom upstairs. "Since I found the one I want to spend forever with. That's one of the signs that what you're feeling is real, Evan. I noticed you didn't fire Alfonso until he insulted Liv."

I nodded. "That was the last straw."

"Maybe she doesn't realize how much you care about her." His jaw cracked in a huge yawn. "I need to head to bed. I'm driving the dive boat tomorrow. For what it's worth, firing Alfonso wasn't a bad move. It'll cost us more, but Stella was willing to take a smaller salary for a few months until she's established. It'll all work out, little brother."

I wish I could believe that.

After returning up the hill at a much slower pace than I'd raced down it, I opened the kitchen door quietly and stepped into the dark room.

"What are you doing skulking around in the middle of the night?"

Startled, I whirled toward Nona, who stood at the counter pouring boiling water into a mug. "I was talking to Gabe. Couldn't sleep?"

She set the kettle on the stove and dipped her teabag several times. Her snowy hair was loose and fell down her back. "No, so I made a cup of chamomile tea. Come keep you old woman company while I drink it."

As much as I wanted to fall into bed and sleep, I padded over to the table and sat across from her. "I wasn't skulking, either. Just a brotherly conversation."

"At this hour?"

"Yeah, it's been quite a day. I fired Alfonso today."

She blew over the rim of her cup to cool her tea, a faint smile rising. "Did you? Good riddance. Insufferable man. Though that does seem to leave us with a rather large problem."

I smiled. "Not anymore. That's what my meeting with Gabe was about. Get ready to be very happy. You've got another grandchild coming home. Stella accepted the position as executive chef of Orchid tonight."

She froze, the cup an inch from her mouth. "Really? Stella is moving back?"

"Yes, though I don't know what her living arrangements will be. Whether she'll want her old room upstairs or move into one of the family cottages like Maia and Wyatt. Or live in Dove Key, for that matter."

I smiled as a wide grin broke over my grandmother's face. "That's wonderful news! We got rid of one problem person and will now have nearly the entire family together again. How about that!"

My smile fell at her words. "Yeah. Almost the whole family. That seems to be the pattern. Hunter showing up here has changed a lot of things."

She inspected her fingernails. "Oh? What kind of things?"

Her mild tone didn't fool me for a minute. "Several people have told me it's time to make peace with Hunter."

Setting her cup down, Nona rested her gnarled hand over mine. "That wouldn't only make me very happy, Evan. I think it would bring you peace too. *Please* try to mend your relationship with Hunter."

"I'm going to try, okay? But I just don't know how."

"Sometimes it's not a how, child. Sometimes it's a who."

I raised my eyes to hers. "You're talking about Liv."

"Yes. I witnessed a rather remarkable change in you while she stayed with us. Liv was very good for you."

A small, reluctant smile rose on my face. "Which was all the more remarkable considering our relationship was pretend to begin with."

"Whatever are you talking about?"

I laughed, unable to hold it in. "That night in the kitchen when I blurted out that we were dating? We weren't, in any way, shape, or form. But Liv overheard us talking in here and wanted to help. So she pretended to be my girlfriend."

Her eyes narrowed, her face becoming shrewd. "But along the way, things changed?"

"Yeah. Big time. Especially for me. Until I blew it all when Hunter showed up."

Nona squeezed my hand. Her touch had always represented safety and love. That at least hadn't changed. "Maybe you didn't blow it all. I saw how she looked at you, Evan. I'm starting to wonder if both of you cared more than you wanted to let on." She let go of my hand to take a sip of tea.

"Maybe. I hope so. I loved being with her. I love her."

"Did you ever tell her that?"

"No. In fact, I said some pretty awful things to her that night. That was why she left. I've tried to apologize, but she won't hear me out."

"Maybe you haven't tried hard enough."

I fidgeted in my seat. "What am I supposed to do? Fall to the floor and beg forgiveness? Send her roses every day for the rest of her life?"

"A big gesture is always a nice touch, but I'd say most women simply want sincerity. If you screwed up, Grandson, you need to make sure she understands loud and clear that you know that. And that it won't happen again."

"How do I do that when she won't talk to me?"

Nona frowned at me, a touch of exasperation showing on her face. "Surely you can find a moment to get the woman alone? And kindly ask her to hear you out? You do speak English fairly well."

I laughed softly. "I don't know about that. I get pretty tongue-tied around women."

Draining the last of her tea, she stood, a smile on her face. "And that can also work in your favor, young man. Women like it when men get flustered in their presence. Just be yourself, Evan. You two might have started out pretending, but she fell for *you*. Remember that."

After Nona went to her room, I stayed at the table, running the situation over in my head. I needed to talk to Liv somewhere where she'd have to talk to me. Somewhere public. In a flash, it came to me. I knew the where. All I needed to know was the when.

I rose and headed to my room to find out.

Chapter Thirty-Three

Liv

I SIPPED from my glass of white wine as Brenna Coleridge went around the living room, passing out next month's book. She handed April and me our copies before sitting next to April on the couch.

Pam, who hosted the meeting, readjusted her dark-blond hair in its clip as she sat nearby. In her thirties and divorced, she was the unelected leader of our group. She formed the wine and books club as a means of branching out after her divorce. She smiled at April and Brenna. "It's very nice to see you two sitting together. Now that April is officially a Markham, I was afraid you two might have to end your friendship."

April laughed and shook her head. "Hardly. And I don't think some feud from the nineteenth century has any bearing now."

Brenna grinned and raised her glass to April. "I agree. But don't tell my brothers that. They still feel otherwise."

"Yeah, I know," April said more quietly, but the two women touched glasses.

"All right," Pam called, standing up and holding the book in one hand. "We'll meet four weeks from today and discuss this second-chance romance. Have a great month everyone!"

As the others in the room started to file out, I leaned forward to speak to Brenna on April's other side. "Is this feud thing real, or do the townies just like to stir the pot?"

She shrugged. "A little of both, but gossip always reigns around here." She alternated her gaze between us. "I have to ask. Is it true that Evan got into a huge fight with Hunter at your wedding, April?"

"It wasn't a huge fight," I replied quickly, not giving April a chance to answer. "They had some tense words, but it blew over quickly and things are back to normal." I bunched my fist on the material of my skirt, pissed at myself for defending Evan. Why should I care if some neighbors saw him in a negative light?

April shook her head. "It didn't ruin our wedding or anything like that. And I don't think anyone could take on Hunter if he wanted to fight back." She barked a laugh and took a drink of wine.

"I went to school with Hunter," Brenna said softly. "We were friends and used to hang out at the library. My parents weren't thrilled about it, but we got along great. We liked the same books."

April blinked. "Gabe said Hunter always used to have his nose in a book. It's hard to believe the man who showed up at our wedding is a bookworm."

"What do you mean?" Brenna asked, cocking her head to one side.

I smirked. "Hunter is a giant and could probably bodyslam a rhinoceros. He looks more like a hired bodyguard than a librarian."

"That's what I've heard," Brenna said, and there was something sad in her tone. She stood. "I'd better get going. Congrats again, April. See you guys later."

After saying goodbye to Brenna, I turned to April. I wanted some alone time with my friend. "You want to go back to the shop for a coffee?"

"Ooh! I'd love a private tour of the new bakery."

Ten minutes later, I brought two cinnamon lattes from the espresso machine to a table in the empty bakery.

"Thanks," April said as she surveyed the area. I'd gone with a soft gray-and-pink palette. Tables had comfy gray or pink chairs, some seating two and others four. "I love it! Everything looks so fresh and modern, though you kept the same wall art. So that ties together the old bakery and the new."

I laughed weakly as I stared at the framed prints. "It wasn't intentional, believe me. I salvaged everything I could."

"It's been a lot quieter at the resort since you reopened here."

I sat back in my chair, surprised. "I can't imagine Local Grind is struggling. Even without Dylan's excellent barista skills."

"I don't think it is, but I'm sure sales have slowed some. They couldn't not." She leaned forward. "Just between you and me, your pastries are *so* much better. The staff was visiting the coffee shop a lot while you were there, and they've stopped."

"Well, it's nice to know someone misses me."

April eyed me over the rim of her pink ceramic mug.

"Evan's miserable, Liv. It's obvious to all of us. He really regrets what happened that night."

"Good. He should. It was your *wedding*, for God's sake. I'm amazed at how calm you are about it."

She smiled and gave a small shrug. "I'm just glad Alex stepped in before things got any more heated between Evan and Hunter."

"I wondered about that. How did he know Hunter was in the military? Alex called him soldier."

"I asked him about that before he and Hope left. He said it's a military thing, and that he can spot ex-military on sight. Plus, Alex was an officer."

I sighed and set my mug down on the table. "You're right, though. Things could have gotten even worse that night."

"In some ways, I think their altercation might have been a good thing."

"April, you are truly a saint. How could that have possibly been beneficial?"

She blew on her latte, then took a sip. "It's forcing Evan to deal with his feelings toward Hunter. To try to mend this rift in the family."

I tried to keep my voice mild. "And he's doing that? Reaching out to Hunter?"

"I'm not sure. He's trying to figure it out, though. I think he could really use someone supportive in his life. Are things really over between you? You can't forgive him for what he did that night?"

I sighed and stared at my coffee, the spicy hint of cinnamon reaching my nose. "It's more than that. I'm hurt, April." I lifted my gaze and pointed at the Hammerheads poster above us. "I love baseball. Evan and I bonded over it. He helped coach Dylan. Early on, Evan told me point blank that he was nothing special, just a high school player. It wasn't until he blew up after your wedding that I found out he was headed toward the Major Leagues. That's a pretty massive detail to keep from me."

She smiled sympathetically. "I know, but I don't think he did it to hurt you. His baseball career is part of the whole Hunter-trauma thing. He never talked about it. The rest of the family was shocked when he started helping Dylan and the other players. I think it's a good sign that he's starting to open up about it more."

I smiled. "You like Evan, don't you?"

"Yeah, Liv. He's a great guy. Who's been terribly wounded, inside and out. According to Gabe, you're the first woman he's really been involved with since his accident. Over a decade ago!"

"He doesn't want anything serious with me. He said so very clearly after the wedding."

"He said a lot of things he regrets."

I shrugged but didn't reply.

"What do you want him to say, Liv?"

I glanced around the bakery, considering my answer. My gaze settled on April. "I want him to tell me he feels the same way I do. I love him, April. But I don't want to be in a relationship with a ghost who can't exist in the present. I need to know he's willing to get past what happened to him." I shook my head and took a sip of coffee. "I haven't really talked to him, though. I think because I'm afraid of what he'll say."

"That he wants to be with you, but can't forgive Hunter and move on?"

"Yeah, that pretty much sums it up. Though it looks like he's not the only one who's afraid, is he? Guess the next time he wants to talk, I need to be more open."

"I think you two sitting down and clearing the air would be a really good idea."

I reached across the table and squeezed her hand. "Thanks. And thanks for hearing me out. It helps."

She glanced at her watch and downed her coffee. "I'd better run. I have an appointment at my gyn in Marathon."

"Nothing wrong, I hope?"

April broke into a brilliant smile. "I'm having my IUD removed. Gabe and I are going completely commando now."

I laughed. "Congrats. Though that might be premature."

"He's thirty-seven and I'm thirty-three. We'd both like a kid or two, so we'd better get cracking on it. What are you doing tonight?"

"I'm going to a Hammerheads game. Dylan made the main team and tonight's the final game of the developmental season. He's starting, so I want to be there."

"You're a good friend, Liv. He's lucky to have you."

"He's a great kid. I'm so happy and proud he made the team, but I won't deny I'll miss having him around here all the time. I've just hired a new gal to take some hours when he's traveling with the team. But extra help around here might free up time for me too, so that's a good thing."

I TOOK a deep breath of fresh green grass, trying to feel good about being here. Dylan's pitching was lights-out tonight and the Hammerheads were ahead three to zero. He'd left the game in the seventh inning to a standing ovation, and my heart had almost overflowed as I applauded. Now it was the top of the ninth, and the last chance for the team from Homestead to score.

Evan had also worked with the relief pitcher, but he didn't have Dylan's control. There were two outs as the batter stepped back to the plate, the count at two and two. The entire stadium was humming, feet drumming against the floor. It was thrilling, yet all I could think of was the empty seat next to me. And my empty apartment. The people around me were also season ticket holders, and we'd struck up a casual friendship over the season. When they'd asked about Evan's absence, I'd brushed them off with a smile and said it was just me tonight.

The crowd roared as the batter took a mighty swing at the ball and missed it completely. Strike three and game to the Hammerheads. The developmental season was over. With smiles and laughter, the crowd rose around me and headed toward the aisles.

I sat in my folding green seat, not eager to leave. Not eager for the half-hour drive home. My bed might be brand-new, but it was also empty and cold. I didn't want to go to games alone. I didn't want to go without Evan, and not just because of how much he'd taught me about the game over the season. I didn't even pick up a scorecard tonight. As the Hammerheads filed out of the dugout and lined up to high-five the other team, I stared absently at the field. The announcer droned on, encouraging fans to secure their season tickets now for the upcoming season. I sat there without moving, miserable and alone.

The air next to me warmed as someone sat in the empty seat.

When I turned and saw Evan, my heart almost stopped.

He wore a Hammerheads T-shirt and was freshly shaven, his hair neatly combed. He was breathtakingly handsome, that granite jaw on full display. Those warm blue eyes were focused solely on me.

After stuttering a few times, my heart pounded, reverberating in my ears. "Evan?"

"Hi, Liv."

"What are you doing here?"

"I've been trying to think of a way to talk to you. Somewhere we wouldn't be distracted. I got here before the game started, and I've been sitting at the back of this section. Originally, I was going to come down here during the seventh inning stretch, but I didn't want us to get interrupted by the game. I really want to speak with you."

The area around us was now deserted. Workers hadn't come out yet to clean up, so we had the section to ourselves. I gave him a shy smile, pleased he'd gone to so much effort. "You could have just texted me to meet at Conch Republic or something."

He shook his head, his eyes traveling around the field. Then he met my gaze again. "It needs to be here. This is a baseball stadium, Liv. Hallowed ground to me. More than anywhere else in the world, I faced down my fears on a baseball field. I need you to understand."

"Need me to understand what?" My hands trembled, and I clasped them together in my lap.

"That you were right. That awful night, when I said what we had together wasn't real. You called me out on it right then and there. I've been crazy about you almost from the first moment I saw you. And a fake relationship was a way to be together without me having to worry about... not being enough. That you only saw a shadow of a man with a bad limp."

He stopped to swallow. A current ran through my body at his words, but I didn't interrupt him. After a moment, he continued. "I didn't count on things getting emotional, though. And that night, I was such a mess. I'm so sorry for what I said to you, and for what I did. To you... and to Hunter. He wasn't there to cause a scene, but I didn't care. I just wanted to hurt him the way he hurt me."

An artery throbbed in his neck and one hand bunched into a fist on his thigh. "That night brought to a head that I can't go on like this. I need to find a way to forgive Hunter and move on with my life. To accept the man I am now. I need to figure out how to start again." He stopped again, his mouth opening and closing. His imploring eyes bored into mine. "Liv... I don't think I can do that without you."

Tears sprang to my eyes, and I reached out to grasp his hand. His skin was much cooler than I expected as he clasped back tightly. "Evan, you are anything but a shadow of a man. Maybe you're not a pro ball player, but you're so many other things. You're the glue that holds everything together. And the only one who can't see that is you."

He shifted toward me in his seat, our knees touching. "I'm trying. Please give me another chance. I miss you so much. I miss everything about us. I love you, Liv, and I want you back."

"I love you too."

At the same time, we leaned toward each other. Our lips met, and I slid mine across his, that familiar, soft warmth. That sense of being home.

Evan slipped his hand around the back of my neck. He ended the kiss and pressed his forehead against mine. "Thank you."

I felt a thousand percent better than I had just a few minutes ago, but I still needed to know more. "Will you answer something for me?"

"Anything. Whatever you want to know."

I straightened and took his free hand in mine. He softly cupped the back of my neck, keeping us close. "Baseball is so deeply a part of you, and yet you kept that piece of yourself from me. That was what hurt me the most. It made me feel like I didn't matter enough to tell me about this huge aspect of yourself."

He clenched his eyes shut. "I know, and I'm really sorry about that." Blinking his eyes open, his gaze drifted around the mostly empty stadium before settling on me. "That first Hammerheads game we came to? That was the first time I've been inside a stadium since my accident. It was rough. I went through some ups and downs that night, and I wasn't ready to talk about it yet. But I was here, because of you. Then, when I saw Dylan pitching in the field on the Key, another piece fell into line because I knew how to help him. Again, because of you."

Removing his hand from my neck, Evan enfolded both of mine within his. "I feel terrible about how my past came out. I was in a really bad head space the night of the wedding. You tried to help, but all I was interested in was pushing people away. I never meant to hurt you by not telling you about my baseball career... I just couldn't. It hurt too much."

"I understand that, and I'm glad that's changed. I guess I'd better ask, is there anything else you're not telling me?"

He smiled that shy, crooked smile I loved so much. "No. No more secrets. I promise."

With the last residual tension draining out of me, I laced our fingers together. "I certainly haven't gone through the pain and trauma you have, but I know a thing or two about picking up the pieces and starting over. You mentioned you can't figure out how to start again. But you already have—you're here, aren't you? And I'll be by your side to help however I can."

His eyes were glassy as he stared at me, and a muscle moved as he flexed his jaw. "I really need you, Liv. Everybody tells me how much better I've been getting since we were together. They're right. Can we start again? For real this time?"

My wounded heart stitched itself back together, whole again. "Yes. Starting right now."

He pulled me to him, and our mouths met again. This time more urgently. His kiss was firm, confident, and made my blood hum. A quiet moan rushed from my lungs as our kiss deepened. This time, I broke the kiss, speaking in a rush. "I've got a brand-new bed in my apartment, but it's cold and lonely. Maybe you can help warm it up for me?"

"No maybes about it. Let's get out of here."

As Evan led me by the hand, we marched out of the stadium. I watched the play of his broad shoulders moving beneath his shirt. His stride was long and confident, his steps assured. He barely limped, and I hardly ever noticed the hitch in his gait anyway. How could this magnificent man ever feel he wasn't good enough?

I had a feeling we'd make the half-hour journey in record time.

Chapter Thirty-Four

Evan

I TAPPED my fingers rhythmically on the wheel as I studied Liv's Tahoe ahead of me, willing the miles to pass faster. When I'd first arrived at the stadium, she'd looked so achingly beautiful in the stands, it had been all I could do not to rush down and blurt out my declaration of love. She wore a Hammerheads jersey and ball cap, her curly ponytail pulled through the hole in the back. To anyone else, she would have been a pretty woman enjoying a baseball game. To me, she was my greatest wish.

My greatest wish now confirmed. For real this time.

The drive back to her place seemed endless. I couldn't wait to get inside her apartment. To plunge my hands into her thick hair. To kiss those full, delectable lips and stroke my fingers over all that lush, creamy skin. That would make a nice beginning.

We parked in the alley behind Sweet Dreams and entered the building. As soon as I shut the door behind me, I couldn't deny myself any longer. Grabbing her hand, I yanked her toward me and slammed my mouth to hers. Wrapping her long ponytail around one hand, I pulled gently, keeping her face tilted up.

"God, you're everything to me. Do you know that? Do you know how you affect me?" I thrust my hips hard against her, grinding to make sure she knew.

Liv gently laughed against my mouth, then slowly dragged her fingers down my chest and abdomen. Then her hand reached the front of my shorts and she squeezed.

Hard enough to make me growl.

She stepped back to slowly raise my shirt. I sucked in a breath as Liv's eyes blazed, radiating heat. I ripped the shirt all the way off, throwing it aside. She slowly let her hands explore my body, stroking down from the top of my shoulders. Every touch felt like a million tiny sparks shooting through me, increasing in urgency and intensity with each passing second.

Liv's lips traced the length of my jawline and then trailed down to find the sensitive spot just below my ear. I shuddered as her fingertips moved over every inch of me, igniting an explosive reaction. I couldn't hold still any longer. I grabbed both of her shoulders and walked her backward into the prep area. Sliding my hands under her ass, I lifted her and set her on top of a stainless-steel island.

A breathy giggle exploded from her lungs, making us both smile. "I guess you mean business," she said, her voice deeper, throatier. Sexier than hell.

Parting her legs, I stepped between them and raked my mouth over hers. I bit down on her lower lip, not enough to hurt but enough to prove my point. I let go to whisper in her ear, "Does that answer your question?"

Her only response was a deep, long moan as I removed her shirt and bra. Slowly, I glided both hands up her thighs.

The heat radiating between us left me trembling, and I dove in to kiss her neck. She smelled like the bakery around us, warm and sweet. It was a comfortable, familiar scent that made me feel like I'd been there before. She smelled like home.

After whisking off her shorts, I focused on exploring every inch of her skin, feeling goose bumps rise on her soft skin wherever my tongue touched. I slowly caressed Liv's body, savoring every inch of her incredible curves. Lowering to my knees, my fingertips traced delicate circles over her abdomen, immediately followed by my mouth. I moved lower still, my hand curling around one hip bone as my thumb brushed across her inner thigh, sliding under the silky material of her black panties.

My tongue lingered, teasing before reaching the place where she wanted me the most. Liv gasped softly as I continued exploring the delicate skin along her inner thigh, lightly tracing circles around her most sensitive areas. Letting my lips linger here and there until we were both panting. She shifted against me, pushing herself into my touch as desire coursed through me.

"Evan..."

Pushing to my feet, I watched her. Her ribcage rose and fell with her rapid breaths, and her eyes were half-lidded as she stared at me. The peaks of her full, round breasts pointed straight at me, and the sight of those black panties made me want to explode. They were all that separated us now. I ripped off the black, silky material with one hand, tossing them behind me. Dropping to my knees once more, I plunged home, my tongue taking a long swipe as she cried out.

She grabbed the back of my head, pulling me tighter,

closer. I circled my tongue in long, rolling swirls, tasting and teasing her until she could take no more.

I smiled as she screamed my name into the dark, empty room.

Rising upright, I pulled my wallet from my back pocket and withdrew a condom. She watched me as I rolled it on, slowly moving one bent leg back and forth. A tiny smile played at the corners of her mouth.

Parting her legs even farther, I positioned myself at her entrance and leaned over her until our faces were inches apart. "Do you know how many times I've thought about this the last couple of weeks?"

She shifted position, rubbing against me. "As many as me?"

"More. I want you. Now."

I slammed into her, enveloped in her warmth as her hands raced to my back. As she raked her nails up my skin, the incredible mixture of pain and pleasure rocketed through me.

I panted against her mouth, my breath coming in rhythm with my thrusts. "Do that again."

She did, hard nails over bare flesh that ignited me like I'd never known. I grabbed a handful of her thick hair, pulling tight. Pulling her hard against my mouth. Our breathing became labored. I moved deeper, pushing us ever closer to the brink as Liv clung to me. Her body began to shake, and she was making sharp, breathy noises.

My heart pounded in my ears and my vision blurred as I lost myself in her, unable to think of anything other than this moment. Our movements became more urgent, harder, and faster. I felt her muscles contracting around me, and the sensation sent me over the top. Together, we both cried out, tumbling into the abyss.

I collapsed on top of her, feeling every beat of her heart against mine, until finally our breathing returned to normal. We stayed like that for what felt like forever, me bent over her with my head resting in the hollow of her neck. Nothing else mattered in the world.

My lips were pressed against her tender skin, and I traced a slow line of kisses to her ear. "Do you understand how much I love you? I can't live without you, Liv."

"I love you too. I've missed you so much."

We kissed again, and this time it was soft, tender. A signal that we were something new now. And there was nothing fake about it.

She danced her fingers over my back, and I moved slightly at the stinging. Her smile was slightly wicked. "I might have left some nail marks on your back."

I shifted position, enjoying the slight pain. "Mmm. I'm not complaining."

Laughing, she glanced around the kitchen. "We never even made it to the bed."

I lifted to rest my head in my hand, my elbow on the hard counter. "The night is still young, my love."

Liv's alarm went off at 3:00 a.m. As she rushed to silence it, I groaned and rubbed my eyes. "God, how do you do this every morning?"

Her lilting laugh came through the darkness. "I'm used to it. It's much harder for me to stay up late."

As she padded to the bathroom, I threw back the covers. After turning on the lamp, I pulled on my underwear and the clothes I'd worn to the game.

Liv stopped short when she reentered. "What are you

doing? You don't have to get up at this ridiculous hour, sweetie."

Warmth flooded into me at the endearment. Smiling, I pulled my sneakers on. "I don't mind. I want to help."

Downstairs, she put on a pot of drip coffee after I refused a handmade one. "Nope. Just follow your normal routine."

I helped her remove some premade items kept in the refrigerator and turned on the ovens and the fryers. Just watching her as she moved efficiently around her domain, getting ready for the day, brought a warm wave rolling through my chest.

We were deep into the day's work when Dylan showed up just before five. Noticing me, his brows flew up. "Hey, Evan. Haven't seen you here when I've come in."

"Well, things have changed."

He grinned. "Good. I'm glad to hear that."

Liv arched a brow at him as she rolled out dough for buttermilk biscuits. "And what does that mean?"

Dylan shrugged as he tied his pink Sweet Dreams apron. "You've both helped me a lot, and I want to see you happy. You two are good together. Does this mean you're a couple again?"

I darted my eyes to Liv, who smiled. "We are."

The fryer timer went off and I removed the basket of apple fritters, setting them out to drain. "I'm surprised you didn't want this morning off, Dylan. The night after the final home game is usually pretty late. And boozy."

Dylan laughed. "I had one beer with the guys at Salty's, but then I went home and to bed."

"You're very dependable," Liv added as she used the cutter to shape the round biscuits. "I'm almost sorry you made the team. *Almost*."

Dylan got busy placing pastries inside the display racks. "I think I might be making *less* money from now on, which kind of sucks."

I laughed. "Get ready to work your ass off. The Minor Leagues can be pretty brutal."

Dylan shot me a glance. "What level of the Minors did you play?"

"All of them. I only played one season after high school, but it was a real whirlwind." I paused, realizing I was enjoying the conversation, finally able to talk about what I had experienced and not what I'd missed out on. Both Dylan and Liv scurried around the kitchen as they prepared to open, so I stepped back. "I'll get out of here so you two can work without a third leg in the way. See you later, Dylan."

Liv followed me out the back door. Stopping next to my Explorer, I cradled her face in my hands and bent to brush a kiss over her lips. "Call you later?"

"You better. If you start ghosting me now, we're going to have problems, mister."

I smiled and pulled her tight. "No chance of that. It might be the opposite. You'll probably start telling me to go away and leave you alone."

Liv winked at me. "That's not going to happen either."

I sobered, tucking a curly lock that had sprung free from her ponytail behind one ear. "Thank you for giving me another chance. Maybe we can get together tonight, and I'll show you how much I appreciate it."

"Ooh! Something to look forward to. Now I can get through my day."

After a trip home to shower and change, I spent most of my morning meeting with contractors who were starting the garden cottage remodels. Like the beach cottages, I'd blocked all the inventory so we could finish the project as quickly as possible.

I spent several hours in my office working on staffing levels for Orchid. I'd had to write up a couple of staff recently for disciplinary actions, but now that Alfonso was gone, I was confident employee issues in the restaurant would dramatically decrease. My gaze drifted to my prized baseball, and with a sigh, I picked it up. My fingers automatically found the seams of the ball.

I had a lot of work to do with forgiving Hunter and possibly repairing our relationship. One thing I knew was that staring at reminders of what I'd lost wasn't going to help. Picking up the display stand, I crossed my office and opened the door to my closet. I moved some boxes aside on the top shelf and gently pushed the baseball to the back. I wasn't about to get rid of that ball—it was a huge part of who I was. And maybe someday it might be a part of my future. But I needed to concentrate on the man I was now. My shoulders were lighter when I closed the door and returned to my desk, and a heaviness left me I hadn't realized I'd been carrying.

THE TREES SURROUNDING Orchid were throwing long shadows when I pushed through the back door and entered the kitchen. The sound of laughter greeted me. Stella stood grinning in the center of the kitchen, her long, almost-black hair curled into a neat bun at the nape of her neck. Her black slacks were crisp and her white chef's coat gleamed as she raised her arms straight out from her sides. "Luis! You suck!"

The sous chef bent over at the waist, laughing. "What can I say? My talent knows no bounds."

Stella stirred a large stock pot and took a sip of the contents. "Yeah, but when Gabe railroaded me into coming back here, he didn't say a damn thing about my sous chef being better than me."

Luis grabbed a tomato and sliced it on a cutting board. "I don't think you need to worry about that. I've heard nothing but compliments on our new menu."

"That goes for me too," I said, smiling as I crossed the room. "We had several guests here during the transition from Alfonso to you, and they mentioned the quality at Orchid is noticeably greater."

Stella took a small bow. "Thank you. And thanks to Luis too. He picked up my changes very quickly. We could really use a second sous chef, you know, even after I'm done working both here and at Blue Nirvana."

I nodded as I watched Luis exit the kitchen, leaving us alone for the moment. "I really appreciate you helping us. It means a lot to have you back. Anyone you have in mind for the job?"

"Yeah. Rea."

My eyes widened. "Really? I knew she wanted to concentrate more on desserts, but I didn't realize she wanted to go the chef route."

Stella shrugged as she went back to stirring. The rich aroma of bisque drifted to me, and I took a deep sniff. She elbowed me. "Keep your schnoz out of there. I don't want you drooling in the soup." Ignoring my grin, she continued, "Rea wants to keep her options open. I told her I'd see if you could get someone else to do the morning baking, so she could shift her hours later. Since you already know a baker..." She arched a dark brow, giving me a pointed look.

I smiled and leaned back against the counter. "Okay, I can take a hint. I'll talk to Liv, though it might need to wait a bit so I can concentrate on getting the remodel going. But an idea is glimmering in my mind. I think I can find a way to make everyone happy."

Stella clasped my upper arm and patted my shoulder. "You're good at that, Evan. You've got a big heart, and you handle people really well. I'd really like to see you apply that to one person in particular."

I did my best not to stiffen. "I'll do what I can to get along with Hunter, and not just because you made it a condition of working here. I'm just not sure what that looks like."

"None of us expect you to fall into his arms expressing brotherly love. But maybe Hunter comes down for a dinner or an overnight trip. All I'd like to see is you two jumping in the pool voluntarily and not snarling at each other."

"I can do that, sis."

Her eyes grew warm. "I love you, and I love Hunter too. We all do. You two were so close growing up! I just want you to try to work it out with him and recover some sort of relationship. Whatever that looks like."

"It won't happen overnight, but I'll try. I promise."

As I walked into the bright afternoon sunshine, I stopped and closed my eyes. The sun warmed my lids and my cheeks. And for the first time in years, I thought of the future and smiled.

Chapter Thirty-Five

Liv

THE WATER WAS STILL and stunningly clear as I paddled above it. A multitude of tiny fish darted about, hiding in the thick roots as I glided overhead. Evan had explained that the saltwater mangroves were nurseries for the reefs farther out to sea, but it still amazed me to see it with my own eyes. The marsh was a magical area any time of day, but the early mornings were extra special, maybe because I didn't get to see it very often at that time.

Evan pulled up beside me. He was shirtless in the March morning, a comfortable temperature either way. And I definitely preferred the view. A week had passed since our reconciliation, a week where we'd been inseparable except for working. I let my paddle rest on my kayak just so I could watch the play of his bare shoulders and back as he maneuvered his paddle. With a grin, I hurried to catch up.

"Your new hire's working out well?" he asked.

"Yes, and I need someone else anyway, even without

Dylan needing to cut back his hours. He said the coaching is going very well, by the way."

Evan laughed. "I wouldn't go so far as to call it coaching. I just give him some pointers. I don't want to elbow in on the pitching coach's job."

"You could probably have that job if you wanted it."

He reached out a hand to clasp mine as we glided along under the canopy of trees and mangroves. The water ruffled here and there by a soft breeze or an inquisitive split-tailed kingfisher seeking out its morning breakfast. "I don't want the job. Too much travel—that's a hard life. The season is six months, not counting preseason prepping. Too much time away from you."

I squeezed his hand and let go to paddle again. "I'm glad to hear that, though I don't want you to hold back on my account."

"I'm not," he said mildly. "This isn't the life I'd planned when I was in high school, but it's a good life. Especially with you in it."

"I agree. I never pictured myself anywhere but the Boston area, but now I never want to be anywhere else. Or with anyone else," I added with a wink.

He laughed and we entered the hidden lagoon. White egrets roosted in the trees around the perimeter, adding a splash of vivid contrast to the green trees.

"After reopening, I increased my advertising budget substantially," I said. "It was a gamble financially, but it's paid off. We're busier than we were before the fire. Which would have been the end of the bakery if not for you."

"It worked out for both of us." He stopped paddling and rotated his shoulders to face me. "Speaking of the bakery, I have a business proposition for you. I've been meaning to talk to you about it, but we've had other things on our minds."

I tipped my head back and laughed. "No argument there. What's your idea?"

"Rea wants to concentrate on desserts and cross-train to be a sous chef, so she wants off the morning shift. Which leaves me without a pastry chef."

My smile remained, but inside, my stomach tightened as I started worrying. My pop-up bakery had saved my business, but the shop on Main Street was my focus. "Sounds like a dilemma. What's your solution?"

"We're planning the remodel of the lobby, Dorado, and the coffee shop. So this sounds like a perfect time to make some changes."

"What changes?"

"I was thinking about a total rebrand of Local Grind, and I'm not averse to giving up the name. How would you like to open up a Sweet Dreams satellite? You could go back to calling it Sweet Dreams Mini, or whatever you want. How about I provide the premises and coffee facilities, and you provide the pastries? We'd be partners, you at fifty percent and the resort at fifty percent."

I stared at him, stunned. Goose bumps pebbled my arms. I'd always dreamed of expanding, but my business wasn't ready for it yet. Unless I had a partner. "I wouldn't have to give up the main shop?"

Evan's mouth dropped open. "After everything you've gone through? I'd never ask that of you. Plus, I don't think it's in your best interest anyway. That shop should be your flagship. Like I said, this is a business deal. We both benefit."

I beamed. "I love the idea! I could hire someone to bake at the main shop every morning, then take the inventory over to Calypso Key and work the rest of their shift there."

"See? Already figuring it out, aren't you?"

I laughed, and the sound echoed off the water around us. Then we were distracted as several shapes glided toward us. My smile remained, and a thrill ran through me as Evan pulled out his Thermos of water and poured it into Betty's mouth. I shifted in my kayak for a better look. "Elmo's already getting bigger! He's so cute." Earlier in the week, Evan had taken me on a sunset paddle into the lagoon, but he'd left the new manatee addition a secret. I'd been delighted beyond measure at seeing the youngster.

Now, the baby manatee approached next to its mother and Evan carefully poured it a drink. We didn't actually know if it was male or female, but Evan had asked me to name it, and I'd decided on Elmo. When the mammals had emptied the Thermos, Evan screwed the lid back on and returned it to the bottom of his kayak. Without water to entice them, the group of manatees drifted away.

I took a deep breath of the sharp, salty air. "I'm so glad I got to come out here this morning. I love what I do, but days off are important."

"They are. You've been sleeping over here a lot. Why don't I spend the night over at your place more often? I hate to make you wake up earlier than you have to. And I sleep like the dead—you won't wake me up."

I smiled and shook my head. "I don't mind. And the drive is nothing. I only get up a few minutes earlier. My commute when I lived in Boston was much longer. It's not a problem, I promise. I love it here."

One side of his mouth twitched. "How about you stay here more often, then? How about you move in with me?" He held out a hand to forestall me. "I know it's sudden, and we've only been back together a week. But I don't want to be apart from you anymore. I was miserable without you, Liv. Please—"

"Evan, stop. I'd love to move in." I didn't even need to think about it. I knew what I wanted. Him.

And the gigantic smile that lit his face was all the confirmation I needed. "Really? I expected a harder sell."

"You already won me over, remember? I felt the same way when we were apart. Like the best part of my life was missing."

"If living in the Big House with my father and Nona is too much, we could move into one of the family cottages like Maia and Wyatt did. That would give us more privacy. I don't want you to feel uncomfortable."

I burst into laughter. "Uncomfortable? Your family made me feel welcome from the first moment I arrived! I love that house and your father and Nona. And if you think I'm turning down a completely private suite that comes with regular housekeeping and a private chef, you don't know me very well, Mr. Markham."

He grinned and we started paddling toward the exit. "Just know the offer is there if anything changes."

"You know, we have Nona to thank for us getting together."

Evan winced. "I'm not sure thank is the correct term."

I couldn't resist a laugh. "That night, the look on your face after she left was priceless. You were banging your head on the table."

"I was trying to figure out how to get out of the mess."

"Instead, you got even further in. Regrets?"

"Not even the slightest bit."

"Me neither."

As we neared the narrow canal, we came across the

manatees again. The youngster lifted his face out of the water, regarding us curiously.

Evan rested his paddle as he scanned the peaceful scene, his expression serious. "When I discovered Elmo, I knew I had to do whatever it took to get you back. We spent so much time waiting to see if Betty was pregnant, and when he finally arrived, I was alone. It didn't mean anything." He turned to stare at me. "Because you weren't by my side. I won't make that mistake again, Liv."

I reached out and our hands met, holding tight. "We belong together. We're partners. In more ways than business."

"Much more." A grin cracked his face. "And who knows? Maybe I'll ask you about another partnership sometime in the future."

I pulled against his hand, drawing my kayak next to his. Our lips met in the soft morning air. "You have excellent ideas. I can't wait to see what the future holds."

Evan glided his paddle, letting me take the lead in the narrow channel. The sun glinted through the trees, throwing dappled sunlight over the still water. Together, we headed back toward the resort. Back toward our lives and a new promise.

Epilogue

Liv

SEPTEMBER

Nerves fluttered in my stomach as I stood behind the chain link safety fence next to April. Gabe stood on her other side, watching intently. I tried to follow the movement as Dylan threw a fastball and it made a satisfying *whack* in the catcher's mitt. The sun had just set, and banks of lights around the stadium lit the field in sharp relief as the players warmed up. The two stadium bullpens were past the dugouts and positioned so fans could watch the pitchers warm up while staying safe behind the fence. Burly security guards ensured the crowd didn't get too boisterous against the players.

Not that Dylan needed to worry about hecklers at the Hammerheads stadium. He had graduated to first in the rotation. Starting this final game of the season, he had just received the news from the team manager that they would work with him over the off-season so he could move up to AAA ball next spring.

I lifted my gaze to my banner in the outfield. It still hung in left field, but I'd increased my sponsorship level and my new advertisement was bigger. And it promoted both Sweet Dreams locations, Dove Key and Calypso Key. Sweet Dreams Mini was now a permanent fixture at the resort and a hit with both guests and staff.

I'd moved into Evan's suite, and we'd settled into a new phase of our relationship and our lives. We were a very compatible couple, and for the first time, I understood people who said being with the right person changed every-thing. I loved every moment we spent together, day and night. I longed for him when we were apart.

We'd watched Skye, now over a year old, several times. As I held her, I couldn't help wondering what a child who was a mixture of Evan and me would look like. Would be like. I loved sharing the house with his father and Nona. She was teaching me to play poker, though I didn't think I'd ever match her skill at the game.

Dylan threw another fastball, breaking me out of my reverie as another powerful *smack* emanated from the catcher. He fielded the pitch without even moving his hand.

"That was better," Evan said, and a smile crossed my face.

He looked magnificent in his Hammerheads uniform. It stretched across his broad shoulders and his jersey was tucked neatly into his pants. He'd proved so popular with the pitchers that he accepted a job as an official consultant for the Hammerheads, attending home games in uniform but not traveling with the team. He nodded at a man standing in the corner of the bullpen and holding a radar gun. "What was that?"

"Ninety-four."

Evan clapped Dylan on the back. "Nice. Good job. Now try your curve."

"He looks like pro material to me," Gabe said softly from April's other side. "Of course, I don't have a clue how to evaluate players. But Evan's impressed."

I smiled. Evan had told me privately that Dylan had a good enough arm for the minors, but he probably wouldn't progress further. Which made me curious about how good Evan had been. The fact that he'd been ready for the majors before his twentieth birthday spoke volumes.

I leaned in front of April to look at Gabe. "Bring back memories of watching Evan?"

He smiled and wrapped an arm around his wife. "Yeah. Evan was something else on the mound."

"I would have liked to see that," April said. "He's so easygoing, it's hard to imagine him staring down batters."

Gabe laughed out loud. "Oh, trust me. When Evan was playing, he was a completely different person. His nickname was the Enforcer. No one messed with him, and he wasn't afraid to back anyone off the plate. He was a lethal lefty—his fastball was blazing and damn near impossible to hit. I wouldn't even play with him."

Laughing softly, I turned my gaze back to the bullpen. Evan stared at me. He winked and tossed me a smile, which I returned. Then I nudged April. "How's your hiring process going? The dive operation must be doing well if you need another divemaster already."

"We hired someone yesterday. I think she'll work out great."

Gabe's arm tightened around her, and he kissed the top of her head.

She turned an elated smile to me. "But success isn't the only reason we hired someone. I'm pregnant."

I gasped and threw my arms around them in a group hug. "Congrats, you two! That's wonderful news."

Gabe's smile couldn't get any bigger. "We're pretty happy about it, but I think Hailey's got us beat on the excited front."

"Well, you have a built-in babysitter. That's a plus."

April's smile turned rueful. "We're still not sure she's quite old enough, but we'll see. She's great with Skye."

"She's rather mature for her age," I added.

Gabe's smile dimmed as he scrunched his eyes shut. "Don't remind me."

April and I both laughed, then Evan's voice carried to us. "Liv! Don't you have somewhere to be?"

Concentrating on Dylan and Evan had made my nerves dissipate, but now they came roaring back. I swallowed hard, my stomach twisting anew. "Why did I agree to this?"

April wrapped an arm around me. "You'll do great! You've had Evan coaching you, after all."

"If you say so. I'm probably about to fall flat on my face. See you in the stands."

With a final wave to Evan, I made my way through the stadium to the area behind home plate, where Suzanne, the Hammerheads' PR person, stood with her clipboard. Every time I'd seen her, Suzanne's brown hair had been down, and she wore business attire. But tonight, her hair was in a ponytail, and she wore dressy shorts paired with a blouse. She brightened at seeing me. "There you are! Ready for your close-up?"

"No!" I said with a nervous laugh. "Can I change my mind?"

She smiled reassuringly. "Don't worry. Everyone gets nervous. And nobody expects you to be Dylan, after all."

She handed me a baseball and I turned it around in my hand nervously. But it looked like any other ball, pristine white with red stitches. I posed for several photographs, the team photographer busy snapping pictures around me.

"Okay, the catcher is coming out of the bullpen now," Suzanne said. "Head on out to the mound."

As I took the field and tried not to fall on my face walking to the pitcher's mound, the announcer's voice boomed overhead. "Throwing out tonight's ceremonial first pitch is major Hammerheads sponsor Liv Jacobson, owner of Sweet Dreams Bakery."

I waved as the crowd applauded, surprised at how loud the sound was from here. Dylan smiled and waved to me as he rested his arms on the dugout wall. The catcher kneeled behind home plate, punching his fist into his thick catcher's mitt.

I stood a good fifteen feet in front of the mound, my feet sinking into the grass. Evan had given me plenty of instruction and encouraged me to shorten the throwing distance to increase my confidence. I also took comfort in the knowledge that the Hammerheads' catcher was known for catching wild pitches.

Oh boy. Here goes nothing.

With my heart in my mouth, I wound up and pitched the ball as I'd been taught. It wasn't a perfect throw, but I'd seen worse. The catcher only had to rise to a half crouch and hold his mitt out slightly to one side to catch it.

Pride and happiness soared inside me as the crowd cheered. I waved to the full stands as the tension drained away. A big, smug smile rose on my face as I took in the moment. The catcher strode toward me, twisting the ball in his hands. He seemed much bigger than when he'd stopped by the bakery and Dylan had introduced us.

I guess all that gear makes him seem larger.

I waved to the crowd again, then turned back as the catcher stopped a few feet from me and lifted his mask, letting it fall to the ground.

It was Evan.

I burst into laughter. "Where did you come from?"

"I wanted to be part of your special night. And here's your game ball. I even autographed it for you." He held out his hand and dropped the ball into my palm.

"Oh, I'm keeping this!"

I disregarded his autograph comment. I'd held the ball since Suzanne gave it to me, so I knew it was brand-new. Still grinning, I dropped my gaze as I spun the ball around. Then I stopped. Something was different. Evan's handwriting was clear on the ball.

But what he'd written stopped me in my tracks.

The noise of the crowd disappeared. Everything disappeared except the simple sentence he'd written: Will You Marry Me?

My heart threatened to explode, and happy tears pricked my eyes. A huge smile lit my face as I threw myself against him. "Yes!"

The crowd roared to life, impossible to ignore. This wasn't the polite applause I'd seen before. As Evan held me tight, I glanced at the giant display screen above the scoreboard, where a still photo of the ball and his scrawled proposal was displayed. Elated and stunned in equal measures, I glanced around the packed stands. Everyone was on their feet now, cheering, and a rhythmic chant began.

It took a moment for me to understand their repeated, "Kiss! Kiss! Kiss!"

Laughing, I moved my head to press my lips to Evan's. He boosted me up so we were at the same height, and the crowd roared even louder. I was laughing and crying at the same time, but I tried to concentrate on our kiss. His lips were warm and firm, and I could feel him smiling. Finally, I pulled back, and he set me back on my feet.

Evan reached into his pants pocket and withdrew a small box. The roaring increased yet again when he slid a solitaire diamond ring on my finger. With our arms around each other's waists, we waved to the crowd.

"That was a bold move, mister," I said, grinning as I lifted a brow. "What if I'd said no?"

"Then I would have been in for a world of hurt," he said with a laugh. "Thank you for sparing me the embarrassment."

We walked toward the sideline, still with our arms around each other. I waved to April and Gabe in the stands, whose grins rivaled mine and Evan's. "Were they in on it?"

"Nope. The only one who knew was Dylan, since I had to change into the catcher's gear after you left the bullpen, and the big screen operator. Dylan snapped that picture of the ball and texted it to him."

"Very nicely done, sir. Now we need to start working on the guest list. We might just have to invite the manatees to our wedding."

We made our way to our seats next to April and Gabe, enduring the good-natured catcalls sent our way by the fans. Dylan took the mound and threw a ninety-five mile-per-hour fastball.

I think the Hammerheads won the game, but I couldn't say for certain. I found it hard to concentrate. As much as I loved baseball, the game was suddenly much less important. All I could think about was the man next to me and the ring on my finger. And the future we were about to begin.

THANK you for reading BECAUSE OF YOU! I loved writing about Evan and Liv—their story was funny, poignant, and heartwarming. Keep reading for another chance to learn about them.

There is still a lot of the Calypso Key story to tell, and the series continues with MEMORIES OF YOU, which is Stella and Aiden's story!

MEMORIES OF YOU: A Small Town Second Chance Romance
CALYPSO KEY SERIES

As I claim my dream as a chef, my old flame returns to claim me.
How can he possibly be my missing ingredient?

STELLA:

I've worked my entire life to become the executive chef of my family's fabled restaurant. Then Aiden Mitchell resurfaces, shattering my well-ordered world. Gone is the awkward boy, replaced by a gorgeous, small-town doctor when we meet face to face in his clinic—in the worst way possible.

My first love, the man who left without a backward glance, tries to assure me he's changed. As our cautious trust becomes pulsing heat, mysteries start unraveling, tossing family strife into my carefully laid plans. More than my heart is on the line—my family is at stake.

I want to focus on my career, not the way his touch sends me reeling. Despite the fire consuming us, finding the recipe for our second chance might be my toughest challenge ever.

Will this unexpected reunion upend the future I've worked so hard to build?

MEMORIES OF YOU: A Small Town Second Chance Romance

I HAVE A **BONUS SCENE**, featuring Evan and Liv, available for BECAUSE OF YOU! Sign up for my Beach Read Update, and as a thank you, I'll send you a glimpse of their happy future. Click below to sign up:

Beach Read Update
(www.erinbrockus.com/because)

My Beach Read Update subscribers hear about all my free content, plus exclusive offers and sales. I'd love to have you along!

Plus, you'll stay up to date with cover reveals, sneak peeks, and exclusive content about my books!

If you're already on my list, I've got you covered! At the bottom of each newsletter is a link to all my free content for subscribers. Just find your last email from me to read this bonus, as well as any others you might have missed. Or you can simply sign up again—you'll have your bonus in a flash.

CALYPSO KEY SERIES:

Main Novels:

Visions of You: A Small Town Single Dad Romance

Because of You: A Small Town Fake Relationship Romance

Memories of You: A Small Town Second Chance Romance

Shades of You: A Small Town Forbidden Romance

Associated Short Stories and Novellas:

Traces of You: A Small Town Rivals to Lovers Romance*

* Subscriber exclusive

HALF MOON BAY SERIES:

MAIN NOVELS:

Finding Hope: Half Moon Bay Book 1

Defending Hope: Half Moon Bay Book 2

Rising Hope: Half Moon Bay Book 3

Forever Hope: Half Moon Bay Book 4

Half Moon Whim: Half Moon Bay Book 5 (Standalone)

Half Moon Ember: Half Moon Bay Book 6 (Standalone)

Half Moon Aqua: Half Moon Bay Book 7

Crowning Hope: Half Moon Bay Book 8

ASSOCIATED SHORT STORIES AND NOVELLAS:

Tropical Dawn: A Half Moon Bay Prequel Novella

*Tropical Chance**: A Second Chance Half Moon Bay Novella

*Tropical Hope**: A Half Moon Bay Prequel Short Story

* Subscriber exclusives

STANDALONE BOOKS:

In Too Deep: A Second Chance Romance

Beached in Bali: A Friends to Lovers Romance

About the Author

Dive into steamy small-town romance, where passion meets paradise!

Erin Brockus writes steamy small town romances that transport readers to exotic, tropical destinations, and provide a perfect beachy getaway from everyday life. Her mature, relatable characters are impossible not to root for, and she weaves breezy romantic adventure into her stories, emphasizing scuba diving and the ocean.

Drawing on her twin passions for diving and travel, Erin infuses her characters and narratives with a sense of excitement and passion. Her idea of the perfect day involves sipping a cocktail on the beach after exploring the ocean depths.

Erin lives in Washington wine country with her husband, who is also a scuba instructor. She is currently hard at work on her next island adventure. When she's not writing, you might find her out for a run or cycling through the countryside on the next quest for adventure.